Her Ghosts Reborn

HLF Book Two

Patricia Elliott

ISBN 978-1-7380272-5-5

First published in 2024 by Patricia Elliott

Her Sweet Addition Copyright 2024 Patricia Elliott
Cover design Copyright 2024 Amy Queau / Q Designs

Chapter One

"It has to be here somewhere," Ebony growled anxiously as she dumped out another drawer from the luxury designer desk in the living room.

If Seth Peters didn't know better, he'd say a burglar had torn through his home and not his young mistress racing around in front of him. Normally, she displayed poise and control. Not today, though.

She was in hunt mode, and as a result, there were only a few things left in the house that hadn't been turned upside down. The newspapers in the basket had been picked apart, couch cushions tossed into the corner, and now the contents of three drawers were strewn across his floor. And she was marching her way toward the planters.

"You could at least help," she snapped. "You have as much to lose as I do."

He glanced at his watch. "I would, but I have to get to the hospital. They said tonight could be the night."

"Maybe you can get the old bag to tell us where it is before she croaks."

"Why are you so sure there's another will? I was there with her when the last one was made."

"Exactly," Ebony said sharply as she picked up a ceramic planter, dumping the entire contents, dirt and all, onto his pristine beige carpet. He cringed.

Seth took a breath and looked over at the maid huddling in the corner, her eyes downcast and her hands clasped tightly in front of her. "Clean this up when she's done. I don't want to see a speck of dirt in this place when I return."

"Yes, sir," she said timidly, still not looking at him.

The young maid, who was only in Canada because of him so she could support her family overseas, was a sharp contrast to the woman who was tearing up the living room. One obeyed. The other couldn't be tamed. And he didn't mind. Ebony had brought excitement into his dull life. She took guff from no one, including him.

"Damn it! Where the hell is it?" Ebony stopped in the center of the room, hands on her hips, casting him a look filled with impatience. "You must know whether she had a favorite hiding spot."

"She didn't hide things from me," he said.

Ebony laughed that haughty laugh of hers. "You don't know much about women, do you? We all hide things."

Judith, his wife, didn't have the guts to go against him, not even when the shit hit the fan after Joanne, their daughter, had her accident. He still couldn't believe his own flesh and blood had betrayed him by marrying his enemy's son. That made him pause for a moment. Maybe Ebony was right. If his daughter betrayed him, was it possible that his wife could do the same?

Seth shook his head. During their entire marriage, Judith never questioned his decisions, wouldn't even open her mouth to offer her thoughts. Not even when he specifically asked her. She would just say, 'whatever you think, dear.' God, she was boring. But he had to admit that a pussy-whipped woman allowed him to have more freedom to do as he pleased, so there were pros and cons to their odd family dynamic.

"I still think this is the only one," he said, sticking to his guns as he held up the envelope containing his wife's Last Will and Testament.

She picked up another plant and dumped it out, examining the pot. "No, it's not. There's another one. I can feel it in my bones."

"What makes you think so?"

Ebony stopped her path of destruction and looked at him, her eyes blazing with anger. "I can see it in her eyes every time we go to visit her. Now stop questioning my intuition, or I'll leave and never come back."

"Okay, okay," he said, holding his hands out. "I just don't think we have anything to worry about. Everything she has belongs to me anyway. I paid for it. So, I don't want you to worry your pretty little head. It isn't healthy for you or our unborn son.

She waved her hand in dismissal. "I'll be fine, but we're running out of time. We need to find it and get her to rewrite it before she dies. I have the solicitor on standby."

Seth sighed. Ebony wasn't going to let this rest until she found it, or until she destroyed his entire house in the process.

"Women are crafty, especially a scorned one," Ebony warned him.

"I gave her everything she ever needed. Why would she be scorned?"

"Uh, how many women have you cheated on her with?"

"We had an open relationship," he argued.

"Open according to whom?"

He opened his mouth to answer, but then realized he had nothing to refute her with. It wasn't something he and his wife had ever discussed. They just stopped having sex years ago because she was never interested. And after being refused so many times over, it seemed like the only logical decision. What else was he supposed to do to get his needs met? Once he made that decision, he never bothered to hide it. Not like some other weak ass men he knew.

"She never had an issue with it," he said, chuckling. "And she wasn't going to leave even if she did."

"Maybe not, but women plan for the worst, so don't put it past her. And she has a soft spot for her kid. Now go on, get out of here," she said, shoving him toward the door. "See if you can get her to tell you anything. And don't come back until you know."

"If it were me, I wouldn't worry about it until there is something to worry about," he said, shrugging his shoulders.

"Good thing I'm not you."

He laughed as he put on his shoes, then pulled her close to kiss her forehead. "I'll let you know if I find out anything, but she wasn't very lucid the last time we were there."

"Careful, you'll ruin my makeup, and I have a shoot later."

"Break a leg," he said before heading out the door. Things were about to get interesting. Very interesting indeed.

❧

"Hi, Laryssa, I'm Nathan Mitchell," the stranger said. "Your father's brother."

Joanne Richards found herself captivated by his bright chocolate-colored eyes, encircled with a ring of black around his irises. She barely heard what he had to say because his eyes were locked on hers, too. She had been struck dumb.

"That's impossible," came a voice from behind her, breaking the temporary spell. "I don't have any family left."

Joanne stepped back and placed her arm around a shaking Laryssa. They never spoke much about Laryssa's past. The only things she knew about Laryssa were that her parents had died in a boating accident, and she'd spent the remainder of her childhood in and out of foster care. She had also been the wife of her late son, Aidan, and was currently the wife of her other son, Alex, Aidan's twin. Life couldn't get more bizarre than that.

"Why don't you come in, and we can continue the discussion in the living room," Alex suggested as he held his hand out to him. "Hi, I'm Alex, Laryssa's husband."

Nathan gripped his hand in a firm handshake. "That sounds great, thank you."

"I'll go put on some coffee," Joanne said, eager to put some distance between the newcomer and herself to ease the flutter in her stomach. She was too old to get butterflies over a guy. Besides, who would want a woman with a limp anyway?

"Sarah, can you handle the kids?" Alex asked their nanny.

"No problem, sir," she replied.

Joanne watched as Alex guided Laryssa with a hand on the small of her back to the living room, with Nathan in tow. She couldn't help but notice the man's wide shoulders and his smooth gait. One she wished she still had. His crisp dress shirt and tailored black dress pants spoke of a man who cared about his appearance. Either that or someone who wanted to put on a good show.

That's not the feeling she got from his gaze, though, but it was easier thinking that way than letting her heart run away on her. Her heart had been broken once, and half of it was still buried in the grave with her husband, Scott. The trouble that ensued from that ordeal was enough to last a lifetime. Taking a deep breath, she reached for the coffee in the cupboard and dumped some into a new paper filter.

"Are you okay?" Sarah asked as she picked up a fussy Justin from the playpen, propping a bottle in his mouth as she moved to sit at the table with Laryssa's young seventeen-month-old twins.

Joanne could hardly believe her son had three kids to raise now. She'd begun to question whether he'd ever settle down again. "Sorry, I just had a very weird feeling about Nathan."

Leaning over, Sarah whispered, "Would that weird feeling have anything to do with how great his ass looked in those pants?"

Joanne's face burned, and she knew it was as red as a tomato. "Really now! We're two almost gray-haired grannies. We shouldn't be looking at a man's butt. That time has passed." Yet, a vision of his hot ass flashed in her mind.

"Speak for yourself. I'm a blonde."

"Salon dyed doesn't count."

"Oh shush. We're not dead yet, and as long as we're alive, we can enjoy a sexy man's ass," the woman said, winking at her. Letting Joanne know she took no offense to her words.

Joanne waved her off. She was still getting used to being a mom and a grandma after hiding it for so long. Adding a man to that would just take away from the time she had with her family. Eighteen months have passed since the news got out that she was Alexander's mom. Hearing him call her mom made her heart leap every time. They were finally a real family now.

Joanne smiled at that thought. He'd forgiven her for keeping it a secret and welcomed her new role in his life. Mind you, he tried to prevent her from working for him as a result, telling her that he'd happily hire a housekeeper, but she liked doing stuff around the house. It kept her busy, and it was what she was most familiar with.

However, her body had begun to plan a revolt whenever she did anything strenuous, like lugging a vacuum up and down the stairs in their monstrous house. They had an elevator, but some areas were only accessible via a staircase. And being sixty-one years old, she had to accept she had limits, especially with a body like hers that still felt the effects of her horrific car accident.

"Say it! Say you thought his butt was hot."

Joanne's eyes widened, and she felt the heat return to her cheeks as she tried to cover the ears of at least one twin. "I most certainly will not say that. We have innocent ears in the room."

The nanny rolled her eyes. "Girl, it's time for you to live for a change."

"Changing diapers is enough change for me."

Sarah shook her head and lifted Justin to her shoulder to burp him. "Go on. Go be with your son and Laryssa. I'm sure Nathan could use a cup of coffee. I've got the kids covered." Just then, Ashley dumped her cereal bowl on Ann's head, and the young girl burst out crying. "Okay, maybe not."

Joanne walked over to the kitchen sink to get a dishcloth and then wandered over to Ann to clean her up. "I definitely prefer toddlers over grown men."

"You need to get a life, Jo!" Sarah sighed, settling Justin back into her arms to finish the bottle."

She couldn't think of a life better than the one she was living right now. She didn't want for anything. Her son hadn't kicked her out of the house when he found out her secret. And her late-husband's parents, Ruth and Mitch, didn't give her any trouble—at least not really.

They were a pretty close family now, and they treated her like a daughter-in-law again. And even though Scott—her husband and their son—had been dead a long time, they told her she would always be family. Her eyes watered as she stood there in the kitchen. She quickly wiped the tears away with the sleeve of her blouse.

Sarah looked at her, her brow crinkling with worry. "Did I over-step my bounds?"

"No, dear. It's fine," Joanne replied, waving off her concern as she gave the highchair one final swipe with the cloth. "I think this little one is going to need a bath."

"She'll survive until the visit is over." Sarah said, nodding toward the coffee pot. "Coffee's ready."

The last thing Joanne wanted to do was impose on a private conversation. *Okay,* she groaned to herself. That was a lie. She wanted to know what was going on, but she didn't want him to look at her again with that steady, unnerving gaze.

One would think by her age, she'd have this man thing down pat, but she'd been out of the game for so long she wouldn't even know what to do with one...like a dog chasing a car.

Taking a deep breath, she picked up the tray and carefully walked with it into the living room, concentrating hard, trying not to spill the coffee with her limp. She wished they would have been able to fix her leg when she was younger because now it was getting harder to move these days.

Joanne glanced around the room. Alex was sitting beside Laryssa in the middle of the couch. Nathan was by himself on the love seat, leaving the other cushion open beside him. The only other available seat was the recliner, but it had clothes covering it that she hadn't gotten around to folding yet.

Nathan patted the cushion beside him. "Please, sit. You look exhausted."

"I really shouldn't. Sarah needs help with the kids."

"Please stay, Mom," Alex said, gesturing toward the loveseat and consequently toward Nathan. The tenderness of his tone, and the use of a word she never thought she'd ever hear come out of his mouth, made her throat clog. She didn't think she'd ever get used to it.

"My dad never mentioned that he had a brother," Laryssa commented.

"You were probably too young to remember," he replied, his voice gentle and serene. "You were only four when it all happened."

"Why didn't you ever come for me?"

"In all honesty, it all happened so fast, and I wasn't in a position to adopt you at the time. My life had gone off the rails with the loss of my brother, and by the time I managed to get it together, you were gone, and no one would tell me anything. If I wouldn't have seen the article of your wedding in the paper, I wouldn't have found you.

Joanne was glad she'd encouraged the newspaper article after the danger of Laryssa's stalker had passed. She had a feeling Laryssa had family out there. The girl deserved a full family after all she'd been through. It took a bit to convince Alex to go for it, but she was glad he eventually did.

Nathan seemed genuine. But as soon as those words fluttered through her mind, he turned and looked at her. His eyes locked with hers, and it was like the room disappeared. If she wouldn't have been sitting, she'd likely have swooned. Heat rose to her cheeks again, and she fanned herself with her hand.

"Is it hot in here?" she asked the others, certain that someone had turned the thermostat up. Not even her worst hot flash was hotter than this.

Her son and daughter-in-law shared a knowing glance, and Joanne watched Alex squeeze Laryssa's hand, and it made her blush all the more. She knew the type of stuff fluttering through their newlywed minds.

They'd been married just over a year and were still very much in love. It had eased the ache in Joanne's heart that she bore for Alex ever since the loss of his daughter. He deserved his happily ever after more than anyone.

"So, does anyone want to introduce me to this wonderful lady?" he asked them, sending a brilliant smile her way.

"Nathan, this is my mom, Joanne," Alex said.

"It's nice to meet the one who raised such a marvelous man for my niece."

She opened her mouth to correct him, but Alex spoke up instead. "I wouldn't be who I am without her or Laryssa."

"I firmly believe behind every good man is a good woman," Nathan replied, letting his knuckles brush Joanne's shoulder.

Goosebumps appeared on her arms as a warm shiver rustled through her body, making her leg stiffen painfully. She'd missed her morning dose of medication, which helped with the pain.

"I couldn't agree more," Alex said. "Would you like a coffee or a beer?"

Joanne made a 'tsk' sound. "It's too early to be drinking, and he might have to drive somewhere." She leaned forward and poured everyone a cup of coffee. After losing her husband to a drunk driver, she wasn't about to let anyone in this house drive after drinking.

"Where are you staying?" Alex asked him.

"I actually just got into town, so I haven't had a chance to scope out any areas."

"Hey, why don't you—" Alex started to say, but Laryssa interrupted him.

"Wait here a moment. I have to talk to my husband."

Her son was probably going to suggest that he stay with them. He had a habit of bringing stray puppies home. That was what he had done with Laryssa when they first met. He felt like he had to help everyone in need, and while Joanne was normally okay with that, *her needs* were currently going in a different direction. To avoid temptation and to give herself a moment to breathe, she got up to follow her son, but the man took her hand.

"Won't you keep me company?"

The warmth of his skin against hers made her pause, and she recalled the first rule of hospitality, which was to make the guest feel welcome. Biting back a groan, Joanne sat down, folding her hands on her light purple slacks. "Do you live near Vancouver?" she asked him.

"In all honesty, I only have a motorhome. I sold my place a long time ago to travel."

There was a hitch in his voice that was barely perceptible, but it was there. "Don't you need a physical address?"

"I have a spot for my RV in Alberta, but I travel more often than not. Would you like to see it? It's parked out front."

Joanne swallowed hard. "Maybe when they get back, we can all go take a peek."

"You're a cautious one, aren't you?" Nathan said, grinning.

"Well," she said, shrugging her shoulders. "You don't get to be our age by being stupid."

The smile disappeared from his face, and his hands closed into tight fists as he looked away, his eyes taking on a despondent look.

Joanne looked toward the hallway where Alex and Laryssa disappeared, hoping they'd be back soon. She had a feeling there was a lot more to be discussed.

Chapter Two

About ten minutes later, Alex and Laryssa returned to the room, and Joanne decided to take a breather by running out to the mailbox to see if anything had arrived. It was approaching Christmas time, and she had ordered a few things for the kids. Who knew the internet could be so handy? She wouldn't have to brave the crowds in the stores. Mind you, she still felt a sliver of fear putting her credit card information on websites, so she only used legit big-name stores she felt were safe.

Walking by Alexander, she put a hand on his shoulder and whispered, "He has secrets."

She felt strange saying that because she herself had lived a secret life for most of her son's life. Was that why she felt the way she did? Maybe he was fine, and this was just her gut playing games on her, but there was no harm in playing it safe, especially not when it came to family.

Slipping on her flats, she grabbed her winter jacket from the hook on the wall and opened the large front door. Snow hadn't yet touched the ground, but sparkling frost littered the grass that lined the walkway.

It was quite the trek to the main gate, but she loved the walk. It helped loosen her tight muscles and kept her relatively limber. She grabbed her cane and shut the door behind her.

It was only recently she'd begun using one for long walks. Alex had suggested buying her a motorized scooter, but she'd hit him on the shoulder and jokingly asked him if he thought she was old or something.

There was no doubt about it. She was feeling her age these days, but she refused to get a scooter. The minute she did that, her body would get more used to being lazy and that, in her opinion, brought her one step closer to the grave. And she had no plans to die anytime soon.

Joanne glanced at the mermaid fountain. Icicles hung from the woman's outstretched hands, but water still flowed from them into the small pond below. Walking alongside it, she watched the goldfish swim around in the slightly heated water that prevented it from freezing. They seemed rather comfortable.

Nathan's motorhome was parked along the other side of the fountain, almost close enough to touch it. The vehicle was on the larger size, probably a thirty-six-footer by the looks of it. A lot of space for just one man.

She was tempted to go inside, but she didn't want to intrude on his personal space. Leaving the RV alone, she continued to the main gate. She loved how she could walk outside and not have to fear for her life. The walled compound kept most of the unwanted away and security met those who tried. That didn't happen often, thankfully.

"Good morning, Doug." Joanne waved to the guard, who was making his morning rounds.

"If you keep walking this way every morning, dear lady, I'm going to start thinking you have designs on my body," he said, smiling at her as he offered his arm.

"If only I was thirty years younger," she said, winking at him. "Has the mail arrived yet?"

Doug reached into his jacket and pulled out a wad of mail,

including a large Manilla envelope. "I had to sign for this one."

Flipping the big manilla envelope over, she saw her name on the front and then glanced at the address. It was from a lawyer's firm in Ontario. And, just like that, a nasty chill raced through her, making her shiver.

The guard helped keep her steady as she swayed to the side. "Are you feeling okay?" he asked.

She waved him off. "I'll be fine. Don't you worry about me."

"May I walk you back to the house? I don't want you fainting along the way. You look as white as a ghost."

She had every reason to be. The lawyer's firm was exactly the same one she fought against when she tried regaining custody of the boys after she recovered from her accident. Why would they be contacting her?

Unless her family found out where she'd been all these years and learned that the truth had gotten out. But why would they care now? Surely, they had other fish to fry. They'd already destroyed her life before. What would they benefit from doing it again?

All she wanted to do was live the rest of her years in peace, however long she had left. Her legs shook beneath her, making her sway again. Doug slipped his arms around her, and she gratefully accepted the feeling of security he offered as they walked back to the house.

"Thank you," Joanne said.

She didn't think she'd survive the walk without him, not with her entire life weighing down on her heart. Her family had power. They could make her life miserable if they wanted to. Her stomach rolled with the nasty intent of making its contents known. She swallowed hard.

"You'll be okay, ma'am," the guard said reassuringly.

"You don't have to call me ma'am, Doug. Joanne is fine."

He may be thirty years younger than her, and a member of the staff, but having lived on both sides of the fence, she preferred everyone being on the same playing field.

"Okay." The young man smiled as they made their way up the front steps to the door. He opened it and motioned her forward with a flair of his hand. "Here you are Ma—Joanne."

She patted him on the cheek and then turned to walk inside. He really was a good boy, much like her Scott had been. He kind of reminded her of him, too.

Instead of joining her family in the living room, she returned to the kitchen and was relieved to find it empty. Sarah must have taken the kids into the playroom or back upstairs.

Opening the drawer beside the sink—known as the junk drawer—she pulled out a letter opener. Slicing open the top of the envelope, she pulled out the contents.

Dear Ms. Richards,

We regretfully inform you of the passing of your mother, Judith Andrea Peters, on November 11, 2009.
Upon discovery of a will, dated the 1st day of the 10th month of 2009, it is her request that you join the family for the reading of the will on the 1st day of the 12th month of 2009. The reading will take place in the office of Harrison and Levi, located at

Harrison & Levi Law Firm
2315 Ontario Drive
Toronto, Ontario
V6T3W1

Please contact us at your earliest convenience to confirm your attendance.

Thank you,
*   Frank Harrison*

. . .

A shaky Joanne plopped herself in a chair at the table, letting the paper fall to the floor. Her mother had died. A woman she hadn't spoken to for almost thirty-three years, not since the day they forced Joanne to leave their property by threatening to commit her to an insane asylum. She wasn't sure how to feel about the news or about the fact that they chose to contact her.

Why were they writing to her? Didn't they know she'd been disowned? There had to be a mix-up somewhere. She was no longer their child. Something she'd come to terms with a long time ago.

She was still sitting in the same spot when Alex came into the room.

"You look like you've seen a ghost," he said.

Joanne glanced down at the paper on the floor. "In a way, I guess I have."

He leaned down and picked it up, his eyes skimming over the letter. "Hot damn! What are you going to do?"

She shrugged her shoulders and shivered. "I haven't the foggiest."

He placed a reassuring hand on her shoulder. "Well, I say screw them. You don't need whatever they have to give."

If only it were that simple. She knew what could happen if she ignored a request from her family, especially now that they knew where she was and with whom she lived.

She squeezed his hand. "Maybe like you, it's about time I faced my ghosts. I've lived with them long enough."

"More like demons," he muttered.

That would be an accurate description of her parents. She prayed that no other child in the world had to face what she did. If it wouldn't have been for Ruth and Mitch, she would likely would have lost her mind.

For all intents and purposes, they had become her family, even if she hadn't been allowed to call them that until recently. They treated her better than her own family did.

Joanne took the letter and read it again. It made no mention of her dad, Seth. Was he still alive? What of her one and only sibling,

Isaac? She could only hope that he hadn't turned out like their father. She pressed her lips into a firm line. Seth was the hardest person to please. He had the coldest heart on the planet and was the king of bearing grudges.

Alex released her shoulder and held out his hand. "Come on, let's forget about the letter for now and see how the meeting is going with Laryssa and her uncle."

He helped her up, and they walked, arm in arm, back into the living room. Nathan and Laryssa were sitting side by side, looking at his phone. Laryssa glanced up at them.

"He has some pictures of me from when I was young," Laryssa told them, her eyes glistening.

Nathan looked at Joanne, studying her. "Are you okay?" he asked.

Astute fellow! "I'm fine," Joanne replied. She wasn't about to detract attention away from the two of them by bringing up her own troubles.

Laryssa, being the sweetheart that she was, turned to her and said, "Mom, spill it!"

Joanne shook her head and tried to glance over Nathan's shoulder at the picture of Laryssa on a tricycle. "This is supposed to be a happy moment. Your moment. I don't want to impose."

Laryssa wasn't having any of it, though. "Really, it's okay. What's going on?"

"My mother just died. There is a reading of the will scheduled in December."

Laryssa stood up and enveloped Joanne in a hug. "I'm so sorry."

"It's fine, my dear. They stopped being my family a long time ago."

"That doesn't make it any easier," her daughter-in-law said solemnly, her own sadness fluttering through her eyes.

Laryssa had faced her own loss. First her family and then her husband, Aidan. Even though Aidan had been abusive, that didn't stop the pain of losing someone. Of course, the pain was more about the loss of what could have been than the loss of what was.

What would it have been like had her family not pulled the crap that they did? What if the twins had stayed together? What if Scott had survived? Would their families have found a way to make peace?

The 'what if' train was a long, bumpy ride. One she usually tried not to board if she could help it. Occasionally, though, unseen hands pulled her aboard, and she found herself thinking about the life she could have had. Not that the one she had now was bad, but that didn't change the wish that remained on her heart that things could have ended differently for her and Scott.

Would she have married Scott if she knew what was going to happen? What if he wouldn't have had to drive her to the hospital that night? What if they would have taken the route he had suggested, instead of hers? She squeezed her eyes closed and pushed the thoughts away.

"What are you going to do?" Laryssa asked.

"I'm not sure yet."

The answer should be easy, but it wasn't. She didn't care about the will, but she was curious as to why they wanted her there. Was it to pull her into their lousy web again? Make her go all the way there, thinking they had accepted her back into their family, and then, in the end, have them laugh in her face?

It could go any number of ways. Goodness, what she wouldn't give for a glass of whiskey right about now! Joanne gasped. Her face paled, and her legs buckled. Before Alex had a chance to help, Nathan jumped up and steadied her. She went into his arms without question. She didn't care that they belonged to a stranger.

"Mom," Alex said, his voice full of alarm. "What's wrong?"

Nathan coaxed her to sit on the loveseat beside him, still keeping his arm around her shoulders.

"I..." She didn't even know how to answer her son. The very fact that her first thought had been to have a drink made her stomach roll. She made a promise after Scott died to never have another drink for as long as she lived. "I think I need to lie down."

Chapter Three

Joanne tossed and turned restlessly in her sleep, pulled into the mother of all nightmares as she went back in time to the worst moment of her life.

"Where are my babies?" she demanded in a weaker voice than she'd been expecting. "Give me my babies!"

Hospital staff surrounded her bed, and at the foot of the bed stood the doctor and her father, who was signing her life away as she lay there.

"They'll be well taken care of, Ms. Peters."

"My name is Joanne *Richards*." She tried to push herself to a sitting position, but her body wouldn't listen. "Please, bring me my babies."

The doctor handed the clipboard to her father, Seth. He was a tall, bald man, with no love in his eyes as he glared at her. "It's for your own good," Seth said.

"You have no right to make this decision for me."

"I'm your father. I can do whatever I damn well please." After he finished signing the paperwork, he spun and walked out of the room as quickly as he had walked in. No, I'm sorry. No hug. No love. Nothing. It was like she didn't exist anymore.

Her mother hadn't come to visit, probably because her father wouldn't let her. And Joanne knew if her mom wasn't loyal to him, then she would get the bum's rush out as well. But her mom should have been there to fight for her and her recovery, instead they were fighting against her. They didn't care that she almost died, or that she'd lost her husband. And now she was losing her babies, too.

"I'm not unfit," she cried. "Darn you!"

"Then get up and walk," her father dared.

Using all the strength she could muster, she swung her legs over the side of the bed and stood up. She had every intention of walking out the door, going to her family's house, and getting her babies back.

But the minute she took a step, she fell flat on her face, but not before she caught the smug look on his.

He kneeled to her level. "Now you're going to know what it feels like to be betrayed."

With her body aching and tears filling her eyes, she looked up at the doctor, pleading with him. "You know me. You've known me my whole life. How could you do this to me?"

The man wouldn't even look her in the eyes, mumbling a set of numbers over and over to himself. Probably a donation for the new hospital wing, provided generously by her father.

"Please, give me my babies."

She wrapped her arms around her flabby belly, bile rising dangerously high in her throat. They had ripped her children from her womb, and now they were being ripped from her life. *No!* This couldn't be happening.

Joanne rested her hands on the floor, her head bowed low. "Scott," she cried, voice full of pain and tears. If he were here, he'd help her. "Please, why won't someone help me?"

Her throat clogged. She struggled to breathe, her body hurting everywhere. She tried to stand but failed, so she started crawling, her right side failing to cooperate as her arm hung limp as did her leg.

Seth laughed at her attempt.

"You can't stop me," she said weakly. "I will come for them."

"You should be like your mother. She knows how to listen."

Joanne raised her left arm and wrapped her fingers around the collar of his shirt. "I hate you."

He pulled himself from her grip easily and stood up, nodding at the doctor. Two orderlies picked her up and placed her back on the bed. She tried to fight them, but the nurse injected some medication into her IV.

"No. Don't do this. Let me see my babies, please."

"Please..." Her voice grew weak, and her eyes closed as the people in the room became nothing more than shadows in the dark. Ghosts that would forever plague her heart and mind.

Joanne bolted upright in bed, letting out a cry of anguish as she broke free from the nightmare. Her nightgown wet with sweat, her hair clinging to her face. Her breath came in short, frantic gasps. The door flung open, making her jump. As her eyes adjusted to the light, she saw her daughter-in-law standing there.

"Joanne, are you okay?"

"I...uhh..." She glanced around the room and took a deep breath, letting it out noisily. It was just a dream. That's all. "It's nothing, dear. I'm sorry to wake you."

Laryssa came over and sat beside her on the bed. "I heard you cry out."

"Just an old woman having a nightmare."

Laryssa picked up Joanne's housecoat off the floor. "Why don't we go grab a hot chocolate and sit by the fire?"

"I don't want to keep you up. You need your sleep."

"You stayed up enough with me. Now, it's my turn." Laryssa held out the bathrobe for her to put on.

Joanne slipped her arms into the white furry bathrobe and snuggled into its warmth, her body shaking.

The two of them walked to the door.

"Let me just go check on Justin, then I'll meet you in the kitchen," Laryssa said, giving Joanne's arm a squeeze before walking away.

Joanne watched her leave and smiled. She was the daughter she'd always wanted. The girl had a heart of gold, despite having been through a nightmarish past herself.

It was a strange and sad circumstance that brought them all together. She hadn't even realized Aidan had moved to Vancouver, away from her parents. It hurt her heart that he'd become as abusive as her dad had been. Laryssa didn't deserve that, and Joanne felt partly responsible for not fighting hard enough, even if it would have put her in the insane asylum. But there was no going back, and she was glad the young twins didn't have to put up with that abusive behavior from her dad or their own father.

Poor Laryssa had been so scared to death when she first met Alex that she had trouble trusting him. But Joanne was happy it worked out for them in the end. She'd never seen Alex so happy and carefree.

Moving through the house, Joanne went into the kitchen and started boiling some milk. Hot chocolate was nothing without milk. Water just wasn't the same. Reaching up into the cupboard, she pulled out the mini marshmallows.

By the time their drinks were ready, Laryssa walked into the room with her young son resting in her arms. She smiled at Joanne. "He was awake and wouldn't let me leave the room without him."

They made their way into the den, and Joanne stoked the dying embers back to life again while Laryssa made herself comfy on a beanbag chair next to it, the baby resting against her chest.

"You're wonderful with him, dear."

Laryssa smiled in a way only a mother could as she gazed at her little one. Her maternal bond with him evident. "I don't think I'd be half as good if I didn't have all of you helping me."

Why couldn't her own family have been like that? Working together to make things better instead of letting themselves get buried in hate from a feud that should have died eons ago? They should have been able to let things rest, make peace with the things that couldn't be changed. That's what she and Scott had tried to do, but her dad wouldn't let go.

"Do you want to talk about it?" Laryssa asked as she blew gently on her drink, making sure none of it landed on the infant.

Joanne watched the flames flicker in the fireplace, letting herself get lost in their wild dance. "I thought my ghosts were dead and gone, and that I'd made peace with it."

"The past has a way of sneaking up on you," Laryssa said. "I mean really. Who would have thought that my uncle would show up after all this time?"

"Do you think he's the real deal?"

"A part of me says yes, but a part of me feels like this is Aidan rearing his ugly head again..." She let her voice trail off. "Sorry, I don't mean to talk bad about him."

"It's all right. I know you went through a lot with him," she said, sending a small reassuring smile Laryssa's way. "With my family raising him, it's not surprising that he turned out the way he did."

"But you didn't turn out that way."

"I had my moments in my teen years where I wasn't a pleasant person to be around. I think I lost more friends than I kept."

"What changed?"

"Scott. He's the one and only person who never gave up on me. Did I ever tell you about the time he saved my life?"

Laryssa took another drink before placing it on the side table and cuddled Justin a little closer to her chest. "I don't think so."

"I'd snuck off to a party that I should never have gone to. My boyfriend at the time convinced me to go. The kid's parents were going to be out of town, so the entire school was invited. We spent the night drinking and other things I won't mention."

Laryssa's eyes widened, and her mouth formed an O shape. "You? You seem so uh..."

"Prissy?" Joanne asked with half a grin.

"I was going to say proper. So, what happened?"

"My boyfriend, Victor, wanted to leave and started to pull me toward his car. He couldn't even walk in a straight line, and me, like the stupid kid I was, went along with him. Just as I was about to climb into the car, Scott took my arm and pulled me away."

"How old were you?"

Joanne's brow furrowed as she tried to remember. "Sixteen I think."

"What happened?"

"I screamed and yelled at him to let me go, but he wouldn't. He kept telling me it wasn't safe. I continued to swear at him to let me go. Even spat in his face," she said, cringing. "I think I apologized over and over for that one later."

"Did you get in the car with the guy?"

"Thankfully, no. Victor saw Scott grab me and tried to hit him, but Scott was like this immovable mountain. Eventually Victor gave up and said, *Fine, you can have her. She sucks in bed anyway.*"

"Ouch," Laryssa hunched her shoulders and buried herself a little deeper in the beanbag chair. "That's what Aidan always used to tell me. Did you ever see that guy again?"

"Nope. He never made it home."

"Oh." There was a finality in her 'oh' that told Joanne that Laryssa understood what she meant. "I'm sorry, Mom."

"If it wouldn't have been for Scott, I would have died, too. Any time I tried to act out and do something stupid, Scott was there to stop me. My dad should have been, but he was too busy to care about what I was doing."

"Scott sounds like he was amazing."

A loving smile warmed Joanne's face as she remembered their first kiss weeks after that horrible accident. "He really was. It's because of him I learned what love was. I was so horrible to him, but he didn't bat an eyelash."

"I'm glad he was there for you."

"Me too." He'd been her lifeline. Her path out of the darkness. And he continued to be that guide, even after the accident that claimed his life. Just knowing his twins carried his blood gave her a reason to smile.

"I have always wondered, though. Did you ever remarry?" Laryssa asked.

"No. I was too focused on helping Ruth and Mitch raise Alex."

And she always felt like a family curse followed her wherever she went. First, Victor died while drunk driving and then Scott died by a drunk driver. She was a bad luck charm, and it was best to be alone. Laryssa's eyes were suddenly twinkling, and she opened her mouth to talk.

Joanne held up a hand. "Don't even think about it."

Laryssa raised her free hand, palm up. "Whatever do you mean?"

"I know that fix-me-up look, young lady."

"I thought no such thing. I was just thinking about how much fun it would be for you and I to spend a day out on the town. Make-overs, the whole works."

Joanne quirked an eyebrow. There was more to that look than just shopping. "Then what?"

Laryssa glanced down at her naked wrist and then over to the clock on the wall. "Oh, geez, will you look at the time. We better try to sleep."

"Laryssa," Joanne warned. "Don't be getting any ideas. Dating is for people in their twenties."

Getting up from the chair, her daughter-in-law walked over and kissed the top of her head. "Relax, Mom. You have nothing to worry about."

Somehow, her words didn't relax her in the slightest. She rested her hand against her forehead and groaned. "Heaven help me."

Chapter Four

While Sarah and Laryssa were upstairs with the kids, Alexander and Joanne were in the kitchen preparing breakfast.

"Have you decided what you're going to do?" Alex asked.

"About?"

"The letter."

"Oh." She'd been trying to forget about it. What was the point of going? It wasn't like she was set to inherit anything. They made that abundantly clear decades ago. "Sometimes I think I should go, but then I wonder whether I should bother."

"You should," he said, flipping over a pancake in the skillet.

"I don't trust them."

"Don't trust who?" a male voice asked from behind her.

Joanne jumped and the knife she'd been using slipped, cutting her hand. "Ouch!" She hadn't even heard Nathan coming up behind them.

Their guest raced over to look at her hand. "I'm so sorry for startling you," he said, flipping her hand this way and that as blood filled the wound. "Looks like it might need stitches. If you'd like, I can drive you to the hospital."

Joanne grabbed some paper towel that hung beside the sink and cringed in pain when she pressed it against the cut. She really had to learn to stop using sharp objects.

"You'd have a hard time parking that RV in the hospital lot," Alex said. "I'll take her, but you are welcome to tag along if you'd like." Her son reached under the sink and pulled out a first aid kit and helped wrap her hand for the trip.

"Sounds good to me," Nathan replied.

Her heart skipped a beat as his deep baritone voice made her vibrate internally. "I'm sure I'm fine," she replied. "No need to fuss over me." She didn't think she could handle sitting with Nathan for a few hours while she waited to see the doctor.

Nathan watched her eyes lower to the ground as he studied her. They told a story that he desperately wanted to understand. He wanted to smooth out the wrinkles that marred her soft skin whenever she looked at him. She was wary about something, and that bothered him. He wanted her to feel comfortable in his presence.

He tucked a strand of hair behind her ear, letting his thumb caress her cheek. "It's best to get it looked at." If there was one thing he knew, it was when someone needed stitches.

"I'll go pull the car around," Alex said, walking by Laryssa as she walked in. "We have to make a trip to the hospital."

"Why?" she asked him. Joanne held up her hand, and Laryssa rolled her eyes. "Again, Mom?"

"Shush, child!" Joanne said, admonishing her for saying anything.

"I take it this is a common occurrence?" Nathan inquired.

He chuckled when Joanne shrugged her shoulders, her cheeks turning red.

"Did you want me to come?" Laryssa asked.

"I'm more than happy to take her so you guys can finish cooking breakfast. They'd probably kick us out if we all go," Nathan said. He kind of liked the idea of spending time with Joanne, even though he'd officially come to see Laryssa.

"Mom?" Laryssa inquired again.

"I'm okay, hun. You should go spend time with your kids." Joanne looked down at her bandaged hand. "We might be a while."

Her voice was like the finest wine, smooth and delicate, but what he found most intriguing were her eyes. They held a fire that she kept under bridled control. A fire he was sure she hadn't unleashed in a long time...if the eye glances she gave him were anything to go by.

He was beginning to wish he wouldn't have waited so long to stop by, but he knew the reason he did. How do you tell the only child of your brother that you're the reason for the boat accident that killed them?

Recent revelations, though, had brought him to this point. He didn't have much time left, and he knew the past had to be made up for. Somehow. Someway. He hadn't been himself back then, and it took him forever to get his life back on track. And go figure. Just when everything was going well, another monkey wrench had to be thrown into his life-long plans.

"Come on, let's go," he said, offering his arm to Joanne.

"Are you sure you don't want me to come along?" Laryssa asked again, eyeing Nathan suspiciously.

He smiled. Laryssa obviously cared for her mother-in-law a great deal. You don't usually see the in-laws getting along. But he had a sneaky suspicion this wasn't a normal family, living the usual family life. There was a back story—a big one. And he could bet one hundred percent it revolved around Joanne.

They climbed into Alex's black Lexus and drove in silence to the Hospital. Alex and Joanne sat in the front seat, which Nathan insisted, and he sat in the back. Alex kept eyeing him in the mirror.

He had a feeling the man wouldn't hesitate to toss him on his butt if he so much as looked at his mom the wrong way. Her son was protective, and that was both unnerving and welcoming. He knew Laryssa had found a family worth being a part of.

That was something he'd given up hoping for. Who'd want him after his stupid mistake? He wasn't worth the effort. As soon as he found a way to tell Laryssa the truth, he'd be on his way because he was certain they'd toss him out on his ass once it all came to light. That didn't mean he couldn't enjoy the company of Joanne in the meantime, though. It might help him remember what happiness was like for a brief moment in time.

After about 20 minutes, they pulled up to the emergency room doors, and Alex stopped to let the two of them out, saying he was going to find a spot to park the car, and he'd meet them inside.

Nathan climbed out and then went to open Joanne's car door, offering his hand to help her.

"Thank you," she said softly as her fingers curled around his, her cheeks showing a hint of color. He smiled. There was something gentle and quiet about her. She didn't act all haughty, like a woman with a bunch of money, despite living in a mansion.

They walked into the hospital and up to the counter. "How can we help you?"

"I accidentally cut my hand with a knife while I was trying to make breakfast."

After she finished checking in, they went and sat down with the other patients, who were all waiting for their names to be called.

"I'm sorry for distracting you earlier."

"It wasn't you. I have a habit of getting startled," she said with a chuckle. "You'd think I'd learn by now not to hold anything sharp,"

"Well, I'll do my best not to startle you next time. I wouldn't want to mar your other beautiful hand," he said, brushing his hand against hers.

Again, she blushed. The color suited her. From then on, he decided to make it his mission to make her blush as often as possible.

"Then you have your work cut out for you," she replied.

He laughed. "Would you, by any chance, let me take you out to dinner to make up for my blunder?"

"Oh, I couldn't encroach on your time with Laryssa, but that's sweet of you to offer."

"Pretty please," he said, giving her puppy dog eyes. "It would be an honor to have dinner with you."

"You're a sweet talker, aren't you, Nathan?" she said, her eyes sparkling.

"I try."

She patted him on the knee. And that made him chuckle. It was something you'd normally do to placid a youngster, but he wasn't a kid.

"So, will you?"

"What?" she asked, looking up at him, like a doe caught in the headlights.

"You are so cute, you know that?" he said, laughing.

Her face turned a fire engine red. He had a feeling that she didn't receive compliments often. "I...uh," she stammered. "What did you ask me again?"

"I asked if I could take you out to dinner to make up for starling you."

"Oh, right." Joanne looked down at her wrapped hand, uncertain of exactly what to say. It had been ages since a man asked her to do anything. But that could partly be her fault, she supposed. Other than her weekly visit with her girlfriends, she really didn't get out anywhere to meet men. And what was the point? She wasn't this young, vibrant woman who could spend hours on the dance floor anymore and hadn't been for a long time.

"You'd make this man very happy if you'd accompany him," he said, resting his hand on hers.

The warmth of his touch sent a shiver through her body. And that reaction made her feel uneasy. This was Laryssa's uncle, her daughter-in-law's uncle. That had to be wrong somewhere, right?

She watched his thumb caress the back of her hand, mesmerized by the feel of it, her parts tightening in ways that she hadn't thought possible anymore. *Oh gosh.* Her mouth formed an 'o' shape. She was hot for him. Literally. It was like someone took a heater and held it up to her face.

"Joanne Richards," the nurse called.

Phew. Saved by the nurse. Or so she thought. Nathan got up to follow her inside. Alex came in the door at the same time and was going to follow them inside.

"Please wait out here," the nurse told them, escorting her inside the tiny examining room. The woman took her weight and then checked her vitals again. Her lips pulled to one side. "Do you usually have high blood pressure?" she asked.

Joanne shook her head. She'd always been known for having low blood pressure. Well, it was a little higher now that she was older, but nothing abnormal. She looked over at Nathan sitting in the chair beside her son. Was it a coincidence that it went up when he arrived?

"Do you want to tell me what happened?" the nurse asked.

"Just me being clumsy," she said, desperately wishing that someone would turn on the air conditioner. "Do you think it needs stitches?"

That's the last thing she wanted, especially when they had such a busy household. She'd feel so useless with her hand wrapped. The knife sliced the fatty part of her hand between her thumb and index finger.

"It's possible. Do you want some numbing gel just in case?"

"Yes, please."

The nurse applied the gel and then put clear plastic wrap over the top. "Hopefully, the doctor won't take too long to see you."

"Thank you."

"Feel free to have a seat on a chair out in the hall."

"Can't I stay here?" she asked, not wanting to make a fool of herself with Nathan.

"Afraid not," the nurse said, pulling open the curtain.

Joanne glanced out the door, and Nathan turned to look at her, her nerves automatically tickling her senses, like a warm breeze on a summer day, making her shiver. Should she go to dinner with Nathan? The answer was still unclear in her mind.

Knowing she had no choice but to leave the room, she got up and walked toward the two men. Nathan automatically stood up when she got close, and he helped her into the chair. Not that she needed it.

"What'd they say?" he asked.

"Not much. I have to wait for the doctor. Did you guys want to go get coffee or something? It could be a while."

"I say she is trying to get rid of us," Alex said jokingly as he looked over at Nathan.

Joanne lightly bopped him on the shoulder and hushed him.

He laughed. "Did you want anything, Mom?"

"I'm good but thank you."

Letting out a breath, she almost sighed in relief when her son stood up. "Would you mind staying with my mom?" Alex asked Nathan.

"I'm f..." Joanne started to protest, but her son cast her a look, and she stopped talking. He had that usual stubborn look of determination. One she never usually won against because he knew how to get what he wanted. That determination served him well in the family business, where he was the boss.

"I'm not leaving you here alone, and I know the area better than Nathan. I'll be back soon."

Joanne slumped in her seat. As much as she loved the company of a handsome man, he made her body act like a stranger, and she didn't like it.

"So, about my earlier question."

His words opened the fountain inside her, deep in her womanhood. A spot she preferred to stay asleep. Life was complex enough already. Joanne shifted uncomfortably on her chair, an unfamiliar burn pulsating between her thighs. She'd almost forgotten what it felt like to be aroused. And she didn't like it was happening now, in a hospital of all places, with a man that looked like he could grace the cover of a magazine as the sexiest silver fox alive.

Joanne shook her head, trying to get the spicy thoughts out of her head. She wasn't sixteen years old anymore. "What about your question?" she asked, swallowing hard.

"Come to dinner with me. I promise to treat you like a queen."

She had to laugh. She could remember her son trying to convince

Laryssa to go out to dinner, too. The two of them had had a rough ride, but it worked out amazing in the end for them. But those years had passed for her. She had married once, and in her mind, it was for life. He was her one and only.

"I'll get you back in time for bed."

The minute he said the word, an image of the two of them in bed popped into her head, and she had to fan herself. *Oh dear!* She really was losing it, and she hadn't even hit her head. Maybe the doctor should do a CT scan or something.

"Fine, I'll go to dinner. Just, please, don't say the word bed."

He let out a deep, sexy chuckle. She could almost feel the rumble in her chest as the butterflies in her stomach flapped viciously.

He leaned in closer. "Bed," he whispered, his breath tickling the hairs on her neck.

Joanne shivered deliciously.

Oh, my dear sweet heavens!

She was in trouble.

Chapter Five

Joanne stood in the middle of her bedroom with her hands on her hips, clothes littering the floor and the double bed. She couldn't even see the bedspread. Nothing seemed suitable. What do you wear on a dinner date?

Oh gosh.

A date...with a man. Her?

It felt strange, like it wasn't really happening. Maybe that's why she couldn't figure out what to wear. She needed help because she could swear her brain lost a few brain cells, but she wasn't due to meet with her girlfriends for a few days. Picking up her cell, she dialed Colleen's number.

"I know you're likely busy with the grandkids, but I need your help," Joanne said quickly.

Her friend wasted no time responding. "Your house or mine?"

"Mine." She'd never felt so disorganized in her life. Finding something to wear was not normally a challenge for her. She often would grab whatever clean outfit was on the hook, but she was drawing a blank. Should she put on makeup? What about her hair?

Her stomach screamed in discomfort, making her race to the

bathroom. Maybe this was a bad idea? Why should they go out when she could whip something up here? She'd rather be in the comfort of her home than out in public, where she could embarrass herself. Here, if necessary, there was always her family to intervene.

Another hour passed, and she still hadn't gotten any closer to solving her dilemma when her friend, Colleen, breezed in through her bedroom door.

"Have no fear. Colleen is here!" she said, pulling her light blue silk shawl off her head, resting it on her shoulders. It meshed nicely with her white and blue pantsuit. "What's the problem, hun?"

"I have a date."

Her friend's eyes widened as she fanned her face. "Oh, my word, I was waiting for this day. The others said it would never happen."

Joanne placed her hands on her hips, pretending to glare at her. "Gee, thanks."

"Sharon and Grace are on their way over."

"But I never called them." She didn't want the whole troop there. Not for this.

"No, but I did," Colleen said, grinning. "And I'm glad I did. This is a huge deal. It's not every day our prim and proper friend has a date."

Joanne's face heated. "Oh, shush!"

"So, what's he like? Is he that handsome man in the living room?"

She reddened even more.

"I take that as a yes. Okay, let's see what you have here." Colleen wandered over to the bed and picked her way through the pile. "Nope. Nope. Nope. What else you got?"

"Other than these, I only have a few dresses stuffed in the back of my closet that I haven't worn in years."

Her friend moved toward the nearly empty closet, but Joanne stopped her. "The last thing I want to do is give him any more ideas."

"He has designs on your body already, eh?"

That and then some! But she wasn't going to let her friend know that. She didn't want to be the talk of the honey hive—a group of older women who got together once a month and to chat about books and gossip. One of their members got nicknamed Cougar because she had a habit of attracting younger men. Joanne, though, was quite happy blending into the background.

"Perfect." Colleen clapped her hands with glee.

She crossed her arms over her stomach, butterflies fluttering away. "No! Not perfect."

Her friend pointed to the closet again, determined to get inside. Eventually, Joanne stepped aside to let her check out the dresses in the back. She doubted she'd fit into any of them.

She cringed as the hangers scraped against the rod. It was almost as bad as nails on a chalkboard. Her friend let out a squeal when she pulled out a sexy red number.

Joanne held up her hands, palms out. "Oh no. No way."

"At least try it on." Colleen shoved it toward her as her other friends walked in.

"Oh my gosh. We haven't seen that on you in years," Sharon said, eyes sparkling.

"Ya, not since I was like thirty-five."

"Who's the hot guy downstairs?" Grace asked. She was the youngest of their group and still very much active in the dating department. She was the only one who never got married, but that's because she loved the lifestyle of fleeting from one man to the next.

"That's her date," Colleen announced.

Grace let out a low whistle. "You scored a sexy one. If things don't work out, let me know."

"There is nothing to work out. We're going out for dinner because of this!" Joanne held up her bandaged hand.

"He hurt you?" Sharon asked, her eyes narrowing.

"He startled me by accident when I was preparing breakfast, and well, you know me."

Grace rolled her eyes. "I think you need to start watching more horror movies, so you get used to the jump scares."

Joanne pointed a finger at her friend. "Don't you dare suggest a movie to him." She'd never survive in a movie theater. Dark corners were where people did naughty things, and her sitting next to him would have her thinking all about stuff she used to do.

"That's a great idea," Sharon said. "The new IT movie is playing."

"Oh, heck no. No. No. No." Joanne shook her head.

"If you shake your head any faster, it's going to fall off," Colleen observed, laughing.

She clasped her hands together in a prayer-like fashion against her chest, begging them to play nice. "Will you guys just help me decide what to wear, please? Something that will not make him want to rip it off me."

Sharon grinned. "If you didn't want him to rip it off, you wouldn't have called us."

"Shushy, shush, shush!" Joanne groaned as she flopped back on the bed. This was not going as planned. She should have put on her black two-piece and have been done with it.

"Stop being so uptight for once and let yourself have some fun," Grace said, shoving the clothes off the end of the bed so she could sit down.

"My body is in no shape for fun."

"Honey, cleaning this house has kept you in better shape than any of us," Sharon pointed out.

"You girls aren't helping." Joanne picked up a pillow and covered her face. The thought of him taking her clothes off was already making her heat up down below. She was quite happy when her body went dormant because she was able to focus on other things instead of sex. Now, it decided to wake up, and she wanted to shut it off.

"Girl, you aren't going to live forever. It's time to show the world what you've got while you've still got it," Colleen said, holding out the dress.

"But I don't got it. I haven't had *it* since my accident."

"Oh, pish tosh," Grace said, pulling Joanne up off the bed.

"You've always had it. You just stopped believing it. Now get dressed."

Joanne stared at the full-length red sequin dress in Colleen's hands. "But I can't wear heels."

"Stop making excuses. You didn't wear heels the last time you wore it either," Sharon said, shoving her toward the bathroom.

Sighing, Joanne disappeared into the bathroom and shut the door. She held up the dress and frowned. Maybe it wouldn't fit. Taking off her shirt and pants, she stepped into the dress and pulled it up, slipping her arms into the sleeves.

It was slightly tighter than before, but nothing outrageously so. The girls would have to pull up the zipper, though, as her arms didn't bend that way anymore. Joanne turned toward the mirror and tilted her head as she studied her appearance.

"Holy mother of God. Please tell me my face wasn't that red in front of them." She covered her face with her hands. *How embarrassing.* They knew her as the calm and collected one. The one that everyone could come to for advice. Now she was standing there in a dress made for women in their thirties. Could she wear the dress out in public? People knew that red was a color associated with luck and sensuality, worn by someone hoping for more than just a romantic dinner encounter. She couldn't do it, couldn't wear it.

"Can't you girls pick something else out?" she yelled from the bathroom.

"Come out. Let us see you," Colleen yelled back.

Biting her bottom lip, Joanne stepped into the limelight, desperately wanting to go back into hiding.

"Oh momma, you look fine!" Grace said gleefully, covering her mouth with her hands.

"I can't wear this. He's gonna think I'm a hussy. A floozy."

"Or he might think you are the sexiest woman alive," Sharon said.

"Please. I'm sixty-one years old. Who's sexy at sixty-one?"

"The man downstairs," Grace said without hesitation. "You have to match his sexiness. You'll be the talk of the town."

"But I don't want to be. I just want to eat dinner and come home."

Grace held up her hand and did a little spin with her wrist. "Turn around so I can do up your dress."

"You guys are really going to make me do this, aren't you?"

"One of us has to live," Sharon said. "I haven't had a date in forever."

"Well, duh, girl, you're married," Joanne huffed, but she turned around as she was told. This was not her plan. How was she supposed to look at him, knowing what was going to be going through his mind?

"What time is the date?" Colleen asked, looking at her watch.

"Our reservations are for six tonight."

"So, a little bit of time to get your hair and make-up done."

"Isn't the dress enough?" Joanne whined.

"Nope," the three women said in unison.

"If I get lipstick on my teeth, I'm going to blame you."

Colleen grabbed Joanne's arm and pulled her to the vanity dresser, sitting her in the chair. "Suits us just fine."

Nathan sat with Alex and Laryssa in the living room. "Maybe we should join you for dinner," Laryssa said, taking her husband's hand in hers.

"Excuse us, while I talk with my wife," Alex said as he pulled them to standing. This was the first time he'd ever seen his mother go on an outing that wasn't with a woman from her group. She needed a little freedom from them all.

"You can't seriously be okay with her going out with Nathan?" Laryssa said, placing her hands on her hips. "We don't even know him."

"This is the first time my mother has been on a date for as long as I've known her."

"Don't you want her to go out with someone you know instead, then? I don't think I'd be okay with my mom going out with a strange man."

"Isn't that what most dates are? Two people who don't know each other going out to get to know each other."

Laryssa stuck her tongue out at him. "Alright, mr. smarty pants. But I still say that we should go with them."

"Would you want a chaperone on our dates?"

"Aren't you supposed to be like the protective son or something?"

In most cases, he would be, but he hadn't seen her eyes sparkle and twinkle like that in a long time. And he had a feeling Nathan wasn't a bad guy. He also knew that he couldn't keep her locked away in his home forever. She deserved to find happiness of her own.

"Our chauffeur is driving them. I've asked him to keep an eye out," Alex said.

His wife let out a breath of relief. "And here I was, beginning to think you didn't care."

Alex pulled Laryssa into his arms, nuzzling her neck. "If he has half the wayward thoughts that I did and still do, I'd be crazy not to send someone. But I don't plan to share our night with anyone."

"Our night?"

"Yes. Don't you think it's time to add another addition to our family?"

Laryssa pulled back and put the desk between them. "Are you nuts? Justin is only a few months old."

"Truth is, I want to feel myself inside you," he said, walking around the desk toward her, like a predator stalking his prey. "Bare and free."

"Nu uh. I'm not getting pregnant so soon."

"We can always try the pull-out method."

She quirked an eyebrow at him as he neared her. "Nice try, bud. But he stays sheathed for now."

Alex groaned. Having sex with a condom took away half the fun. There was nothing like gliding into a woman, warm and wet as she closed around him. Just thinking about it was enough for his member to harden. Moving a little faster, he caught her arm, and she laughed as she struggled to get away but no such luck. He lifted her up, sitting her on his office desk.

"We have a man to interrogate," she said half-heartedly when his hands slipped under her blouse, playing with her breasts.

"I imagine my mom is going to take another twenty minutes to get ready. We have time."

"But he's in the other room," she said with a moan when he ran his thumb over her sensitized nipple.

"Then I guess we better be quiet."

"Alex."

He pressed a knee between her legs to open them and moved in between them, letting his other hand press up against her mound through her clothes. This was his favorite thing to do with her, and he'd do it more often if they could. But with three kids, it was rarer than he'd like. They had to sneak a few moments here and there when they had the chance.

And right here, right now, was one of those moments. And after waiting six weeks to have sex when Justin was born, he had a lot of time to make up for.

Grabbing her hips, he pulled her to the edge of the table, tight against his cock. She was still the most beautiful woman in his world and had the ability to turn him on merely by walking into the room. He hoped his reaction never grew old, and that they'd still be lighting up each other's worlds when he got to be as old as his mom.

Laryssa reached for his zipper and pulled it down, touching his straining cock. "I love knowing I still turn you on." She let her finger run the length of him.

Just when he was about to suggest that they move on to round two, they heard his name being called.

"Alex?" Joanne called again.

"Mommy calls," Laryssa said, straightening out her clothes.

"No fair!"

His wife laughed, patting his erection. "Poor, baby. Don't worry. I'll make it up to you later."

She hopped off the desk and started to walk by him. He growled, tapping her on the ass. Laryssa shrieked and raced toward the door, giggling.

"Women!" he grumbled good-naturedly. Maybe they would eventually get another man in the house, and he wouldn't be so outnumbered.

Walking back into the living room, Alex stopped in his tracks, his jaw dropping. His mother was standing there in a formal gown that accentuated her figure. When he turned to look at Nathan, he appeared to be speechless, too. The look of a hungry predator flashed in the man's eyes, making Alex suddenly weary.

"Well, how do I look?"

Chapter Six

Sweat beaded under her armpits as she waited for everyone to respond, but they stood there in what looked like shock. "Geesh, I must look hideous."

"Of course not, Mom." Laryssa rolled her eyes at the men. "You look breath-taking. I didn't even know you had a dress like that."

Behind Joanne, her three friends gathered with amused expressions on their faces. "See! We told you it would do the trick," Grace whispered.

"We'll show ourselves out," Colleen said, taking the other two women by the hand and guiding them to the door. "Have fun, Joanne."

She resisted the urge to stick her tongue out at them. Maturity and sophistication were her plans for the evening. "I wish you guys would say something at least," she begged.

Laryssa leaned toward her, kissing her on the cheek. "Be careful."

"Always."

"I've put pepper spray in your purse just in case," Laryssa stated.

"I'd rather not go to jail tonight, my dear." But with the way Nathan was looking at her, pepper spray may definitely be needed.

Alex called for the driver to bring the car around and gave his mom a hug. "If you have any trouble, please call me."

"I'm sure I'll be fine. It's not like he's taking me to the black lagoon."

Concern marred Alex's brow.

She smoothed his worry lines and gave him a kiss on the forehead. "Don't worry."

She sounded braver than she looked and for that, she was grateful. But inside, she was trembling, and she wasn't sure whether it was from excitement or dread, or a mixture of both. It was her first date in decades, and it felt both wrong and right at the same time.

Nathan finally gathered his bearings and walked over to her, offering his arm. "Ready, beautiful?"

Joanne ducked her head to hide her face, which she knew would show her embarrassment from the nickname. She wasn't beautiful. She was just her. A woman not even her own father and mother could love.

She knew Alex's family loved her, but her own parents hadn't been able to. And that still drilled a hole in her heart. What did she do that was so wrong? All she did was care about someone who made her feel like she mattered. Someone who didn't care about family feuds or hate. Scott didn't have a hateful bone in his body, except for those that tried to do her wrong.

Joanne's eyes misted as the recently placed picture of Scott resting on the mantel caught her eye. Did he approve of her date, or was he churning in his grave? Maybe she should have fought against it a little more. She began to question her acceptance and backed away from Nathan.

"What's wrong?" he asked.

"I'm not so sure about this," she answered honestly.

"Don't worry, hun. We're just two friends going out and having fun," he replied, bringing her hand to his lips to kiss it.

"Friends don't do that," she whispered.

"I'll be honorable. I promise," he said, crossing his fingers over his heart.

Her family stood back and watched the exchange. She kind of hoped they would butt in and tell her not to go, so she'd have an excuse to change her mind. But they didn't.

Joanne looked up at Nathan, losing herself in his yummy chocolate eyes. "Promise?"

"Yes." After saying that, he placed her arm in his, and they began their trek to the door.

"I have eyes everywhere, Nathan," Alex warned.

Nathan smiled at him. "I'll treat her as though she's the most precious jewel in the world. You have my word."

Finally, they stepped outside the door and into Alex's car. They rarely drove around with a chauffeur, so Joanne had a feeling that Alex placed him there to watch out for her. The two of them settled into the backseat, and the driver waited until they put on their seatbelts before putting the car in drive.

"I didn't want to say this inside, but you look absolutely ravishing tonight."

"You don't look half bad yourself," she replied. He wore a nice three-piece jet-black suit, with a sky-blue dress shirt. But what caught her attention the most were his eyes. They were intense as they stared at her, making her insides roar like the ocean waves. It left her a little unsettled, so she moved closer to the door and was grateful when he didn't try to close the distance again.

"I take it this is the first time you've been out in a while?" he asked with amusement and genuine curiosity.

"You could say that." The last time she went out was with her female friends. They went to the Silver Mountain Club last week. Guy dates were non-existent.

"Do you remember how to dance?"

"I'm afraid my leg doesn't allow me to dance much," she said.

"Do you mind if I ask what happened?"

Yes. She did mind. The memories were already too close to the surface, and she didn't relish the idea of stirring up the dirt again. Every time the memories surfaced, so did her bad dreams, like ghosts in a closet.

"I was in a bad car accident when I was young."

That's all she chose to say. He didn't need to hear her whole sordid life story, and thankfully he didn't press for more details. She was grateful for the momentary silence which allowed her to gather her thoughts and her body, which was still trying to run away from her as he sat there, with his woodsy marine scented cologne drifting her way.

He smelled better than the sea breeze that she loved so much. Had her friends told him she loved the sea? She wouldn't be surprised if they slipped him that info when she wasn't looking.

"Where are we going?" she asked.

"I know a place down by the water from when I was here last," he said.

"But if you've been to Vancouver before, why haven't you stopped in to see us?"

His lips snapped shut, and he turned to look out the window. It would seem they each had a story they'd rather not share. But given that he'd respected her wishes, she gave him space. She itched to know more about him because she knew that if a family member of hers was in the foster care system, she'd do whatever she could to make sure they came to live with family, and not some stranger. But he allowed Laryssa to grow up in the system.

She studied his profile as they drove down the road. He had a softness about him, yet the pain in his eyes spoke of a deep routed pain that he himself had to bear. That was something she could relate to.

"Your son looks very happy," Nathan said out of the blue when he turned back to look at her.

"Very much so. I thank Laryssa for that."

"They have the three kids, right?"

"Well, technically speaking, they have one. Justin. The twins belong to his brother, Aidan."

He turned in his seat, resting his right leg on the cushion between them, his eyebrows raised. "Well, that doesn't happen every day."

Joanne gave a sad chuckle. She hadn't planned on going into details, but he sucked that one out of her. "Nope."

"I'm sensing a convoluted story here."

"You, sir, have no idea."

"I like the sound of that *sir*," he said, winking.

The car pulled into Stanley Park, the road twisting this way and that as they drove up to a fancy restaurant on the hill overlooking the beach. She always had dreamed of walking the Seawall, but that was not in the cards with her leg.

Walking into the restaurant, they stood at the entrance while they waited for the hostess to return. This was the type of place that you brought someone who you were hoping to romance into your bed. Across the room, there was a fancy gold and marble countertop bar. The candle-shaped chandeliers hanging over each linen-covered table brought a certain romantic allure to the place, providing just enough light to walk and read a menu.

There were no families to be seen, only couples. Phones were tucked away as they focused on each other. The same way her date was focusing on her right now. What was going through his mind as he looked at her?

"I'm the luckiest man here," he said. She blushed in response.

Nathan could hardly believe he was standing by her side. He thought for certain she would back out. There were moments during their drive that he had thought she'd get the driver to turn around, but she didn't.

He smiled as he let his gaze take in the full sight of her, not phased in the slightest by the scar on her cheek; it added a certain intrigue to her beauty. Maybe it was because she hadn't let it destroy who she was inside. A warm, bright and funny woman who left him wanting in ways he hadn't expected. All he had planned to do was come and talk to Laryssa until he met Joanne. Now, spending time with this delightful beauty had become important, too.

Nathan wasn't under any delusion that it would develop into anything, especially not when he revealed the news of his past. Once he spilled the whole truth, they'd probably have him escorted off the property by the police. He knew he had changed a lot over the years and wasn't the man he used to be, but his past still trailed along with him wherever he went.

The biggest question that remained was whether Laryssa was his child or his brother's. He couldn't leave the world not knowing the truth. But how the heck was he supposed to broach that topic? Was he just supposed to say, 'hi, ya, there is a possibility I might be your dad'?

People usually spend their entire life believing certain facts, and it never goes well when they find out it was all a lie. When his brother found out Laryssa might not be his, he was devastated, and look how that ended up.

He didn't want that to happen to Laryssa. Maybe he could steal a piece of her hair and get it sampled, so he wouldn't have to reveal any sordid details. She only had a few memories of her parents, and who was he to spoil them? He grimaced.

"What are you thinking so hard about?" Joanne asked him.

"Nothing really. Just dazzled by your beauty."

"Mhmm," she replied, giving him a disbelieving look.

It was too heavy of a topic to delve into on a night like tonight. He wanted to be able to enjoy her company before everything went nuts.

"Right this way," their hostess said, finally returning to the front where they were waiting.

He held out his arm to Joanne, and she willingly took it, smiling up at him. She was a few inches shorter than he was. Her brown and gray hair had been swept up into a loose bun, and she wore a very subtle pink lipstick.

The hostess stopped at a corner booth, placing two menus on the table. They sat across from each other.

"Can I get you anything to drink to start off?"

"Water, please," Joanne said.

"I'll take a coffee."

"I'm surprised you didn't order a beer," she said with a half-grin.

He strummed his long fingers on the table, trying to figure out how to answer her comment that didn't open up another discussion about his past. Man, he hadn't realized how ashamed he was of who he used to be. No matter what thought came to his head, it always seemed to lead to something he wanted to forget.

"I'm finding as I get older, my stomach doesn't handle alcohol like it used to."

Her eyes brightened, and a smile broke across her cheeks. "That's such a relief to hear. I've hated drinking ever since..." She let her voice trail off as she quickly picked up the menu, hiding her face. "I wonder what's good here."

He reached out and slowly lowered the menu so he could see her. "Are you okay, Joanne?"

She placed the menu on the table and sighed, her eyes losing a little of their usual twinkle. "You know how I was talking about my accident?"

"The one that injured your leg?"

She nodded. "We were hit by a drunk driver, and my husband was killed."

He let out a long breath with a slight whistle. Wow, talk about heavy dinner talk. "I'm sorry for your loss."

"You know. Sometimes I wish people could find a different response for a change," she mumbled, picking up her menu again.

"Sounds like you hear that a lot."

"More times than I cared to hear. It's usually what people say when they can't think of anything else."

"I'm so—" He closed his mouth when she frowned at him. "Let's start this evening again, shall we? Hi, I'm Nathan," he said, holding out his hand.

"Joanne," she said, sending a tender smile his way as she placed her hand in his. His fingers wrapped around hers, and he brought them to rest on the table, keeping a firm grip on it, not letting her pull away.

"It's a pleasure to make your acquaintance," he continued. There it was. A little bit of that sparkle came back into her eyes, and it set his insides ablaze.

"This is so silly," Joanne said.

"Well, then we'll be silly. I think we've lived long enough to get away with it," he said, winking at her.

She giggled, giving her head a quick shake. "You really are something, Nathan Mitchell."

He locked eyes with her while he played with her palm. Her pupils dilated, and her cheeks glowed a healthy pink color.

"I'm glad you think so," he said.

"Uh, shouldn't we be looking at the menu?"

"I am."

She pulled her hand away and hid her face behind the menu again. "Sir, I'm not a dinner choice."

"I think you could be a very delectable choice."

Joanne wished he didn't have that rumbling baritone voice. It echoed through her system, like bass from a subwoofer. "Our waitress will be back soon."

He chuckled, obviously loving her discomfort. She couldn't understand how her body could react to someone she had just met when it had been dead for years. Heck, she thought her libido died with Scott.

Nathan kind of reminded her of him. He had much of the same demeanour, and he even looked like how she imagined Scott would have looked if they had been given the chance to grow old together. She lowered the menu so that her forearms rested on the table.

"You've got that *I'm thinking* wrinkle between your eyes again," Nathan commented.

"You remind me so much of my husband," she said and then

snapped her lips closed before she said any more. She hadn't meant to say that.

"He must have meant a lot to you."

The tears that filled her eyes surprised her. "He was my world."

Nathan pulled the hankey from his pocket and handed it to her. "He was a very lucky guy."

It was a once in a lifetime love. At least, that's what she'd thought at the time, especially when she couldn't seem to get aroused by anyone but him. Mind you, she hadn't meshed with anyone romantically since then, either. Although, that was possibly because she never gave anyone a chance. She'd been too busy with her family.

"Oh look, our waitress is coming back," she said.

And she hadn't even read a single thing on the menu.

Chapter Seven

It took a while, but they finally ordered their food and had it delivered to the table. Nathan ordered a typical guy meal with steak while Joanne ordered a chicken parmesan.

"It smells incredible," she said when they placed it in front of her. She was glad to have something else to keep her hands occupied.

"The steak is cooked beautifully," he said as he cut into it with his steak knife. "This restaurant has never failed to impress me yet."

The amount of food on the plate impressed her. Usually, expensive restaurants give you a piddly amount for a ridiculous price. "I'm beginning to think I should have ordered the senior portion. I doubt I'll be able to finish this whole plate."

"Well, that might call for a nightcap in my trailer then."

Joanne giggled nervously as she looked at the nearby tables, wondering if they had heard him. The couples showed no indication that they were even paying attention to their discussion, which was surprising considering all his sexual innuendos.

"How long do you plan on staying in the Lower Mainland for?" she asked, trying to keep off the topic.

"I haven't quite decided yet. That's the one joy of living in an RV.

Freedom to go or stay for as long as you like." He stopped for a moment to take a bite of his dinner, then started again. "Tell me, if there was one thing that you could do—one thing on your bucket list —what would it be?"

She sat back in the booth and contemplated her answer, happy to have a new topic to discuss. There were a lot of things she wanted to do, but never found the time to do.

"I'd love to do a cross-country trip in the United States. There are so many things to do and see."

"Ever been to the States?"

"Not in years."

"I could take you."

"That's sweet of you to offer, but I can't take off on my family. They need me."

Nathan finished chewing another piece of his steak, not taking his eyes off her. She couldn't seem to stop looking at him either, watching as his tongue swept across his bottom lip, sweeping away the juicy steak morsels that remained.

"I think they are more self-sufficient than you think. Come on, it would be fun."

"I couldn't do that. We just met. What would people think?"

"That we're two old geezers that deserve to have some fun?" he said, scooping up some potatoes and holding them near his lips, grinning.

"Hey, speak for yourself."

Nathan laughed. "We do deserve to have fun, though, don't we?"

"I couldn't, even if I wanted to."

"Why not?"

She cleared her throat as she tried to come up with another excuse. "I don't have time. I have to go to a reading of my mother's will in a few weeks."

"I could take you."

She could have face palmed herself. She walked right into that one. Now what was she supposed to say? Who runs off with a man they recently met? Glancing up at him, she studied his deep brown eyes, searching for any sign of deceit or malice.

His eyes were soft, and his smile was warm. He was leaning back against the cushion in the booth, seemingly without a care in the word. Relaxed was the only word that came to mind when she looked at him—other than the electricity that crackled between them.

Joanne cleared her throat and focused once again on her food. "I couldn't impose."

"No imposition at all. I'd be quite happy to help you out."

"Why?"

"Because I like to help," he said. "And I won't lie. I want to get to know you better, and this seems like the perfect way to do that."

Joanne dug her fork into her pilaf rice and took a bite, contemplating how she should answer. She didn't want to be rude and turn down his kind request, but she also didn't want to come across as stupid and naïve by accepting.

Slowly, she chewed her food as thoughts raced back and forth between her synapses. He was handsome, with his gray hair brushed immaculately to the side, and the mustache that added extra sophistication to his look. There was an air of confidence about him. He was a man who knew what he wanted and wasn't afraid to go after it. And she was certain he knew how to please a woman with hands that had years of experience.

"I can't do it, not yet."

Nathan looked down at his digital watch. "Well, I guess I have at least a week to convince you before it gets too late to leave."

Her heart did a triple flip before coming back down for a landing. "You plan to stay a week?"

"I don't really have any other place to be."

She couldn't understand how a man had so much freedom. What did he do for work? Was he retired? Didn't he have other family members to visit? "What about your family?"

"You mean like a wife?"

Her mouth formed an 'o' as she dropped her fork onto the table. "Oh gosh! Are you married?"

Nathan let out a deep chuckle, and her face burned with embarrassment. Why the heck hadn't she asked that before they went out?

"I wouldn't be out with you if I was."

Joanne pressed a hand to her chest and let out a visible sigh of relief. "Don't do that to me."

"So, you *were* hoping this was a date?"

"Honestly, I didn't know what this dinner was going to be," she replied with a shy smile, her heart still galloping along.

"Well, your first inclination was right. It is a date."

Joanne once again busied herself with her food. A regular conversation was easy to have. But how do you have a conversation with someone you might be interested in? Was she interested?

Her body appeared to be, and she found herself wondering what it might be like if the date went a little further than dinner. Joanne shook her head, trying to clear away the wayward thoughts and images in her mind.

"What are you thinking right now?"

"I think I'll keep my thoughts to myself," she murmured.

A bed-like smile spread across his lips. "I bet I can guess."

Joanne frantically looked around the room, her insides bubbling like mad. "Don't you dare."

"Why not?"

"Because it's...it's not appropriate."

Nathan pushed back his near empty plate and folded his arms, resting his elbows on the table. "Are you always appropriate, Ms. Richards?"

She growled under her breath. She was so tired of everyone thinking she was a goody goody. But in a way, she supposed she was. Being a caregiver always had a way of doing that to you. Oh dear, was she boring?

Her life had once again become one of diapers, bottles, and kids. And she was still learning how to be Joanne, the mother of Alex and not Joanne, the housekeeper. It almost filled her with an identity crisis. She wasn't even sure how to be a woman anymore.

That's it. She made her decision, then and there. Placing her fork down on her plate, which was only about half empty, she folded her arms across her chest. "Okay."

"Okay?" he asked, lifting an eyebrow.

"Let's do it."

"You need to be more specific, hun."

"I'll go with you cross-country. It'll be cheaper than flying anyway and less nerve-wrecking." Okay. She wasn't sure about the last part, but she wouldn't have to worry about turbulence. However, when heat flared in Nathan's eyes, she realized that the ride with him might be even more interesting than a seat on the plane. "On two conditions?" she said.

"Anything."

"Don't tell my son yet, and I need my own bed." She dropped her shaking hands to her lap and fought to keep control of the rest of her body. The very idea of going with him placed a very naked image of him in her head.

The vague smirk on his face told her he knew exactly what she was thinking. "While my bed is big enough for us both and as much fun as I know that would be, the table folds down into another bed if you so desire to sleep alone."

Her womanhood screamed in protest, begging her to remember what joining with a man felt like. The Passion. The moaning. The feel of their cock sliding in and out, hitting her sweet spot. She groaned again, and her cheeks heated.

By the look in his eyes, he knew exactly what she was thinking about. She wanted to bury her head in the sand. "Sounds good, thanks."

"If you change your mind, my bed would welcome you."

"The table will be fine."

"That might not be very comfortable for what I have in mind."

"Now I know what they mean when they say one's mind is in the nutter." Her eyes widened in horror. "I-I mean gutter."

Nathan laughed and smacked his hand on the table. "You, my dear, are priceless."

"Shush," she whispered as she looked around at the nearby tables. "Everyone is staring."

"Ah, let them stare. I'm having a blast."

Didn't people know it was rude to stare? One look at her, and everyone would know what they were talking about. Now she was wishing she wore her hair down instead of up so she could hide her face.

"Don't be embarrassed, sweetheart. It's a natural discussion."

"It's bedroom talk."

"We could always continue it in my bedroom."

"I'm...uh...going to go powder my nose." She needed to find a way to cool off, and that meant taking a break from her handsome, charming date. Without waiting for his response, she got up and moved across the restaurant toward the washroom. She hoped she was going the right way, because she'd be embarrassed if she had to go back the other way and cross his path again.

Joanne crashed into the bathroom door, shoving it open. It almost hit the woman behind it who jumped out of the way. "Oh my gosh. I'm so sorry. Are you okay?"

She was a tall, skinny, and to-die for blond. "Trying to escape, are you?"

"Is it that obvious?" Joanne asked her.

"I could feel the intensity between the two of you all the way across the room."

Joanne raised her head toward the ceiling and groaned. "And here I thought I was handling it okay."

"Girl, if you had a handle on it with a guy like that, you'd have hormones of steel. Want my advice?"

The woman appeared to be in her early thirties. She wore a short black number, her blond hair curling around her shoulders. She had the look that told Joanne she'd had a lot of conquests in her short lifetime.

Joanne gave a slight nod of her head as she headed over to the sink to tidy up. Her hands were sticky from eating.

"Don't forget to breathe."

Joanne laughed. "Duly noted."

Even now, she struggled to take a deep breath. He kept robbing her of it. His smile. His eyes. Even his hands as his fingers flexed on his fork.

"It should be a sin to be that handsome," the woman said.

"Don't I know it."

"Just go out there knowing your own worth, and you'll have him eating out of your palm before you know it."

Joanne glanced down at her hand, which tingled the minute she thought about his lips against her skin. *Oh, holy gosh.* Sweat droplets formed under her armpits as she fanned herself. Her body's heat thermostat had to be broken.

The lady laughed. "Have fun."

"Gee, thanks," Joanne said sarcastically. Wasn't she supposed to be able to control herself by now? After spending so many years alone, she thought that was something she had perfected.

Within twenty-four hours, that man had turned her world upside down. And it should have had her running for the hills, but instead, she washed her face with cold water and returned to their table, where he had been waiting for her patiently.

On one hand, she had hoped he would follow her into the bathroom; but her other half berated her dirty mind for thinking that way. What woman nearing retirement would make out in a public restroom? Shaking her head again, she took her seat across from him and met his knowing gaze.

"A little bit hot, were you?"

"Shush up," she muttered.

That made him do a deep husky laugh, which made her insides

giddy. She felt very much like a young girl again, discovering things about her body she'd forgotten existed.

"Stop it!"

"What?" he asked, his voice filled with a fake innocence.

"Being a guy."

"Oh, I didn't know you swung the other way."

Joanne smacked her forehead. She was not winning this conversation. Instead, she was putting her foot in her mouth. Never in her life had she had such a strange conversation.

"I...uh...I'm—"

"Don't worry, I'm just joshing with ya."

"Now that's a phrase I haven't heard in a while. Are you older than you look, Nathan?" Happy to turn the joke back around on him.

"Regardless of how old I might be, everything still works."

"Good to know," she murmured. Now she was going to be envisioning his manhood all night.

"Come on, let's dance."

Chapter Eight

With her leg throbbing from an evening out, Joanne shoved her key in the lock and opened the door, then turned to face Nathan. "Are you sure you don't want to sleep inside? It's chilly tonight."

"Are you inviting me into your bed?" he asked.

She went to answer him when the door flung open behind her, and Alex's tall frame filled the doorway.

"No, she isn't," he replied, his eyes glowing with distaste, as he pulled his mom into his protective arms. "Good night, Nathan."

"Alex, don't be rude," Joanne admonished, pulling away from him. "Go back inside. I'll be there in a minute."

"But—"

She gave her best *don't give me any trouble* look. "I'll be fine. Now scoot."

He looked between the two of them, his lips pressing into a firm line. The last thing she wanted was a fight, and she knew Alex would protect her from anything he perceived to be a danger. And right now, that appeared to be Nathan.

But after spending the evening with him, she couldn't help but like the man, despite his forwardness. He made her feel like she was the last woman on earth. He didn't even turn his head when a sexy woman half her age walked onto the dance floor in a short, skin-tight black dress, and her hair as blonde as blonde could be.

Joanne knew she didn't look like a Victoria Secret Model anymore, not that she ever had. Scars riddled her body, and her old injuries gave her the appearance of a doll that had been sewed together multiple times, rather than a flawless model. But for once it was nice to have a man's eyes on her and her alone. Even in this moment, his gaze never left her face.

"I swear if you lay a hand on my mom—"

"Alex, now!" Joanne said, pointing inside. He let out a growl and then turned on his heels and walked back inside. She let out a breath. How would he react when she finally announced she was taking a trip with him...someone they'd just met?

Even she couldn't understand it herself, but the idea made her feel a bit more alive than she'd felt in a long time. It may not exactly be the most proper thing for a woman to do, but she'd spent a lifetime being proper. And with the reading of her mother's will looming over her head, which made her feel like death warmed over, she deserved to feel alive for once.

She had a feeling it would be best not to tell Alex yet. He seemed to jump back and forth on whether he liked the guy. She'd have to talk to him later and try to find out what was going on.

"I'm sorry about that," she said.

"It's fine, hun. He's your son. He's doing what any son would do in his place. I respect that."

Joanne smiled. He didn't seem offended in the slightest. "Do you want to come in for a drink before bed?"

"I think I should let you have some time with your family. I'm sure you have a lot to discuss."

"Speaking of family. Can we not tell them about the trip yet? I think it's best if we keep that to ourselves."

"Our own little steamy secret?" he said, grinning. "I like it."

Joanne giggled and fanned herself again. The first thing she was going to do was go into the kitchen and get an ice-cold glass of water to cool down her core. It was heating like a volcano.

"Well, I'll head out to the RV and map out our trip. I can show it to you in the morning?"

"I really wish you'd sleep inside, where it's nice and warm."

He took her hand and pulled her closer to him, and she let him. "It's all good. I like my little home. But you can join me out there if you'd like."

Just as when they were dancing earlier, she wrapped her arms around his neck and looked up at him. "My son would have your RV surrounded in minutes."

"Sneak out later?" Nathan suggested, letting his hands rest on the small of her back. He wanted more time with her. The night was ending far earlier than he wanted it to, but he couldn't complain. She was even better company than he had expected.

"I think we'll have to call it a night. Kids see and hear everything."

"I can't wait until I get you all to myself."

Joanne bowed her head, but not before he saw her pink cheeks. He tucked a hand under her chin and raised her face to meet his gaze. She froze for a moment but didn't break eye contact.

"May I?" Nathan asked, glancing down at her lips.

Asking was killing him. He wanted to dive right in, like he normally would when a woman looked up at him so wantonly. But there was something about her that was different. Special. And she deserved to be treated like a queen. No one kisses the queen without permission.

He could see every emotion battling it out in her eyes, like two knights with swords. Soon, she gave him a gentle nod. And that was all he needed. Framing her face in his hands, he brushed his lips against hers lightly. They still tasted like their decadent strawberry dessert.

Her hold around his neck tightened as she pulled her toward him, rising on her tippy toes. They stood there, body to body, lost in the embrace. She was warm, and her taste was like a dream he never wanted to forget. Nathan ran his tongue along her bottom lip, hoping she'd open for him. And when she did, his floodgates opened, and his cock hardened.

She groaned when he pressed his hard length against her abdomen as he pulled her close. Their tongues met in a friendly game of tag. It had been far too long since he'd been with a woman, and if he wasn't careful, this would get out of hand quickly.

He kissed her hard one final time before pulling back, untangling her hands from around his neck. "I shall bid you goodnight before it's too late."

Completely dazed, she stood there a moment, almost like she couldn't focus. Her eyes a little glossed over as though she'd been drinking, but he knew better. Glancing at his lips, she touched hers with the tips of her fingers.

Not wanting to be tempted beyond his weakening control, Nathan took her by the shoulders and turned her to face the door. Before letting her go, he leaned close to her ear and whispered, "I'll be dreaming of you."

"Of me?"

"Of the day I have you in my bed," he said, kissing her under the ear lobe.

She raised a hand to her chest, her breath quickening. "Oh my."

"Good night, my beautiful angel." He couldn't wait for their trip across the country. But here, he had to be careful. Otherwise, her son would wipe the mat with him for the thoughts he was having.

With that, he prompted her to head inside with a slight push forward, and then stepped back himself before turning and walking down the steps toward his RV, humming the tune of Pretty Woman.

Once inside his RV, he shut the door and collapsed on the sofa, running a hand through his hair. His pants unbelievably tight. He didn't usually walk away from an opportunity, but she deserved more than a quick roll in the hay. She deserved flowers, candy, and anything else that would make her smile. She had too much sadness in her eyes, and he wanted happiness to shine inside them.

Whatever she'd been through, he wanted to make it better. That meant taking things slow, so tonight his hard-on would have to fall asleep on its own. He chuckled. He'd probably dream of her and have a wet dream. That wouldn't surprise him in the slightest. He was harder than he'd been in a while.

"Guess I don't need Viagra yet."

It took a bit, but she finally pulled herself away from Alex's third degree about coming back late. Their roles seemed to be reversed now. She could remember lecturing him about his earlier treatment of Laryssa when she first came to stay with them.

The only way she got away from his lecture tonight was playing the mom card. He tried to argue, but eventually gave up and let her go. You don't win when arguing with mommy dearest, she thought to herself with a chuckle.

She really did love her boy and was so grateful for who he was and everything he'd ever done for her. He gave her a home when he was more than capable of living on his own. Even after his daughter died, he kept her around. She couldn't do much, but that hadn't bothered him.

He seemed to find comfort in her being there, and for that, she was eternally grateful. When the truth came out, she half expected to find herself on the street. But his heart was big, despite the pain he had to work through.

Joanne walked over to the bedroom window that faced the front driveway and stared down at the motorhome. The light inside shone through the front window, and she couldn't help but wonder what it would have been like to take him up on his offer.

She shook her head, turning away from the window and from temptation. "Geez, Joanne, you barely know the guy," she muttered. What was she thinking?

Her youthful spirit begged her to sneak out, begged her to follow the desires flooding through her psyche. Eagerly reminding her that even though her body was older, her spirit was still that young, playful woman she remembered in high school. The one who lived on the edge of excitement. Her parents would have given her the tanning of her life if they knew how often she'd gotten into trouble with the boys and Scott. She got into *trouble* with him on a regular basis.

He had made her feel so alive, and for some reason, so did Nathan. She couldn't make sense of it because she had just met him. She had known Scott for years before they got together. They didn't exactly run in the same circles, so it took longer for them to become a couple. And she regretted that now. She could have had more time with him than she did.

Joanne let out a sigh and sat on the edge of the bed. They always warn you about feelings that come on too fast. They make you leap before you think. It's like a bulldozer running you over. And it wasn't right. He was Laryssa's uncle. One that no one knew anything about.

How the heck had she even agreed to the trip? She learned nothing about him at dinner, but somehow, she chose to go on the trip with him. What was her crazy mind thinking? He could be a serial killer for all she knew. They had charismatic personalities, didn't they?

There was no way she could go with him. Not at least until she knew more about him. Should she ask Alex to get him checked out? Joanne bit her bottom lip. That seemed so intrusive. She wouldn't want anyone doing that to her. Suddenly tired, she got up from the bed and wandered into the bathroom.

She brushed her teeth and stopped to look in the mirror. Her cheeks had a hint of red to them, and her parts hummed with energy, even though her spirit was still leery.

Finishing her usual bedtime routine, she went to slip out of the dress and remembered that she couldn't undo it herself. That meant going and finding someone who could help. Sarah would pepper her for information. Her son would begin his lecture again, and Laryssa, she'd probably ask if she'd learned anything about the man.

And she really hadn't. He had learned more about her than she did about him. She couldn't even imagine what was going through Laryssa's mind. The poor girl had been put through the ringer, and they had every right to know whether Nathan was the real deal, and why he hadn't visited her before.

Granted, she'd been sent from foster home to foster home, and he wasn't her father, so Child Protective Services probably wouldn't be as forthcoming with information. But he could have gone the legal route and did what he could to find her.

Why hadn't he? Because the minute Joanne was well enough to look for her kids, she was out there trying to get them back. She understood he wasn't the father, but to not be in the kid's life completely didn't make sense to her.

He seemed like a good guy, and her intuition about people was usually spot on. But she also knew that many people, even good people, had a boatload of secrets. Painful memories that many wanted to keep buried instead. And he looked like a person with a painful past.

But there was something that called to her, even while he was outside in the RV. The very thing that made her agree to a trip with virtually a total stranger. Joanne shook her head as she left her room in search of Laryssa.

As she wandered down the hall, she decided she needed to phone her friends soon and get them to knock some sense into her scatter-brained head.

She hoped that when she knocked on Laryssa's door that Alex was still down in his study. The last thing she wanted to do was walk in on the naughty dance. Walking up to their door, she noticed it slightly ajar.

"Laryssa?" she asked, pushing it open slightly.

The light was on, but the room was empty and the bed still unused. She glanced around and couldn't believe how different things looked. When Laryssa first moved in, it was the first time anyone had used the room since his daughter, Julia, died. It was as pink as a room could be. Her chest tightened, and she brought a hand to her breast.

She'd been such a sweet little thing and was her daddy's world. The stench of death had surrounded them for so long and hung like a dark cloud over their lives. It broke her heart to see her son go through the loss of his daughter, and then his wife, who left him. He'd forgotten how to smile and how to enjoy life. He immersed himself so completely in his job and tried to bury his pain until Laryssa came along. She helped him heal.

And that showed through the change in the room. He painted the pink walls a sky-blue color, one of his favorite colors, and replaced the pink carpet with a navy-blue carpet that spanned the room. They also hung a brand-new marriage photo, which a local artist had painted. Along another wall, he had the cover of Julia's favorite book framed, and underneath that was her favorite stuffed bunny.

Joanne walked over and picked up the stuffed bunny and ran her finger over the missing eye. Her granddaughter never went anywhere without it. Many times, she sat with Julia at nighttime to read a story, with the bunny nestled safely in her arms. Tears pricked her eyes. They'd had so much fun.

Taking a deep breath, she placed the bunny back on the shelf and whispered, "I love you, Julia." She went to turn to leave the room, but a movement in the corner of her eye made her jump as she let out a panicked cry.

Chapter Nine

"It's just me, Mom," Laryssa said as she placed a glass of water on the dresser.

"My goodness, child, don't do that to me."

Her daughter-in-law let out a chuckle. "Sorry, is everything okay?"

"I was able to get into this dress, but it would seem that I can't get out."

"Is that anything like I've fallen and I can't get up?" Laryssa asked with a cheeky grin.

"Oh shush. That happened once, and it was because my chair fell over backwards on a hill."

It happened when they were out at the park, having a family picnic. She went to sit in a chair, and it fell over backwards. She never got hurt, but it took a minute for someone to help her because they were all too busy laughing. Her legs were up in the air while her head was pointing down the hill.

"Come on. I'll help you out," Laryssa said. Arm in arm, they went back to Joanne's room.

"How was your date?" Laryssa asked. "I didn't get a chance to ask yet."

"He was the perfect gentleman," she started to say. "Somewhat."

"Somewhat?"

Joanne walked over to her dresser and pulled out a plain blue nightgown, contemplating how to answer her. "He's quite—how shall we say—suggestive."

Laryssa walked over and helped slide the zipper down, and then she turned around while Joanne changed. "Care to define suggestive?" she asked, prodding for more information.

"I'm a little out of practice, but it's not customary for men to ask you into their beds on the first date, right?" Joanne thought it best to leave out her agreement to go on the trip with him.

Laryssa squeaked and then coughed, hitting her chest slightly. "He didn't?"

"He did."

"I'm going to kill him!" she said, her fingers closing into tight fists.

"Don't say anything," Joanne pleaded. "He was the perfect gentleman. He's just more verbal in some respects than I expected."

"Maybe Alex was right. We should have gone with you."

"It was fine, really. He didn't do anything that I didn't want him to. He didn't even kiss me without permission," Joanne said, smoothing out her nightgown.

"He kissed you?" Laryssa's hands went to her hips.

Oh gosh. She should shut up right now. Why had she even brought it up, especially to his niece? "Sorry, forget I mentioned it."

"I want you to tell me everything he did."

"Everything who did?" Alex asked, walking into the room. He glanced between both girls, and his eyes clouded. "Did he hurt you?"

"No-no. Nothing like that." She took them both by the hand and led them to the door. "Since my dress dilemma has been solved, I'd like to go to sleep."

"Mom?" Alex asked in a warning tone.

Joanne tensed at his tone. "I'm fine. He was fine. Now scoot," she said, pushing them out of the room. When they left, she shut the door and then turned to lean against it. "Well. That went well."

If that was what happened with him kissing her, imagine what would happen if she went on the trip. They'd kick her tail to kingdom come. She'd have to tell him the trip was a no go. The last thing she wanted was to get him into trouble. He was the only person left in Laryssa's family that she knew about, and that needed to mean more than her own feelings.

Joanne climbed into bed and pulled the sheets up to her chin. All she could envision was the two of them on the dance floor. The way he moved her so effortlessly around the slightly crowded room. The way he never took his eyes off her but seemed to see everything at once.

She hadn't planned on dancing because of her leg, but he held her so tight that she barely had to put any weight on her leg. It would be so easy to get lost in his arms. And she did, temporarily, shivering with delight. It felt so sweet to be held again. To feel cherished, even if the moment was brief.

Joanne sighed and rolled onto her side, staring at the picture of Scott on her nightstand in the dim light. A picture she no longer had to keep hidden. Scott had made her feel special, and maybe that's why she'd felt drawn to Nathan, because in the brief time she'd known him, he'd made her feel the same.

How was that possible in such a short time? It was scary and exciting at the same time. She'd only read about instant connections in romance novels. The ones where you felt like you knew someone for their entire lives, when in reality you only just met. Kindred spirits, she supposed.

And her spirit wanted to go back downstairs and accept his offer of spending the night in his RV. Her parts burned with knowledge of what it would be like if she had sex again. It was like a pulsating need that needed to be fulfilled, feeling much like a drug. And they hadn't even done anything yet.

It was quite overwhelming to be wanted by a man after so long. A sexy man, she might add. Joanne let out a breath and willed her body to go back to sleep, so she could relax and get some rest herself.

Smiling, Joanne closed her eyes. She liked this feeling. Very much so. She couldn't wait to get together with the girls and hear what they had to say about her predicament and the trip invitation. Would they help ease her concerns and tell her to go, or would they kill him for asking?

She had a feeling she already knew the answer. And the answer would dance her right into the fire. And with that Joanne covered her head with the pillow, trying to stifle the images and thoughts that jumped into her mind.

Sleep. Sleep. Wherefore art thou sleep?
Oh dear. Triple oh dear.

Joanne and her three friends sat around a glass table by the window at the café in Gastown, across from a mini clock tower. Customers bustled around them, itching to try the pastries behind the display.

"You have to go!" Grace said, excitement written all over her face.

"Darling, she barely knows the man," Sharon said. "A date is one thing, but a week-long trip. Alone. I'm not so sure."

"We could always see if he's on that criminal database thing," Colleen suggested. "My daughter was showing it to me the other day."

"Oh, don't be silly," Grace said. "I've gone on a few trips, and so far, none of the guys have been serial killers yet. And they were some of the best times of my life."

"Better to be safe than sorry," Sharon commented.

"I'm sure my son has already had him checked out," Joanne said. "Nothing slips under his nose."

"Alex probably did that the minute he found out you were going on a date with him," Colleen said.

"See, it's settled. If your son let you go out with him, then he's fine," Grace said gleefully.

Joanne brought her cup to her lips and took a sip of her white hot chocolate. Grace seemed to be gung-ho for the idea. Sharon not so much. And Colleen was somewhere in the middle.

"If you won't go, I will!" Grace said. "I'm starting to go stir crazy staying in the city."

"Oh, heck no!" Joanne exclaimed, and then she slapped her hands over her mouth while all the women laughed. Everyone in the café looked over at the four crazy old women in the corner.

"I think we've already lost her," Colleen said as she sat back in her chair, resting her arm along the back of Sharon's chair.

"You only live once, Joanne," Grace reminded her.

That's where she was torn. She wanted some excitement, and the trip itself held some danger that carried an allure all its own. But was she willing to risk her life on a man she barely knew? Her entire body hummed with a strange vibration that made this feel like a dream.

"Want my advice?" Colleen asked.

Joanne nodded.

"You still have a week left. Spend as much time as possible with him and then decide."

"Or better yet, have him come to dinner with us, and let us decide for you," Grace said. "That way, if you don't go, I can decide if I want to."

"I think I'm good." There was no way she wanted the women to get their claws into him. It might scare him away. And she didn't want to scare him away. Not yet.

Colleen looked down at her watch. She preferred a good old-fashioned watch rather than her cellphone. She hated the idea of having to charge devices. "I better get going. I'm watching the kids this afternoon."

"You guys were no help at all," Joanne said, huffing. They were supposed to help her decide. They were supposed to be all in or all out, but it was a mixed reception. Going on the date had been a unanimous decision, but the trip not so much.

"I know that you'd prefer to drive than fly if you had your way, but I want you to be safe," Sharon said, reaching across the table to squeeze her hand.

With that, her other two friends stood up and said their goodbyes, leaving only Grace and Joanne at the table.

"Do you think it's worth the risk?" Joanne asked her.

"I've never known a woman who has better judgment than you, Joanne. If you don't have a bad feeling about him in your gut, then I'd say it's as safe as any other trip."

"What makes you do it?"

"I'd probably be a little more hesitant if I had a big family to watch over and take care of, but it's just me, and I spent most of my childhood playing the adult, raising my siblings. I guess I like the freedom it brings to be able to make my own choices without having obligations to deal with first. Besides, they often give me my own room."

"I'd be stuck in an RV."

"That could be romantic. You know, going to a campsite out in the country and staring up at the stars. Maybe you'll see a shooting star and be able to make a wish."

"Well, aren't you a romantic soul," Joanne said, staring down at her dwindling hot cocoa as a romantic scene jumped into her mind right then and there. They were sitting around a campfire in a big double chair, wrapped in a blanket, staring up at the sky without a care in the world. And that's all she wanted. To be able to forget and just be a woman with needs again.

But she knew that would only last a short while. Once they neared their destination, and she had to confront her greatest pain, her emotions were going to go haywire. And she didn't know whether she'd be able to keep it together, especially coming face to face with her dad. Did he still have the same mindset that he used to have? He said that she'd hit him with the deepest betrayal that mankind had ever seen. He said what she did was worse than anything any human being has ever done before.

How do you respond to that? It had been a long time since they spoke last, but she didn't mind in the slightest. He was as cruel as cruel could be. A man with no peace. She'd never been his favorite nor ever felt like his daughter, and she could never do anything that made him smile.

Grace drank the final remnants of her coffee and then asked, "What are you thinking about?"

"My dad."

"That cantankerous old fart?"

Joanne chuckled, her hand holding the cup shook slightly. Thankfully, her drink was almost gone. "That description fits him to a T."

"Give me two minutes alone with him, and he'll regret what he did to you."

Joanne didn't doubt it. Grace had a very cunning side to her that made people never mess with her. Maybe that's what made her a good corrections officer in the past. Watching Grace whip her dad's butt into shape would be a sight for sore eyes. He'd never mess with her again.

"In a way, I wish the four of us could go together. What guy would mess with four old women?"

"You're right there, but I promise you'll have much more fun with Nathan," Grace said, grinning and fluttering her eyelashes suggestively.

"I still don't know if I should," Joanne mumbled.

"Honey, you'll be fine. Go. Enjoy yourself. I bet you'll be pleasantly surprised."

"Fine, I'll go," she muttered.

Chapter Ten

It was the night before they were supposed to leave on the trip, and no one had caught on to their travel plans. Joanne had insisted that it wouldn't be a good idea to tell anyone. Nathan knew, at some point, it would come back to bite him in the butt, but who was he to deny her wishes? He wanted to stay on her good side.

"Do you mind if I use the washroom?" he asked as they sat around the dinner table.

"Sure. You remember where it is, right? Go through the living room and down the hallway on your right," Laryssa reminded him as she dug into her Chinese food. "It's the last door on the left."

He pushed his chair back and stood up, touching Joanne briefly on the shoulder. "I'll be right back."

"Do you need anyone to go with you?" Alex asked.

"I'll be fine." He hadn't had any other chance to move around the house until today. And they hadn't been able to discuss the issues that had brought him to their place.

He walked by a knight statue as he neared one of the many adjoining hallways and stopped to look at it for a moment. Alex seemed to own his own personal museum. One could spend ages walking around here looking at the things Alex's family acquired over the years. But for now, he had a mission.

Stepping into the bathroom, he shut the door behind him. The room was about the size of his RV, with a nice Jacuzzi tucked away in the corner, surrounded by steps on all sides. Sweet, teal-colored tiles covered the wall. He walked across sparkling ocean patterned linoleum to the counter.

But the look of the bathroom wasn't what interested him. It was the two hairbrushes resting on the shelf beside the mirror. It was easy to identify Laryssa's comb because her hair was longer and didn't have any gray strands yet. Although with three kids, that would likely happen soon.

Nathan pulled a bag out of his pocket and used a pair of tweezers to pluck a few strands from the brush. Now all he needed to do was mail it off without Joanne finding out. He wouldn't have a chance to hit the post office until they were on their way out of town. Maybe he could go in under the guise of picking up food.

You should tell her.

"Shut up," he grumbled to his conscience. Joanne didn't need to know until the truth was discovered. He would have to tell them eventually, but no one needed to know right now. Not until he had all the information at his disposal. It would help him decide how to best approach the topic.

They'd gotten a little closer relationship wise during the week, and even spent time in his RV talking until the wee hours of the morning. He hadn't done that with anyone before. They spoke about everything under the sun, from sports to news to wish lists.

They had more in common than he had expected. But he'd always avoided the one discussion about why he had been away. He felt guilty keeping this from her, but it was far too early to mention it. He'd be kicked out on his ass for sure, and she'd never let him take her on this trip. There was a burning need to take this trip with her. They needed to explore the connection between them.

Heat had sizzled between them while in his RV whenever their eyes locked, and he desperately to take her by the hand and walk her backwards to his bed, peeling each layer of clothes off her body, but he hadn't. However, he went to sleep dreaming of it, though, and woke up quite turned on.

He was looking forward to driving her and chipping away at all her defenses until she was the one who took him to bed. He wanted her to willingly walk with him back to his bed. That would show him that he'd broken through her shy barrier. He knew how important it was to let her make that decision. The choice had to be hers.

Taking a breath, he turned his attention back to the situation at hand, which was stuffing Laryssa's hair in a zip-lock bag. Zipping the bag closed, he placed it in his pocket and put the brush back where he found it before returning to the table.

"I hope I didn't miss anything," he said.

"Just talking about tomorrow," Joanne said, smiling at him shyly, fully aware of his presence as her eyes dropped to his crotch, causing his cock to jump to life. *Down boy.*

"I can take the morning off to take you to the airport," Alex offered.

"It's alright. Nathan offered to take me."

Alex growled and sat back in his seat. "I'd much prefer taking you."

"You have work, my dear, and Nathan is on his way out and said it would be okay to get a ride with him."

"Fine, but he better drive safely!" he said, glaring at Nathan.

"Always," he assured Joanne's son.

Soon, their dinner was finished, and they all took their own dishes to the sink. He watched as Laryssa and Joanne cleaned up the kids. With how close the two women were, you'd almost think they were a biological mother and daughter. He was so happy that Laryssa had that support.

It was unconventional for parents to still live with their kids after they grew up in Canada, but it seemed to work well for this household. And everyone pitched in and worked together. It was like they were living the perfect dream. He wished his own house had been like this growing up.

His dad hadn't given him the time of day, didn't even care what he got into, and when he died, his mother married a douchebag. Nathan had left and moved in with his friend, who happened to be the brother of Catherine, Laryssa's mother.

Nathan gripped the back of his neck. The Day was still so vivid in his mind. Joel, his brother, and Catherine had had a fight. She ended up staying overnight at her brother's house where he was. Her brother was out of town, and they'd had too much to drink as she tried to drown her sorrows.

If they wouldn't have taken a trip down memory lane while drinking and been filled with nostalgia of when they used to be a couple, it never would have happened. He never did stuff like that. It wasn't who he was. And it had never happened again. Ever. Not even with anyone else. He refused to have a deep relationship with anyone because they deserved better than anything he could give. No one needed a cheater.

It killed him that he broke his brother's trust like that. He couldn't remember too much of what happened, other than finding her naked body draped over his in the morning. After that, he avoided Catherine like the plague, even if that meant never seeing his brother. He never wanted to be a home-wrecker.

Joel voiced his suspicions once or twice over why Nathan never wanted to see Catherine, but it never really came out until the night on the boat. Nathan shook his head as he remembered the flames. His clothes hid the burn marks that scarred him for life. A constant reminder of his transgression when he was twenty years of age.

"Are you okay?" Joanne asked him. He turned and saw her looking at him with concern etched into her features.

"I think the food has made me sleepy," he said, rubbing his stomach. "Do you mind if I retire back to the RV?"

Joanne placed the cloth she was using on the counter and said, "I'll come with you."

"I don't want to impose," he said.

"Nonsense, I'd love to keep you company. Will you guys be okay if I go with him?" she asked her family, who all responded with a less than enthusiastic nod of their head, especially Alex. He looked like he wanted to pop a gasket, but he didn't say anything. Nathan chuckled quietly. It looked like Joanne was the boss around here.

She kissed the top of the kids' heads and then joined him in the entryway. "Let's go," she said.

He bent his arm and tucked hers inside his, resting her hand on his forearm. They made their way through the house slowly, and he didn't mind. That meant more time with her.

"What's wrong?" she asked again as they neared the front entrance.

"I think I'm just tired after such a long day."

"The kids did keep us running around in the snow, didn't they?"

He laughed. "That they did. You really do have a wonderful home and family."

"Thank you," she said as they made their way down the front steps. Snow was lightly falling, creating a halo around the Christmas lights that decorated the outside of the house. They apparently kept them up year-round because it was too challenging to put them up every year since the place was so huge. He could understand that.

"Have you lived here for long?" he asked.

"This place has been in the Richards family for generations."

What he loved about this family was that they didn't seem spoiled, despite having heirlooms passed down to them throughout the generations. Alex worked all hours of the day and seemed like a down-to-earth kind of guy. One who was very protective of his family. Nathan liked that about him, even if Alex might punch him later for disappearing with his momma.

"Was it built by his ancestors?"

"Yep."

"I'm glad Laryssa found you guys. She deserves the stable life that you all have."

"When did you fall out of touch with the family?"

"Pretty much right after the accident."

"Did anyone try to contact you to come get her?"

"Nope. I'd been written off pretty much."

"Why?"

Nathan released her arm as he reached for the door of the RV. "I was the black sheep," he said, shrugging his shoulders. No one would have given him custody even if he'd asked for it. It's not like he deserved it anyway. Laryssa would have hated him the minute she found out the truth about what happened, like his own mother did. His mom even told him his father would be turning in his grave.

What burned him was that she didn't even try to get custody of Laryssa because she said the child would remind her too much of the son she had lost and his own betrayal toward them. Her bitterness killed her fairly quickly after that. And that left Nathan with no one. He had no other siblings, no other family, save Laryssa. Even his friends slowly left him one by one. According to everyone, he had done the unthinkable.

Joanne placed a hand on his shoulder as his head hung low. "I'm sorry. I know what it feels like to be the black sheep."

He turned to look at her, surprised. "You? But you're so sweet."

"My dad didn't think so," she said bitterly.

"Well, then he's a fool," he said, holding out a hand to help her up the stairs.

When her hand closed around his, he felt her tenderness right to the tips of his toes. It made him want to give her the world, but for now, the couch in the RV would have to do as he led her to it to sit down. On the table across from them was a map where he'd been planning their trip itinerary.

"Thank you," she said.

"I'm glad you decided to walk out with me. I've been wanting to have you to myself for the last hour," he said, bringing her hand to his lips.

She lowered her head, smiling shyly. "I'm looking forward to tomorrow."

"Me too," he said, settling back against the couch as a peaceful calm, in his usually stormy life, came to rest over his RV. There was enough room for the two of them to fit comfortably. "Have you thought of the top two places you want to see?"

Joanne tilted her head and stared up at the ceiling, trying to think. "There are so many places I've wanted to see in the States, but funny enough, I never really put the same thought into exploring Canada."

"Since you can't walk too far, we won't worry about anything that takes a hike to get there.

"I can do short walks, but nothing too fast or strenuous."

"I'll keep that in mind."

Joanne glanced around the motorhome. She knew it had been outfitted with winter tires and had chains in the underground compartment, so they'd have no trouble traveling in the snow, which was already blanketing much of the great outdoors. Snow had fallen earlier this year than normal. They almost never got snow in November, but this year was an exception. It was probably trying to make up for no snow last year.

"I've heard of a beautiful lake, Lake Morin?" she suggested.

"*Moraine*, yes. It's just northwest of Banff, close to Lake Louise, which is another spot I'd like to stop. But it depends if we go Northeast or if we cross over the border into the states, which will be a quicker drive."

"That would be perfect. Would Mount Rushmore be on our way if we did that? I've only ever seen it in movies."

He smiled. "We'll be able to drive right by it."

"Oh," she said, clasping her hands together. "Perfect. Just perfect."

He stood up and held out his hand to help her up. They walked over to the map on the table. "I still prefer a good old-fashioned map," he said.

"Careful, someone might think you're from the stone age."

He bumped shoulders with her and chuckled. "Careful, darling, I might have to show you just how young I'm feeling."

And there it was again—the heat...feeling like flames against her face. Joanne cleared her throat and tucked a strand of hair behind her ear. "Behave, Mr. Mitchell," she said, giggling like a schoolgirl.

He leaned over and straightened out the map, letting his fingers run across the back of her hand. "I think you'll find things a lot more fun if we don't behave."

Her body sizzled. "You're going to be the death of me."

"But what a way to go," he said, his voice deep and husky.

He was so close she felt the heat rising from his body. Or was it from hers? She couldn't differentiate between the two.

She moved away and took a seat at the table. He, thankfully, sat across from her. But when she met his eyes, she wished he would have sat beside her. It was like someone had gathered all the passion in the world and placed it in his eyes. They were glowing like fiery embers, heating her body all the more.

Joanne cleared her throat and glanced down at the sideways map. "So, which way do you think is best?"

"Missionary."

She dropped her hands to her lap, trying to bury the rising excitement between her legs. He seemed to have one thing on his mind. And she had to admit, it wasn't very far from hers either. Last night, she had dreamed about sleeping with him. And it was the spiciest sex ever.

They surrounded by tall grass in a field, and across the way, there was a path that led along the water. He'd laid out a blanket, and they feasted on expensive hors d'oeuvres before he had laid her back on the blanket and had his wicked way with her. *Oh gosh.* It felt so good. She could still feel his hands on her body.

"I'm talking about our trip, meathead!"

"Sorry," he replied with a sexy grin. "The hunger in your eyes confused me."

"Oh, shush," she muttered, her face flushing a deep shade of red, which was easy to see when she turned and saw her reflection in the window beside her.

He chuckled. "Okay, I'll curb the discussion for tonight." Spinning the map, he faced it toward her. "I figure we could cross the border at one hundred and seventy-sixth and take the I-Ninety pretty much right across, unless we decide to take a detour. "

"You don't think we'll run into any winter trouble, do you?"

"This vehicle can handle it. I've taken her many places over the years."

"Her?"

"Yep, she's my non-human woman."

"You do realize how creepy that sounds, right?" Joanne laughed.

He did a creepy mechanical evil man chuckle, making her think of Santa Claus being possessed by a mad scientist. *'Tis the season, after all.* Joanne laughed so hard that tears started gathering in the corner of her eyes.

Nathan's eyes sparkled as he sat back against the seat with his arm resting along the back. He was on the side that was adjacent to the kitchen counter. "I love seeing you laugh," he said. "You get cute wrinkles on your forehead."

Consciously, she covered her forehead. "I do not!" She prided herself on keeping her skin young and healthy looking. Oil of Olay bottles lined her dresser, and it seemed to do the trick.

He leaned forward and reached across the table, pulling her hand down. He then ran his index finger across the laugh lines on her forehead. "Right here."

She pushed his hand away, but instead of letting her go, he wrapped his around hers. "I better go," she said, trying to pull away.

He held on tight and momentarily brought them once again to his lips. "Until tomorrow, my darling."

She stood up and made her way out of the motorhome. Once she was safely on the ground, she turned and looked up at him. "I've never met anyone like you, Nathan Mitchell."

"That makes two of us," he replied. "Come on, I'll walk you to the door."

"No, it's okay. You go and relax," she insisted as she turned. "See you tomorrow.

Chapter Eleven

"Mom, call me when you get to Toronto, okay?" Alex said, pulling her into a nice warm hug.

The last time she went away it was to visit her in-laws, Alexander's grandparents, who raised him. His grandfather, Mitch, had experienced a heart attack, and she went to support Alex's grandmother, Ruth.

It was only because of them she got to be with her son. They could have turned her away like her own parents did, but they hadn't. They had kept her from telling Alex who she was, but in the end, it all worked out anyway. And they were closer than ever before.

"I'll call you every evening," Joanne promised, giving him one last squeeze.

"I still don't get why you're going a week early. I didn't think you wanted to spend time with them."

"Lots of things to see and do. I don't want this trip to only be about the will or my father."

She still hadn't found the courage to tell him she'd be traveling with Nathan the entire way. The two men had come to an understanding of each other, but there was still much they didn't know about Nathan, so she knew Alex would throw the book at her if he did or would insist on going with them.

"We better go, Joanne. Traffic could be heavy."

Alex handed the plane ticket to her and the printout of the hotel where she would be staying. "I wish you'd let one of us go with you."

"I need to do this on my own, son," she said, patting him on the cheek. Nathan loaded her suitcases into the motorhome and then waved her over.

She quickly turned and hugged Laryssa and Sarah, giving each of the kids a peck on the cheek. "Behave for Mommy!" she said. It was going to be nice to have no responsibilities for a while.

Nathan took her hand and helped her up the stairs and into the vehicle. They climbed into the front seat, and she did up her seatbelt, then gave a final wave as they drove around the fountain to leave.

"They care for you a great deal," Nathan said, smiling over at her.

"They are my life. My world."

He reached over and squeezed her hand. She squeezed back. There was quite the distance between the two chairs, so he released her hand and placed it back on the steering wheel to better control the moving vehicle.

"I kind of feel bad for not telling them our plans," she said, biting the nail on her thumb. After realizing what she was doing, she placed her hand back on her lap. She kind of felt like a teenager rebelling and sneaking off to a party.

"I haven't done anything like this since I snuck out with my girl-friend in high school and tried to stay in a motel for the night," he replied with a grin.

"You didn't?" Joanne's eyes widened.

"Both our parents found out, and let me tell you, it wasn't pretty."

She laughed. "I wouldn't imagine so."

"Now we're doing it, except in a motorhome."

Her actions surprised even her. She was the practical one. She never did anything out of the ordinary or dangerous. With how busy her life was, she didn't have time to do anything anyway.

"Where's our first stop?" she asked.

"Missoula. That's as far as I dare push it today, and that depends on the wait at the border."

"How long will that take?"

"About ten hours," he said.

She hadn't really accounted for how long it would take to get to Toronto by driving. All she had been thinking about was spending more time with Nathan and enjoying herself before facing her father.

"I'll try not to bore you too much," he said, chuckling at the horror on her face. "We'll get out and stretch our legs at the halfway point."

"Sounds good." Joanne stared out the window and watched as they drove by the houses in their neighborhood and out onto the highway.

"What's your favorite color?" he asked after they'd been driving for about ten minutes. "You know, in case I want to surprise you with something."

"You don't have to get me anything," she said. "Going with you on this trip is enough for me."

"Humor me." Nathan wanted to get to know her better. He had a feeling they'd know each other inside and out before the trip was done.

"Blue. I've always liked blue."

"Any particular shade?"

"Sky Blue. What about you?"

"Teal. My mom suffered with OCD, and it's the color of their awareness ribbon. I grew up watching her and her rituals and wished there was a way to help her."

"Did she ever get help?"

"No, and after she lost Joel, she totally lost herself and her ability to think rationally. She died shortly after. The grief was too much."

"Joel was Laryssa's father, right? She never told us his name."

He nodded, the lump in his throat growing. It wasn't a topic he wanted to touch on, but it always seemed to come back around to bite him in the ass.

"Do you know what happened? Laryssa knows there was a boating accident, but she doesn't remember much."

Nathan cleared his throat, trying to find his voice. "There was an explosion on board."

"Oh, how horrible."

"My brother managed to make it back to shore, but his injuries were too severe, and he died on the way to the hospital. And Cat, she—" His voice broke. It was all his fault. He should have known that Joel was up to something with how hard he insisted that they both go on the trip with Joel. She never tagged along on their boating trips.

"It's okay. You don't have to talk about it," Joanne said softly.

"You would think after all this time it would be easier to talk about." But it wasn't. It was still stuck in his mind almost every minute of every day. How do you get over something that was your fault?

"If you haven't worked through it, then it can feel just as fresh every time."

They sat in silence for a while. He knew that if he opened his mouth, then he'd start blubbering, and he didn't want to cry in front of her. Eventually, the truth would come out, and he'd have to face rejection again. He wanted to put that off for as long as possible. Preferably not until they got back.

Maybe after he found out the results of the DNA test. His friend was meeting him in Missoula. He would have mailed the hair sample, but his friend lived near their first stop, so it was quicker that way. And once he found out his answers, he'd know how to approach the topic.

"My accident still makes me tear up, too. I don't think we'd be human if they didn't," she said.

He opened his mouth to respond, but then closed it and returned his focus to the road. He was almost about to let the cat out of the bag and say, 'well, at least yours wasn't your fault.' But he didn't.

"I'm pretty good now, for the most part," Joanne said. "But every once in a while, especially when I'm alone, I think about what happened and the domino effect afterwards."

"Do you mind if I ask what happened?" He had no right to pry, especially when he wouldn't talk about his own experiences.

"I'd just gone into labor, and Scott was driving me to the hospital. We were stopped at a light and when it turned green, Scott stomped on the gas...nervous, I guess. He didn't see the other car blow through the red light until it was too late. The car hit Scott's door. He never made it to the hospital. Sometimes I wonder what would have happened if I never went into labor that day."

Nathan let out a long breath. The pain in her voice tore at his heart. He knew the pain of the great *what if* questions. They ruled his life as well. If he wouldn't have cheated with Catherine, the fight wouldn't have happened, and they'd all be alive today.

"Were you seriously hurt?" he asked.

"Ya, I was in a coma and came out almost paralyzed on my right side. My head hit the window, shattering the glass."

"And the baby?"

"Babies."

"You were pregnant with twins?"

Joanne nodded. "Alex and his brother Aidan."

"Where does Aidan live?"

She drew in a sharp breath, and that's when he knew the answer would not be good. *Man.* This poor woman had been to hell and back.

"He died a few years back." After the comment, her eyes took on a haunted look. "Oh look, we don't have too long of a wait at the border," she said, pointing to an overhead sign. It said fifteen minutes.

"I'm sorry for prying."

"It's okay. I can't keep the topic sealed off forever, can I? Aidan died in a car accident of his own making."

"Boy, it seems like accidents are our curse."

"Was anyone else on the boat?"

Just as she asked that, he attempted to swallow some saliva that built up in his mouth, but it went down the wrong way. "Water," he gasped as he coughed up a storm.

Joanne reached into the cooler beside her and pulled out a water bottle, opening it for him as she eyed him curiously.

He took a few sips, and his coughing subsided. Well, if that didn't look suspicious, he didn't know what else did. He could see the questions building.

"Sorry. Something went down the wrong way," was all he said.

"Do you know what caused the fire?" she asked again.

Yes, he and his big mouth caused it. He and his wandering hands caused it. But he wasn't about to say that out loud. He wasn't ready to lose what trust he had built with her at this point in their trip.

"The engine malfunctioned," he said simply. That much was true. God, he'd been such a stupid kid. He'd do anything to go back in time and undo the damage he caused. But this wasn't *Back to the Future*. He didn't have a car that could travel through time.

"I guess you weren't in the area to adopt Laryssa?"

He let out a shaky breath. He wanted to ask her whether she would have adopted a child if she'd been the one responsible for the accident? What would you say to a teen who asked where their parents were or what happened to them? Even if he would have had the chance, he couldn't have done it. He wouldn't have been able to look her in the eyes every day and still be able to give her the emotional care she needed, not when he was so broken.

"Unfortunately, I was indisposed of. Adopting her was out of my control."

"How come?"

He gripped the steering wheel tightly, his lips pulling into a thin, tight line. The questions were legit. He knew and understood that, but He couldn't answer. Not Yet.

"I'll tell you everything in time, hun. It's just really hard to talk about." He fought hard to keep his voice even and friendly. She wasn't doing anything wrong. It wasn't her fault he hadn't come to terms with it yet.

"Okay," Joanne said as she turned back to face the front window. There was a little crack in his voice that told her he needed a break.

When they reached the United States border, he pulled to a stop in one line. Neither had a nexus so they couldn't fast track it, but it wasn't that busy anyway.

"Where are you guys heading?" the attendant asked.

"Technically to Toronto but seeing some United States landmarks along the way."

"Where in the States do you plan to go?"

"We're taking the I-Ninety across, stopping in Missoula and then we're gonna see Mount Rushmore," he said, wondering whether they would give him any trouble entering the country. He hadn't tried going into the states for ten years because of his past.

"How long will you be in the States for?"

"About five days," Nathan responded with a smile.

"Do you plan to do a return trip back through the states?"

"We aren't sure yet," Joanne said.

They hadn't discussed what they were going to do after the reading of the will. He was hoping if she enjoyed his company, she would want to spend more time with him after...if Alex hadn't killed him by then.

"Do you have anything to declare?"

Nathan had emptied the trailer of any food that couldn't go into the states and only had some non-restricted food and medication on board.

"No, just medication," Nathan said, showing him the doctor's note.

That made Joanne turn and look at him. Must be some pretty serious medication if he's got a doctor's note for it. But she didn't want to question him at that moment with so much going on.

After a few more questions and given the size of the motorhome, they had them pull over to the side.

"We want to do a quick inspection."

Nathan nodded and pulled over to the allocated area.

Chapter Twelve

A few minutes later, a few border guards walked up to the motorhome and asked Nathan to go inside, and for Joanne to wait with the vehicle while another guard with a dog did their search. Something felt off. She'd been over the border many times, and this had never happened before.

Nathan quickly assured her that everything would be fine, and then he followed the guards inside. Bad butterflies warred in her stomach. Maybe this trip was a bad idea. Should she call Alex? Joanne bit her lip as she watched the men search the motorhome.

"No food hiding anywhere?" the guard asked her.

"Nothing that can't come over the border. We made sure of that," she replied, taking her seat in the front again to keep out of their way. It wasn't long before the search was done with surprising finesse. They left nothing out of place, even though she'd seen that before on the border patrol shows.

As the men were leaving, she asked, "Do you know how long Nathan is going to be?"

"Not sure, Ma'am."

"Why did they take him inside?"

"Just routine protocol."

That didn't sit right with her. "If it's routine, then why not me?"

"If there are any problems, we'll let you know. For now, hang tight," the young man said as he exited the vehicle. Well, at least they had one thing going right. The guards found nothing out of the ordinary.

"Can I go in and sit with him?" she asked the guy before he disappeared.

"No, Ma'am, sorry."

"Okay, thanks anyway." What was she supposed to do now? Joanne looked around the motorhome. It was going to be her home for a few days, so she might as well get acquainted with where everything was located. Wiping some white specks off her slacks, she stood up and placed her hands on her hips. Chances are, she'd be doing most of the cooking. It was the least she could do to pay him back for helping her.

Walking the few steps to the kitchen nook, she started opening and closing drawers and cupboards. In the process, she found the pots, pans, cups, and bowls. Of course, like every house, he had a junk drawer, too. It was filled with the usual crap. Lighters, scissors, screwdrivers. Wait...

"What is that?" she asked, noticing a loose board at the back. She pried it loose with her fingers. How did the border patrol not notice? Inside was a large sum of money, wrapped with an elastic band. "Rainy day money?" As she lifted it out of the drawer, she caught a glimpse of another plastic bag. Joanne pulled it out and held it up.

"Hair?" Why would he have a few strands of hair in a bag, and why the heck would he hide it? It made no sense. A moment later, she heard a noise outside the door and quickly shoved the stuff back inside, replacing the false back. She spun around when another guard walked inside, her heart pounding.

"We're all done. As soon as they're done inside, you should be free to go."

Should she say something about the money? Didn't it have to be declared? Was Nathan doing that inside right now? Joanne glanced at the drawer as the man turned to leave, and he must have caught her apprehensive look because he asked, "Are you okay?"

But she noted that his expression wasn't one of concern. His eyes were narrow and filled with suspicion as he waited for her answer. It made her heart skip a beat.

"I'm fine. You just startled me."

Say something, her conscience pushed. More and more pieces weren't adding up. How many more secret compartments were in his motorhome? After the guard left, she continued her search while she waited.

Little by little, she made her way through the vehicle and only stopped once she reached his bedroom in the back. A small curtain was the only thing separating it from the rest of the vehicle. There was a small walkway on either side of the bed, with a closet on one side and a bookshelf on the other.

Joanne ran her finger along the edge of the books, reading each title. She recognized some of the mystery book titles, which seemed to be his favorite genre. Hers too, but she preferred them to have a romantic element. It was the only part of her life that had any real excitement. Facing the closet, she placed her hand on the handle. Should she do it? Should she open it and see what was inside?

Did she really want to break his trust by searching through his things? The closet was much more private than a junk drawer. She wouldn't want anyone going through her bedroom. Her fingertips itched to open it, to discover more about him...like where had he been for all this time?

But she couldn't do it. She wanted to treat him like she wanted to be treated, so she left the sanctuary of his room and went back to her seat to wait, taking a mystery book with her. She figured he wouldn't mind that. Her phone beeped, letting her know she received a text. It was from Alex.

>*Have you made it to the airport yet?*

>*Don't worry about us, darling. Focus on your family.*

She didn't have it in her to lie. The airplane tickets were sitting in her purse next to her. They should probably be canceled before the flight so they could get their money back. Pulling out her phone, she quickly called the airport and canceled them. She didn't want her son wasting his hard-earned money on a flight she had no plan to take.

Settling back in her tan-colored seat, she kicked off her shoes and opened the book—might as well pass the time somehow. It was a mystery book with a romantic element. It was written by an author she hadn't read yet, despite the fact they had a large library back at the house. Alex wasn't much of a reader, so his ex-wife and Joanne stocked it with books. They even had one entire corner dedicated to kid's books for their growing family.

It's what she did a lot of in her downtime, considering she couldn't get out and exercise much. Reading helped keep her brain sharp and witty, which was exactly what she needed right now. Eventually, after an hour or two of reading, she reached a scene in the book that took place in a woman's apartment. The detective had found some hairs on the woman's pillow that weren't her own, and they didn't match those of her husband.

Joanne's eyebrows knitted together as she glanced at the drawer with the false backing. Was Nathan a detective of some sort? Had her father sent him? That would explain the wad of cash in the drawer.

No. That wasn't possible. He had a bunch of pictures of Laryssa and her family, not to mention he was in a lot of the family photos. But something wasn't adding up. If he had that much money, he had to have a secret job of sorts. Joanne looked down at the book in her hands and decided that maybe reading a mystery book right now wasn't a good idea. She tried to shake the thought out of her head as her anxiety kicked up a notch.

Standing up, she slowly made her way back to his bedroom to place the book on his shelf. She'd just turned to leave when the door to the trailer opened and up the stairs he walked. Joanne froze in place, her hands by her side. Blood rushed to her face when he looked from her to his bed. She knew her cheeks were bright red.

"Already trying to get into my bed, are you?"

"I-uh, I-um," she stammered.

"I'm joking," he said, his sexy grin turning her insides to mush. "Come on, let's get going."

"We've been given the all-clear?" she asked, her voice a little higher pitched than normal.

"Yes."

"Why'd it take so long? I've never had them do this before," she said, hoping he would enlighten her.

"I was their pick of the week, I guess," he said, shrugging his shoulders as he climbed into the driver's seat.

Joanne climbed into hers and did up her seatbelt. There was more to it than that. She was sure of it. The border patrol never kept you there for that long without good reason. She wanted to ask him if he'd declared the money that was in the drawer while he was inside, but every time she tried, her voice box froze. And she couldn't figure out why. He'd never given her any reason to fear him.

"Don't worry. I'm not a serial killer," he said, attempting to lighten the mood.

She chuckled nervously as a shiver rippled through her. "The thought hadn't crossed my mind."

"But you're hugging the armrest like there's no tomorrow." He nodded toward her two hands, which were gripping the armrest like her life depended on it.

Consciously, she relaxed her hands and folded them on her lap. "Oh, sorry. I was reading one of your mystery novels. I suppose it spooked me a little."

Nathan wasn't sure if he believed her, but he gave her a smile and returned his attention back to the road. They had quite the drive ahead of them if they were going to reach their first destination by sundown. He knew that getting through the border would be tricky, but it was a good thing he knew one of the agents on duty today, or he may not have gotten the clearance to go.

This was one of the main reasons he didn't travel outside of Canada all that much. The hassle wasn't worth it. Who wanted to waste hours of their life in an interrogation room? However, this trip was important to Joanne, and he wanted to go, so it was worth the trouble this time.

"We should watch a horror movie later," he suggested, "So you can hold on to me instead."

She whimpered softly. The barely audible sound made his friend wake up, rising to attention. Nathan shifted in his seat. It was the definite downside to being a guy. He couldn't exactly rearrange himself with her sitting right beside him. Hopefully, she wouldn't notice, but, just in case, he lowered the armrest to hide his discomfort.

"I think I'll stick to my drama and mystery shows, thank you," she said.

"What's your favorite show?"

"NCIS." When she said it, she looked back toward the kitchen for a second before turning to look out the front window again. "All the things they can do these days with forensics fascinates me."

Nathan flicked on his signal and changed lanes to turn onto the I-Five. Something in her demeanor had changed since he'd gone into the building. He wasn't sure if it had to do with their delay or if something else had caused her eyes to be filled with a hundred and one questions.

"I prefer the real-life forensic shows," he replied. It's the one thing that had kept him entertained over the years while isolated from the real world. Being inside the border crossing's interrogation room brought back some unpleasant memories.

"I'm so surprised by what they can do these days, like DNA testing on hair," she said, looking over at him, her eyes burrowing into his, with one eyebrow quirked.

"It's a field they are learning more about all the time."

"Have you ever studied it?"

"No." And that was the truth. His friend occasionally gave him interesting little tidbits about the field and was the one that was going to help him discover the truth about whether Laryssa was his daughter, but he wasn't about to let her know that. He had plans to meet up with him tonight. The man needed money and Nathan needed answers, so the wad of money hiding in the drawer would help him find them.

He glanced at her. She still didn't seem satisfied with his responses. Had she found the hidden compartment in the drawer? The fact she was in his bedroom and obviously looking around the motorhome made that highly likely. Her fingers were drumming on her leg, her lips slightly parted, as though she were debating whether to say something. But she didn't, so he wasn't going to either.

It's not that he wanted to lie. He just wanted to have this time with her, uninterrupted by anything that might impede their relationship. Was it selfish of him to want this time with her before hammering a nail into his coffin? It's not like their relationship would last forever anyway. His forever ended when his 'C' diagnosis came in. *God*. He didn't even want to say the word. No point in putting anyone through that pain.

There would be enough pain when Laryssa and her family found out the truth about what happened all those years ago. And he knew he'd get the boot as soon as they found out. It wouldn't even matter whether he was her father. When he arrived, he hadn't expected to find Joanne. She was unlike anyone he'd ever met.

After their odd conversation, there was an awkward silence that filled the car. At least that's how it felt to him. She stared out the window at the passing trees, and he stared down the road as they drove along. In an attempt to break the ice again, he asked, "Any other favorite television shows?"

"I love the old shows. You know, I love Lucy and The Love Boat."

"Lucy, you've got some 'splaining to do!" he said, mimicking Ricky Ricardo's voice.

Joanne chuckled and her lips finally broke into a grin. "You did that pretty good."

"My mom used to love watching that show. It's one of the few times I can remember hearing her laugh. It used to make me smile."

"That's a wonderful memory to have."

"What about you?"

Joanne sat back in her seat and sifted through her memories, good and bad. By the end, there were so many bad ones it pushed aside any sweet ones that she thought she had. Her dad had never been a hands-on parent, except when it came to discipline or ruining her life. Her mom had her moments.

Her eyes misted as she thought of her. "I think my favorite memory was when she used to read to me at night. We had this set of Curious George books. I swear we read through them a million times."

"Sounds like you were close to your mom."

A sad sigh filled the motorhome and her smile retreated. "I used to be," she said sadly. "But that all changed after I got together with Scott." Her relationship with her mom was like any other teen daughter, but after she went against them, that closeness ended. She believed her dad pushed her mom away, threatening her somehow. The woman who raised her wouldn't have acted that way otherwise. In a way, she wished it was her dad who went first, not her mom. Maybe she could have salvaged their relationship somehow.

But now, she would never know, and it made her even angrier at her dad. She could usually push her anger for him aside and focus on what she had, rather than on what she didn't, but the current circumstances of her mother's death brought all her feelings back to the surface.

"I'm sorry. We don't have to talk about it if you don't want to," he said softly.

"I'm going to have to at some point, right?"

"Only if you want to."

Was he giving her an out because he had something he didn't

want to share, or was he being kind? His interaction with her pointed to the latter, but his eyes and the motorhome held secrets he wasn't ready to reveal either, apparently. She had mixed feelings on the matter. Maybe if she opened up, he would, too.

"A secret for a secret?" she prompted.

"Are you suggesting we play *never have I ever?*"

Joanne shrugged her shoulders, her palms facing up. "What the hay. Let's do it."

Chapter Thirteen

"If we play that, though, we need to add some excitement to it. Way back when, we used to do shots, but since we don't drink, we'll have to think of something else," he said.

She brought her fingers to her chin, one finger over her mouth. He could see the gears in her mind working to come up with an idea. His own mind was drawing a blank.

"We could always share a secret if the other person says something we've done?" she suggested.

He wasn't sure about that one because admitting to having done something and then having to reveal another secret seemed like overkill. "How about for everything we've done, we remove an article of clothing?"

Her face turned red as she giggled. "Don't you think people will look at us strangely if we drive down the road naked?"

"Who knows, we might become famous on YouTube," he said, grinning. It would seem his grin made her blush all the more, the color disappearing beneath the collar of her shirt. He would sure love to see how far down her body the blush went.

"I could do without my rolls being seen by the world, thank you," she said.

Chuckling, Nathan flicked on his signal and changed into the slow lane to allow a car to pass them that was quickly approaching from behind. The downside of having a lummox of a vehicle was how slowly it accelerated on hills. But he didn't care how slow it went today. The longer it took him to get to their location, the better, because he'd have more time to get to know her. "I'm sure they are just as cute as the rest of you."

"Oh, shush."

Her cheeks turned a deeper cherry red color. Right then, he made it his mission to make her blush as much as possible. The color suited her. And he found it quite arousing and enjoyable that he could be the cause of such a colorful display of beauty. She was innocent, yet not innocent at the same time. He could see the hidden erotic nature caged in her eyes, waiting to be unleashed. Would he be able to tug on that leash and have it unravel?

"We could always play the game later when we're safely in the confines of the campsite," he said. "Then we could play it whichever way we want."

Joanne fiddled with the hem of her shirt, waiting until she was certain her voice wouldn't betray the giddiness and nervousness building inside her. He wanted to see her naked. No one had seen her naked since the last person she tried to date after Scott died. Once her clothes came off, he took off out the door. Since then, she refused to let any relationship get that far. Her body looked nothing like it used to, and even she didn't like to look at it.

"You'd run for the hills if I got naked."

"Is that a dare?" he asked.

Stunned, she blinked rapidly. Unsure of how to respond. Did she want to dare him? Joanne cleared her throat and struggled with what to say. "You don't want to see me. Trust me."

"Why don't you let me be the judge of that?" he answered softly.

"Because I know the answer."

Not a single part of her body was untouched from the accident. There was no way anyone would find it beautiful. She had watched the last guy's cock soften at the mere sight of her. Her throat clogged and tears formed in her eyes at the memory. Joanne pulled a Kleenex from her pocket and dabbed the corners of her eyes. "Sorry."

"Don't apologize, hun. You've been through something traumatic, and that's something I understand completely. Some things are so bad that it feels like they could haunt us for the rest of our lives if we let them." The tone of his voice was slightly haunted, like he had his own ghosts to contend with.

She tried not to let her past bother her, and her emotions were usually under control until she thought about opening up to someone. But wasn't that the whole point of this trip? To finally let someone in and stop living the life of a prude? She didn't want to live the last part of her life in isolation. She watched her son let someone in and knew that if he could do it, so could she.

Nathan smiled. One that reached up to his eyes. Genuine and caring. "Maybe we could help each other become a little less haunted."

"I'd like that," she said, unable to help herself from smiling back at him. There was something about his character that begged her to let him in. And her body was telling her to go for it. That maybe he'd be different.

"I've got a few games we can play to help get ourselves more comfortable."

She swallowed hard. He definitely wasn't going to suggest Tic-Tac-Toe. "Such as?"

"An adult card game," he answered.

"Strip poker?"

"Something like that," he said huskily.

The look he gave her set her womanhood ablaze, and it tingled with a heated passion. She fanned herself. "Oh dear."

He caught her gaze, and his eyes were filled with the knowledge of what he was doing to her. It's like he could read her mind without her saying a word. That told her things were going to heat up hotter than a red-hot chilli pepper. It was intimidating, to say the least, but very alluring.

"Shall I explain it?"

"Okay."

"We use about twenty-four cards in a pile. One joker, and six sets of four, like four aces, etc. Each set will have a different task. One might be to remove an article of clothing that you choose. Another will have you telling me what article of clothing to take off myself. One will have the option of putting a piece of clothing back on. Another will be to tell a secret, etc."

"And the joker?"

A sly smirk spread across his face and before he even opened them to speak, she knew she wouldn't like what he had to say. But her breasts perked instantly, her nipples pressing against her bra. She didn't even know they could still do that.

"If you pick the joker, you lose or win, depending on how you look at it."

"Why? What does the joker make you do?"

"The other person gets to remove your clothes and do whatever they want to you for 1 minute."

Her body sizzled, and her cheeks flushed. "Oh." She hadn't played that type of game before. She played a round or two of strip poker with a group of friends when she was a teen, but it never went beyond getting naked. Joanne cleared her throat, unsure of what to say. The game held a certain appeal. But what business did she have playing it at her age with wrinkles and scars in places she'd rather not show?

"It's fun, trust me," he said, his voice filled with the same energy as a kid in a candy store. Joanne couldn't help but laugh.

"Whenever a guy says that, you're usually looking for a pregnancy test two days later."

"I don't think we'll have that problem."

"Gee, thanks," she said wryly, even more acutely aware of her age.

"We can have as much fun as we want and not have to be worried about breaking the news to our parents," he said, winking at her.

That was true. No one else needed to know what trouble the two of them got into. They were well into adulthood now. No one to be accountable to, except for Alex, but he had no idea where she was. She felt a twinge of guilt but pushed it aside. He was her son, not her keeper.

"Do you want to know what I'd do if you picked the joker?" he asked, letting his gaze pass over her body from her head to her toes.

She blushed. "Eyes on the road, buster!" Her insides tickled with desire. It wanted to know what he would do.

He laughed. "You are so cute."

"That's what you say to a kid," she huffed.

"Well, Joanne, I definitely don't see you as a kid. I see a brave, wonderful, sexy woman who needs to be reminded of how much fun life can be."

"And you think you can do that?" she asked cheekily.

"If you'll let me."

There was a certain allure to giving him the power to show her how to have fun as a woman again. She'd been so busy being the nanny and housekeeper that she'd almost forgotten the feelings that came with adult fun and doing something for herself for a change.

"Let's see if you have what it takes, then," she said bravely.

"May I make a proposition?"

"What?"

"That you say yes to everything I ask."

Oh dear. That was a recipe for disaster and not something she was quite willing to do, but the childlike pull in his eyes almost had her saying yes. But Joanne was not without her sensibilities. "I promise to say yes if it means no laws are broken, and no unsafe requests are made."

"Deal."

"Wait here," Nathan said as he pulled up to the office of the Missoula KOA campground. She watched as he climbed down out of the motorhome and walked over to the door, disappearing inside. They'd found that many other campgrounds were closed for the winter, and she couldn't blame them. There was a foot of snow on the ground. It was not exactly the time to be camping, but at least they had a motorhome, not a tent. It would be warm, for the most part, as they would have power here.

Trees surrounded them, covered with a dusting of snow. One of them even had multi-colored Christmas lights wrapped around it, shining brilliantly in the moonlight, with decorations hanging off the branches. Reindeer lawn ornaments littered the front lawn of the office. And tucked in the corner was a medium-sized nativity set. Joanne smiled. They didn't forget the reason for the season.

Tire tracks in the snow led deeper into the campground, showing that there had been a bit of activity throughout the day. She stared out the window, watching the snowflakes fall. There was something pure and magical about it, adding beauty to the world.

As she was sitting there, her phone rang. Reaching over, she grabbed it out of her purse. "Hello?"

"Hi Mom, how was your non-existent flight?" Alex responded, a slightly hardened edge to his voice as his words dripped with sarcasm and a slight sprinkle of fear.

She was speechless for a moment. She hadn't expected him to check up on her flight so soon. But she should have known he would. He was meticulous that way. A very *in the know* type guy.

"Please tell me you didn't go with Nathan."

"I can assure you I'm fine, Alex." She didn't exactly want to explain herself right now. There was no way she could, even if she tried.

"Is this why you wanted to leave so early? Where are you now? I'm going to come and get you."

Chapter Fourteen

Joanne sat upright in her chair, steeling herself for a fight. "No. You'll do no such thing."

"He could be dangerous."

She'd contemplated that possibility at the beginning, but after spending time with him, she knew he wouldn't hurt a fly. "Alex, please don't worry about me. I'm fine. He's been nothing but a gentleman."

"How could you lie to me?"

In that moment, it felt like their roles were reversed. She felt like a teen doing something wrong and getting caught red-handed. But it wasn't wrong. She was an adult and allowed to make her own choices.

"I should have told you, but I know you would have run Nathan off the property for even asking to take me."

"Of course, I would. Any guy who asks to take you away this early is trouble."

Frustration bubbled inside her. "Son, I know you're concerned, but Nathan has been nothing but kind since he arrived. And I told him I wanted to do a cross-country trip someday, and he offered to take me."

"If he jumped off a bridge, would you do it, too?"

"Alex, don't be ridiculous. I'm not a child anymore."

He grunted. "You're acting like one."

"Don't speak to your mother that way. I'm an adult, capable of making my own decisions."

"But Mom, you haven't been out with a guy in forever. Now you've taken off with the first one who shows up at our door."

"Weren't you the one who brought a woman home to live with us that you didn't really know?"

"Mom, you're being frustrating," he said in a nasally voice. She knew that meant he was pinching the bridge of his nose. Something he often did when upset. It wasn't her intention to make him mad. But she had wanted to come and see what would transpire. Nathan was making her feel alive for the first time in a long time.

"I promise to stay safe, Alex. If there is a single sign of trouble, I'll call you."

"I hope you know that I'm going to do a background check on him."

"I wouldn't expect any less of you." And she didn't. What surprised her was that he hadn't done that already. That was the first thing she had thought he would do the minute the man showed up at their door. Now that she realized Alex hadn't checked Nathan out, it left a twinge of fear in her gut, but she'd always prided herself on her gut instinct. She knew when someone was a fake, and Nathan didn't come across as one. Just like Laryssa hadn't either.

He may be a man with secrets, but his spirit seemed genuine. Not everyone spilled their whole life story right away. Heck, some kept secrets for way longer than they should. And that was something she knew about. The door chimed beside her, and she looked out her side window. Nathan was walking back toward the vehicle with papers in hand.

"I have to go, Alex."

"Call me tomorrow."

"Will do. Bye, hun." She clicked the end call button and let out a breath. That wasn't a call she'd been expecting so early on in the trip. She had hoped they'd make it at least halfway before he suspected anything.

"Who was that?" Nathan asked as he climbed back into the driver's seat.

"We've been found out," she said, staring at the blank screen on her phone.

"That bad?"

Joanne shrugged. "Nothing that I didn't expect." Well, except for the fact she had no idea if the man she was driving with was Nathan Mitchell or not. For all she knew, he could be pretending to be Laryssa's family, and his last name might not even be Mitchell. He could be the creepy friend in the photos.

Thanks, Alex.

Nathan turned on the engine and pulled away from the office, following the tire tracks from the last vehicle that had arrived. "I have a feeling something else is wrong," he stated.

Joanne tried to give him a reassuring smile, but her insides were in turmoil. "I'm not sure how I feel, to be honest." What would Grace do in her situation? She knew her friend wouldn't care that she didn't know anything about her companion. She'd listen to her gut. But what if your gut was sending you mixed signals? Was that possible?

"Did he give you a hard time?"

"He threatened to come get me," she said, the corner of her lips twitching. That's something a parent would have done had they found their kid at a party they weren't supposed to attend.

Nathan laughed. "What did you tell him?"

"Told him I was a grown woman."

Nathan locked eyes with her, his gaze burning with desire. "That you are," he said huskily. "A mature, sexy one."

There was no doubt in her mind what was going through his. She knew his thoughts were on the bed in the back of the motorhome, but hers were still griping onto the fact that her son hadn't checked him out, and he had a bag of hair hidden in the drawer. Were the strands of hair from each conquest of his or a trophy gathered by a serial killer?

Joanne shook her head. That settled it. No more reading mystery novels during this trip.

Slowly but surely, they made their way to the back of the campsite, endless empty camping spots greeted them. That shouldn't surprise her as it was nearing wintertime, but the silence was unnerving. There would be no one to rescue her if things went south. Why did the attendant feel the need to place them all the way at the back? Had Nathan requested it?

When he finally pulled the big vehicle to a stop, he turned to her. "Should we eat here or walk to the little café that we passed on the way here?"

"Café," Joanne said quickly.

It would give her time to sort her thoughts out and calm her nerves. She could study him a little more in the comfort of a public audience before spending a night alone with him. If worse came to worst, she could book herself into the small hotel near the café.

"Is anything wrong?" he asked again. "Your nerves seem rattled."

"It's so quiet here," she said, glancing around at the trees encasing them on both sides. There was a small gap in between the trees leading to the next site, but it was empty, too.

"Not too many people brave the elements this time of year unless they are full time RV'ers," he replied as he unsnapped his seatbelt. "I'll be right back. I'm gonna hook up the lines."

"I'll get myself ready to go."

The walk through the dark campground had an ominous feel to it, right down to the light mist rising from the snow. High in the sky, the only light visible was the moon, casting shadows onto the roadway ahead of them. Despite Nathan procuring a flashlight from inside the motorhome, it didn't make much of a dent in the darkness. Joanne shivered. Anything could happen out here and almost no one would hear.

"Cold?" Nathan asked.

"Nope. It's just kind of spooky out here."

"Don't worry. If anyone tries anything, they'll have to get through me first," he said as he puffed out his chest with great exaggeration before letting out a chuckle.

She laughed. "I can't believe you just did that. You aren't a peacock."

He lightly bumped her shoulder with his and laughed along with her. "I love hearing you laugh."

A second later, the toe of her shoe snagged on the ground, and she lost her balance. Joanne let out a shriek of surprise. She pitched forward, only to have his strong arms reach out and catch her.

"Careful, Jo," he said.

"Well, isn't that embarrassing," Joanne muttered. She hated being a klutz, but it wasn't always something she had control over. Every once in a while, she couldn't pick her foot up high enough, and it would drag.

After the near miss, he kept his arm around her for the remainder of the walk. Despite all her suspicions, there was something comforting and arousing about his arm around her, tucking her safely against his side. She liked his touch. There was no malice in it. It was light and gentle, like the look in his eyes when he looked down at her.

Upon approaching the café, she saw a man sitting along the wall in tattered clothes, holding a sign. Sadly, homelessness appeared to exist in small towns, too. She reached into her pocket and pulled out a granola bar that she was saving for bedtime, handing it to him.

Surprised, he looked up at her, gratefulness sparkling in his eyes. "Thank you, ma'am," the gray-haired man replied, giving her a smile, his two front teeth missing. She nodded and continued to follow Nathan through the double glass doors.

She was grateful when they finally entered the small, brightly lit twenty-four-hour café. It was reminiscent of a Nineteen-Seventies diner, with its long counter accompanied by red cushioned stools, separating the workspace from the dining area. Along the windows were rows of booths with matching red cushions. It was around ten at night, so they had their pick of the seating. The only other customer appeared to be a trucker tucked into the corner booth as he dug into a big beef burger. His big rig parked outside.

As she sat down, she massaged her bad leg and wished like anything to be young and healthy again, longing for the time she could walk for miles and not get tired. Joanne reached into her purse and grabbed out some painkillers.

"I'm sorry. I should have considered stopping here before going to the campground," he said, his tone remorseful.

"It's fine. After sitting for so long, I needed to stretch my legs."

"Hi folks, I'm Dianna," the waitress said as she placed two menus on the table. "Can I get you something to drink to start off with?"

"I'll have a coffee, Dianna, thank you," he said, smiling up at her before looking at Joanne.

"I'll have water, thank you." If she drank a coffee now, she'd be up all night. Some people could drink anything with caffeine all hours of the day and fall asleep at the drop of a hat, but not her.

"I'll be right back with your drinks."

Joanne watched the younger lady smoothly walk away. No limp in her stride. It was so nice to see someone young dressed decently. No low-cut shirts, and no shorts riding up her butt. She had on a nice white blouse, black slacks, and a tan apron with her name embroidered on it. It reminded her of her younger days when she used to work in a similar place before the accident ripped everything away. Oh, to be young and carefree again.

"You're still as beautiful, you know."

"What?"

Nathan nodded toward the waitress, who was behind the counter now, pouring their drinks. "I don't think you realize that you have a grace and elegance about you that young women could only dream of having."

"Grace?" Joanne gave a hard laugh. "I tripped over my own feet walking here."

Taking one final look at the menu, he closed it and placed it by the edge of the table for the waitress to pick up. "I don't care that you limp or that you struggle when you walk. What caught my attention is how you live with your heart, visible for all to see."

She blushed. If she stayed with him for too long, her ego might pop. Clearing her throat, she asked, "Did you decide what you want?"

There was an unmistakable gleam in his eye as his gaze dropped to her lips before returning to her eyes. "Yep."

Her body heated from her head to her toes, spreading like a wave. She was going to have to invest in a personal handheld fan if she couldn't get her libido to behave itself. "Food, you silly billy."

"You didn't clarify which food."

"I'm not edible."

The corner of his lips curled into a grin. "I beg to differ."

Joanne bit her bottom lip, her panties wet. She glanced around the empty room in search of the washrooms when she saw the waitress returning to their table to take their order. After ordering her clam soup, she stood up. "I have to use the facilities."

Nathan sat back in his seat, proud of his accomplishment as he watched Joanne somewhat waddle to the bathroom in obvious discomfort, trying desperately to be nonchalant about it but failing horribly. He couldn't stop the comments from slipping out. He wasn't usually so blunt, but it was so much fun with her. She was very easy to arouse. If she asked him to stop, he'd have a hard time, but he would stop. Respect meant the world to him.

He sat there strumming his fingers on the table when the bell above the outside door chimed, letting everyone know a newcomer was coming inside. Nathan glanced at his watch. His buddy, Carter, was right on time.

Chapter Fifteen

The man looked around the room and then saw Nathan sitting there, nodding his way before heading to the counter. He raked his hand through his dark brown hair. "Hey Dianna, can I get a large glass of coke?"

"Anything for you, darling," the waitress said, flashing him a smile. "How's Jessica doing?"

"Still in the hospital, but she'd love to see you."

Jessica was the man's sister, who'd apparently taken a turn for the worst while Nathan was in Canada. But even though Carter had his hands full, he still offered to help Nathan with his problem. At first, Nathan wasn't sure how he was going to make the exchange with Joanne there, but her timely bathroom visit helped immensely.

After Carter ordered his drink, he came over to their table. Nathan quickly took the bag out of his pocket and a wad of change, handing it to him before Joanne returned to the table.

"It's going to take at least a week or two to analyze. Are you okay with that?" Carter asked.

"If you could put a rush on it, that would be awesome. I have at least one week left with the family."

"Have you told them yet?"

"Aside from the fact that I'm Laryssa's uncle? Nope. I'm waiting until I know for sure."

"What about..." his friend let his voice trail off.

Nathan shook his head quickly. "Definitely not. They don't need to know that."

"I'm surprised she didn't find out when you crossed over the border, or didn't they give you a hard time?"

"A little, but nothing blatantly evident."

"You do realize that they'll eventually find out you were in jail, right?"

"I know. I know. I just want to have some fun before I nail my coffin closed." On that cue, Joanne emerged from the washroom, still red from his earlier comments. *God.* She looked gorgeous. "Now go. My date is coming back."

Carter—his tall, lanky friend—returned to the counter where his drink was waiting. He glanced back at them momentarily when Joanne sat down in her seat.

She looked between the two of them. "I'm sorry. Did I chase him away?" she asked innocently.

"Nope. He just asked for some directions," he said, unraveling his fork from the folded napkin. She made a noise under her breath that sounded like she didn't believe him, so he continued his story. "I think he got turned around in the dark. He was looking for the highway."

It looked as though she wanted to ask more questions, but then the waitress stopped at their table with their food. "The lunch special for you," she said to Joanne, placing the hot bowl of soup in front of her. "And here's your big sirloin beef burger, enjoy!"

"Thank you," they said in unison.

The aroma from Joanne's soup was like the ocean coming alive in the restaurant. It had been a while since she had a good clam chowder, and this one smelled divine, making her think a pearl might be found inside. It distracted her momentarily from Nathan's friend sitting at the counter. The man occasionally peeked back at them, appearing to be curious.

"It seems like he knows you," she said, inconspicuously pointing to the man.

Nathan shrugged, casually picking up his big homemade burger. "He does seem vaguely familiar. I think I've seen him passing through here on one of my many trips over the years."

"That makes sense. He looks like he wants to talk to you, though. Should we invite him over?" she asked.

"No," he said, a little too quickly and abruptly.

Joanne lifted her spoon to her lips to distract herself from the odd look in his eyes. There were so many untold secrets swimming around inside them that it was becoming very difficult not to inquire about them. She had a feeling they had to do with her family, and the very reason he came to see them. Maybe he'd open up before the end of their trip.

"I'd rather have dinner alone with you," he said, letting his foot brush hers under the table. "It's not every night I have the most beautiful woman gracing me with her presence."

"Just eat your food," she said with a smile, taking another bite of hers.

"Have you thought about the little game I mentioned?"

"Shush, I'm not going to discuss that here," she said, blushing again. The man that Nathan had been talking to wasn't far enough away to be having that discussion. And she didn't want to have to take another trip to the bathroom to deal with her problem down below.

"You could always whisper," he said before taking another bite of his burger, not taking his eyes off her.

Joanne shook her head, chuckling. Boys will be boys. No matter the age. But she was torn right down the middle. She didn't know anything about him, and he had been pretty closed lipped about it. Yet, she still found herself wanting to give in to him, no matter the amount of secrets.

"I believe that some things should always remain behind closed doors," she said.

Although, she had to admit that hadn't always been the case. She'd had her fair share of risqué activities back in the day, the most brazen being in a park in broad daylight, hidden from a pathway by only a few bushes. They'd heard voices, but Scott refused to stop, and when they were right in front on the other side of the bush, she came. She'd never tried so hard in her life to stay quiet in the middle of an orgasm. She knew she had failed miserably when the people burst out laughing.

"Looks like you're having some juicy thoughts there," he said, his voice low enough that the man at the counter couldn't hear.

Joanne took a moment to bring herself back to the present moment by wiping the cracker crumbs off her shirt. Nathan was going to be the death of her sensibilities. In an attempt to change the topic, she asked, "What time are we going to be pulling out tomorrow?"

"That depends how far you want to travel tomorrow and how late of a night we have," he said, winking.

The heat rose from her neck up to her face again, and the spot between her thighs pulsated. Man, her hormones had come out of hiding with a vengeance. And as much as her circumstances should have stuffed her libido back into the box, it was doing no such thing.

"I like that look on you, by the way," he said, pointing his index finger at her while holding his burger close to his mouth.

"What look?"

"Like you mated with a tomato," he said nonchalantly as the waitress walked by. But when their eyes met, she saw blatant need. They had an *I know what I want to do with you* look, full of heat and passion. Joanne's breath caught, and she found herself unable to look away. He put his almost finished burger back on the plate. "I'm done. Dianna. Can we have the cheque?"

"Coming right up, sweetie," she replied from behind the counter as she wiped her hands on her apron.

Joanne didn't argue with the decision. Her body was driving her mad. Might be because she hadn't had sex in more years than she could count, but she no longer cared what they knew or didn't know about him at this point. He'd revved up her motor, and she was going to let him drive it. Besides, she couldn't help but be a little intrigued about the game he suggested.

The walk back may have been silent, but the air was humming with sexual intensity, like electricity arching from one transformer to the next. Her arm was linked with his. His hand covered hers, his thumb drawing little circles on her skin, sending sparks deep within her soul.

The most annoying part was that she couldn't see whether or not he was aroused. The darkness around them enshrouded his lower half, and she wanted to know. Did she dare touch him? Was that acceptable these days?

Gosh.

She was sorely tempted. No one would see it or know it but the two of them. It's not like anyone was watching them with binoculars in the dark. Giving herself to him would certainly keep her mind off the uncertainties of what the end of their week might hold. He did a pretty good job keeping her centered in the moment. And that's what she wanted. Needed. Maybe he knew that.

Once they reached the motorhome, he pulled out the stepping stool and helped her into their sleeping nest for the night. "I'm going to double check the connections. I'll be right back."

The doorway led into the kitchen nook and to the right was a small living room. One side had a sofa, and the other had a table that turned into a bed. Her gaze fell upon the drawer that held the secret compartment. Joanne shook her head and sat on the couch to wait for him.

Nathan quickly walked around to the other side of the motorhome and slipped his hand into his pants to rearrange himself. His cock hardened even more at his touch, pressing firmly against his underwear. Oh, God. Was she really going to let him pull the moves tonight? He thought he'd have to wait a day or two, but she seemed as eager as he was. Checking the hoses and power cables, he found they were all okay.

Almost tripping over his feet, he hurried back around and jumped up the stairs, not even worrying about the stepping stool. He shut the door to keep the heat inside. The icicles could stay on the trees outside, thank you very much. He planned to heat up the trailer to levels it had never seen before. It wasn't every day he had a sexy older woman within its walls. Could the windows even fog up?

Joanne was sitting on the couch, her hands folded neatly on her lap. One could easily tell that her parents had raised her to be a proper lady, but one look in her eyes told him that she often rebelled against it. And he was hoping for that rebel tonight. Walking over to the junk drawer, he grabbed out his deck of cards and then wandered over to her and held out his hand.

"Let's move this to the bedroom," he said in a low seductive tone.

It took a moment, but her hand reached up and took his. He led her back to the bedroom. She sat on one side, and he went over to the other. Swinging one leg up on the bed, he sat down, letting the other hang off the side. "Are you sure?"

She bit her lip and took a moment to ponder his question but then grinned. "Let's do it. Tell me about the game."

"We'll use King, Queen, one, two, three, ace, and a joker."

"What will each of them mean?"

"If you flip over a King, you tell me what to take off. If I flip over a King, I decide what piece of clothing to take off my body."

"Queen?"

"The opposite of the last one. If you pick a Queen, I tell you what to take off. If I do, you get to pick what you take off."

"Guess that's fair," she said, chuckling nervously. "What will the others mean?"

"One will mean that you get to put an article of clothing back on. Two will be a dare. Three will be a juicy secret. Ace of spades is a spank card, and the other aces are simply wild cards. And well, I already told you about the joker."

She had the look of a deer caught in the headlights. Her eyes wide. Her mouth uncertain of what to say. "Did you just say sp-spank?" Joanne stumbled over the words, and it made him grin. That one definitely took her by surprise.

"Ever been spanked before?"

Her cheeks once again reddened at the question. "Only as a kid."

"So never in a sexual way?"

She shook her head as she once again took to biting her bottom lip. An action that he found delightfully hot. He had debated on leaving the spanking card out of the deck, but her reaction gave him all the more reason to keep it.

"Well, then, I sincerely hope you get the card," he said as he began to lay them face down on the bed, five rows of five. This was the moment he'd been waiting for all day. He didn't think she'd be up for his games so fast, but Nathan wasn't about to complain. His intention was to live life to the fullest while he still could. There's no saying how long his body would keep functioning on this level. He held the other remaining deck of cards out to Joanne. "Pick one. We need to decide who goes first."

Chapter Sixteen

Joanne picked a card and looked at it while Nathan did the same. Butterflies attacked her stomach as the word spanked bounced back and forth in her head. Did he really mean he'd spank her if she got the Ace of Spades card? Her nipples hardened at the thought, pressing against her cotton bra. If she didn't calm down, he would see that when her bra came off.

Nathan showed her his card with the number six, and she showed him her card of eight. "That means you get to pick first," he said.

"Oh darn," she said with a nervous laugh.

This was not exactly what she had planned when she decided to come on this trip. It felt like something teenagers or college kids would do at a party, and it reminded her of games like spin the bottle. Some of which she had done in the past. But she'd never gotten into anything super kinky. Scott was straightforward, for the most part.

She glanced at the cards on the bed and then looked up at Nathan, who was grinning from ear to ear as he leaned back against his pillow with his hands locked behind his head. He looked oddly comfortable. "Do you do this a lot?" she asked.

"I've done it once or twice many years ago, but I haven't met anyone I've wanted to *do it* with for a long time."

A delightful shiver zipped through Joanne's body as she picked up on the double innuendo. "I can honestly say I haven't played this one before."

"I'll have to make sure it's a moment you never forget."

If he spanked her, she would definitely not forget about it. Joanne let her hand come to rest on a card and took a deep breath as she picked it up. *Please don't let me get the joker.* It was a diamond card with the number one.

She looked up at him. "What does this one mean again?"

"You get to put an article of clothing back on, but since we haven't taken anything off yet, it's like a free card." Nathan reached over and turned over a king. "I think luck is on your side this round," he said good-naturedly as he looked over his clothes. In the end, he removed his socks.

Not what she'd been hoping for him to remove, but that's one less article of clothing than she had on. Joanne studied the cards, not liking the fact she had no idea where the joker was. It was as nerve-wracking as it was exhilarating. Taking a breath and letting it out, she picked up her second card and flipped it over. It was a two. That was a dare card, wasn't it?

"What did you pick?" he asked as she held it against her chest.

What would he ask her to do if she showed him? Would he make her do something kinky? Because that was the whole intention of the game, wasn't it? "A two."

"Oh goodie," he said, sitting up straight now as he rubbed his hands together. "The question is, should I be nice or dirty?"

She knew she should have set some ground rules before they started because he had a wicked gleam twinkling in his eyes. "Be nice. I've never played this before."

"Okay, I'll go easy on you this time. Look in the cupboard, you'll find a banana. I want you to peel it and pretend you're sucking on it."

"Why?" she asked, and then her eyes widened as her mouth

formed an O shape. The butterflies in her stomach started sparring again. "That's going easy on me?" She'd done that only once before when she'd been teasing Scott on the first night they had sex together. He was trying to keep her virtue intact, and she never wanted him to. That night, she had pulled out all the stops.

"I could pick something more daring if you'd like?" he asked teasingly.

"No. No. I'm good, thanks." Joanne pushed herself up off the bed and went into the small kitchen, checking the cupboard for the banana. "Oh gosh. I can't believe I'm going to do this," she muttered.

She had promised to play the game, so it had to be done. Fanning herself from the sudden hot flash, she wandered back to the room where she found him relaxing back against the head of the bed again. Her gaze dropped to his crotch, where a bulge was evident.

"Stand right there so I can easily see you," he said when she reached the end of the bed. She wanted nothing more than to turn her back and do it where he couldn't watch. The innuendo of such an action made her body heat like she was standing in the middle of a fire.

Joanne peeled the banana and stared at how the fruit curved like a certain appendage, and the spot between her legs began aching for activity. Bringing the fruit to her lips, she stopped momentarily, letting out a chuckle. It was absurd to do such a thing, but the look in his eyes egged her on.

Okay, here goes nothing.

She opened her mouth and welcomed the long fruit, moving it in and out between her lips in slow, agonizing movements, staring at him in the process. Joanne squeezed her legs closed as the telltale sign of excitement seeped onto her underwear. His hands gripped the sheets as he watched, making her think he was doing whatever he could to stay where he was.

"You don't know how much I want to come over and take your clothes off right now," he said huskily, his voice deep.

She swallowed hard with the banana still in her mouth, still moving it in and out, watching his pupils dilate.

He squeezed his eyes closed. "Oh, God! You just swallowed. Stop. Stop, we'll move on," he begged.

Pleased with herself, she put it on a side table and returned to her position on the bed with a big smile on her face. She couldn't believe she did that. Now, she was hoping he'd pick a dare card, but she had no idea what she'd have him do. Her mind was drawing an absolute blank. Suddenly, a brilliant idea flashed in her mind.

"Your turn," she said, rubbing her hands together.

He cocked his head and looked at her. "Uh oh, what do you have planned?"

"I didn't do anything," she replied innocently.

"I know that look."

"You might find out, eventually. Pick a card." She fought hard not to bounce a little on the bed. She could hardly contain her excitement.

Nathan sat up and glanced over the remaining cards, choosing the leftmost card from the row closest to him. He flipped it over and chuckled as he shook his head. "It would seem I might get naked before you," he said, showing her another King.

Joanne clapped her hands in delight. Super happy that she would remain fully clothed. He had only three remaining clothes on, a shirt, pants, his underwear. He had a watch, but did that count as clothing? She sat there waiting while he decided which article to remove.

Nathan settled on his watch, spinning it around on his finger before setting it down. Guess that was her answer.

"Well, that was a safe choice," she said, sticking her tongue out at him.

"I'll take something else off if you will," he said, laughing.

She laughed. "I'm happy fully clothed, thank you.

"Dare to try your luck again?" he asked with a flourish of his hand over the cards.

Hopefully, her luck wouldn't run out. This time, her selection produced her first queen card. "That means you take something off of my choosing, right?"

Nathan laughed. "Nice try, but no. You have to take something of your choosing off."

"Oh, poop," she said. Well, she'd take a play out of Nathan's book and remove the safest option. Her socks. Taking them off one at a time, she rolled them into a ball and tossed them at Nathan. He ducked, laughing, as they hit the curtain pulled over the back window. At least they didn't reveal anything substantial, except her feet. She could live with that. "Your turn."

Nathan brought his hand up and rubbed his chin, thinking long and hard. Reaching out, he went to pick a card, then thought twice about it and picked one from the row closest to her. Flipping it around, he revealed his own Dare card.

"Oh goodie," she said.

"So, what shall I do for mi'lady?"

She was hoping he'd pick it, but she didn't think he'd get one so soon. "It's not so much what you will do, but what I'm going to do. I dare you to give me your phone. I'm going to take it into the bathroom and take a picture."

Nathan froze, the smile dying on his lips. Did she know something was up? Is that why she wanted his phone so she could snoop?

Crap!

He couldn't give her his phone. If she opened it and read his messages, then the cat would be out of the bag, and she would certainly take the next flight out.

But if he didn't give it to her, then she'd really be suspicious. He looked at Joanne, who was staring at him curiously. "Are you afraid I'll find out you're a serial killer or something?" she asked him, her eyebrow quirked.

"Of course not," he replied with a nervous laugh. Oh, God! How was he going to get out of this one? He was the one who chose the game and added dares to the list. They could have easily been left out. "Can I change the rules?"

"Nope, you made me do the banana," she said, and with those words, her cheeks reddened again.

He couldn't help but grin. "That I did, but what are you going to do with my phone?"

"I'm going to take a picture."

That caught his attention, and he leaned forward, resting his elbow on his knee. "What kind of picture?"

"That's for me to know and you to find out."

"I like the idea," he lied, "but it sounds more like a dare for you, not me. What's the catch?"

"You're not allowed to look at it until the end of the game."

He fell back toward his pillows, covering his face with his hand, chuckling. "Oh, that's mean." He didn't think she had that in her, but apparently, she did. "Why don't you think of another?"

Joanne shook her head and wiggled her fingers at him, refusing to release him from the dare. "This game was your idea, remember? I'm just playing by the rules."

"Cheeky woman!" he mumbled. "Give me a second." Unlocking his screen, he deleted the message between him and his friend. No point in letting the cat out of the bag too early.

Her eyes narrowed a fraction, and she furrowed her brow. "What are you doing?" she asked as she leaned over to look.

"Nothing," he replied, moving it away from her. The action made her frown. *Careful, dude, you're making her suspicious.* "I just had some pictures on there that I didn't want you to see."

"Really?" she questioned. A flash of mistrust quickly replaced the joy that was in her eyes earlier.

This wasn't what he had planned when he'd suggested the game. It was supposed to be light, exciting, and end in only one way, but at this rate, it would end with him sleeping outside. "Yes. I'm a single guy," he said, shrugging his shoulders.

"Yuck," she said, scrunching up her nose.

Now it was his turn to be curious. "If you've never looked at those types of pictures, why do you want my phone to take one?"

"Because."

Realizing he wasn't going to win this battle and because it was the name of the game, he had to relinquish his phone into her possession and let her disappear with it. Did he have anything else on there that was incriminating? He looked up at the ceiling, trying to think. But when he couldn't come up with anything else, he relinquished his phone. "Two minutes, then I come find you."

"Thank you," she said, then she disappeared into the small compact washroom, leaving his heart going a mile a minute with worry.

Chapter Seventeen

Joanne closed the sliding door and took a breath. She had begun to wonder whether he was going to give it to her. But what did he delete? Was he being honest about the pictures? She had spent enough time in her own lie to know when someone was hiding something. Glancing at the screen of his cellphone, she contemplated clicking on the message icon. But once she did that, she couldn't take her actions back.

The battle raged within her as she stood there, staring at the home page. Trust wasn't an easy thing to come by and once it was broken, it was hard to earn back. And she never wanted to be that woman, but—*gah*—the phone was in her hands. One quick click of a button and she could have all the answers she was looking for.

"Do I have to come find you?" he called.

"I'll be out in a second."

Pushing the desire to have all the answers to the back of her mind, she decided she couldn't be that person—the snoop—just yet.

"Joanne," he called again. "Ten seconds, and I'm coming in."

Eep!

She clicked on the camera app, wondering what type of picture she should take. Joanne turned the phone this way and that, frowning. Was she really that fat? Her face looked a lot bigger on camera than it did in the mirror. How the heck did anyone make themselves look good in a selfie? Then an idea hit her, and she hit the button, taking a photo.

As she opened the bathroom door, a smirk spread across her face. She intended to have fun, and the picture was the start of that. Walking up to the bedroom door, she saw Nathan stretched out with his hands behind his head, looking strangely delicious. The butterflies in her stomach went haywire with need. She placed his phone on the dresser.

"Can I see?" he asked, holding out his hand.

"Not until the end of the game."

He sat up, folding one leg underneath his other as he eyed his phone. "I might be too distracted to remember."

Joanne grinned and shrugged as she sat down on the bed, ready to flip a card over. Nathan must have seen that as an opportunity and got up to reach for his phone. She pushed his chest, making him fall flat on his back on the bed. He pulled her down with him, making her land on top. Their movements jostled the cards.

He wrapped his arms around her and stole a quick kiss. "This works for me."

Being in the warmth of his embrace felt like heaven. She sighed, resting her forehead against his chest. She couldn't remember the last time she was in the embrace of a man who wasn't family, and that made it hard to pull away, but they had a game to finish.

"If we don't play the game, it will get too late to finish."

"I don't need a game for what I want to do," he replied.

Joanne blushed. "You started it, so we have to finish."

"You really want to torture me, don't you?" he grumbled with a good-natured grin.

"Much more fun, don't you think?" she asked as she set the cards up again. "Whose turn was it again?"

"Yours."

"Darn." Joanne studied the cards and wished she had x-ray vision to avoid the joker. There was no telling how she would feel if she was the one that flipped it over. On one hand, it would be nice to get it over and done with, but on the other, she liked the slow burn. There was nothing like building up anticipation. She picked the card in the middle of the row right in front of her and held her breath as she flipped it over. Giggling, she flipped it around to show him that she'd picked up a king.

He leaned his head back and laughed. "Of course, luck would be on your side. What shall I take off?"

She pulled her lips to one side as she thought about it, bringing her fingers up to her chin. Shirt, socks, or pants? It was time to see whether he was as fit as he appeared. "Shirt," she blurted before she chickened out.

He gripped the sides of his white t-shirt and pulled it over his head, tossing it to the floor. Her eyes involuntarily took a trip from his face down to his torso, where a powerful set of abs betrayed the truth of how old he was—firm and mouth-watering. She pressed her lips together to make sure no drool escaped. When she managed to look back up again, he was staring at her with an amused look on his face, his eyes dancing with heat.

He rested his forearm on his knee as he leaned forward. "Why don't we skip the game and go right to the main event?"

Joanne jerked backwards and fell off the bed. She landed on the ground with a thud. Nathan kneeled on the bed and looked over the edge, with even more amusement playing across his features as he struggled hard not to laugh.

She looked up at him. "Shush up."

Nathan laughed as he held out his hand to help her up. "What? I didn't say anything."

The minute his hand closed over hers, the warmth spread through her like a forest fire. She felt tempted to take him up on his offer, but it was the scars on her body that prevented her from saying the words. If he was going to see them, the only way she'd be brave enough for it was to let the game decide for her.

"Why don't you sit at the head of the bed, so you don't fall off again?"

Joanne stared at the pillows. There would be nowhere for her to run if she sat on that side. He could easily lay her back and have his wicked way with her. "I...uh...I'm fine right here," she stammered.

He chuckled. "You do realize that the pillows won't bite you, right?"

Unable to help herself, she stuck her tongue out at him. "Just pick a card." The game should help keep her focused on something other than his abdomen. It should be a sin for a man his age to look that good. She shifted uncomfortably.

"I guess it's my turn, eh?" he asked.

Joanne nodded and held her breath. The game was going to kill her before the night was over. Would he be naked before her? Was she going to get the joker, or would he? She wished she could see into the future.

Reaching out, Nathan flipped over the card closest to him and held it up to look at it. "I'm beginning to think the cards are stacked in your favor," he said, holding up another king. Since he was only wearing underwear and pants now, he had only one option. Standing up, she watched as he undid his belt, never taking his eyes off her.

"If you keep looking at me that way, I'm not going to be able to wait until the game is over," he said huskily, tossing his pants to the side.

Joanne licked her lips as she stared at his noticeable bulge straining against his sky-blue underwear. She fanned herself. "Oh gosh," she whispered under her breath. He was already aroused. Her heart thumped in her chest. She shifted, trying hard to ignore the damp heat pooling on her underwear. One look in his eyes told her that her excitement was evident to him, too.

He sat back on the bed, with one leg crossed toward his other, which hung off the bed. The skin on the back of his leg looked paler compared to the rest, like he'd been burned in the past. She chose not to say anything, as she wouldn't want anyone commenting on her body either. It certainly didn't take away from how sexy he looked.

"Your turn," he said, his eyes appearing grateful for her silence.

They were getting closer and closer to finding the joker. Her hand shook as she grabbed the card farthest away from her and held it up, forgetting what it meant. "It's a 3."

"A juicy secret. Do you want me to ask a question, or do you want to freely divulge one?" he asked.

She was drawing a blank and as much as she feared any question he could ask, she figured they'd be all night if he didn't ask her something. "You go ahead."

He let his gaze travel from the top of her head to her chest, and then stop between her legs. Despite being fully clothed, she instinctively dropped her hands to hide herself. "Don't you dare," she said.

"Oh, I very much dare," he said with a husky growl, a defiant grin spreading across his face. "Are you wet?"

If her face wasn't red before, it was sure to be now, and he appeared to be enjoying himself at her expense. "You didn't just ask me that."

"I did."

"That's not a question you should ask a lady."

"Well, we aren't playing a lady-like game," he countered.

He had her there. They stepped into the realms of the wild where anything could happen between a man and a woman. What would Grace do? Her brow furrowed as she struggled between staying decent or sharing the truth and feeding it to him on a silver platter. Because that's exactly what he'd want—her on a dinner plate. She could see it in his eyes.

"Let's just say I'm uncomfortable down there," she replied shyly.

"That's good enough for me," he said, chuckling. Nathan realized this was still new to Joanne, and he didn't want to press her too much. He knew the end of the game would be even further beyond her comfort zone, and he wanted her to have fun. The plan was to get her used to the idea of sex before things got that far.

He eyed his phone on the desk once more. There was a picture of Joanne on it, and he was itching to see it. Was she more daring behind a closed door? God, he hoped so. He saw the desire fluttering through her eyes, especially when he took off his pants.

Picking up a card from the third row, he flipped it over and almost shouted with pleasure. He turned it around to show her. "Off comes the shirt, my dear."

Joanne looked down at her white cashmere blouse, the top button undone. Could she do it? Could she take her shirt off in front of a man? Something she hadn't done for as long as she could remember, other than for a doctor? She drew the corner of her lip into her mouth and bit down on it nervously.

"I could help if you like?" he offered.

No way. If she let him do that, she wouldn't want him to stop. "Keep those busy hands to yourself, master." Heat once again rushed up her neck and onto her face. "I mean mister."

"The first one works for me," he replied with a huge grin, the corners of his eyes crinkling with laughter.

Fumbling with her buttons, her fingers shaking, she slowly undid them. Each button revealed her white undershirt instead of a bra. When she slipped the blouse off her shoulders, he groaned.

He looked down at his underwear and then over at her. She was still fully clothed in his eyes. "That's so unfair. I'm at a complete disadvantage here."

"Your disadvantage is my advantage," she said, winking. After placing her blouse neatly on the top of the dresser, she turned back to the bed and eyed the cards on the comforter. Sitting back down, she grabbed the left card in the second row and flipped it over.

"Damn, it's not the ace of spades," he grumbled as he looked at her ace of diamonds.

"That's a wild card, right?" she asked.

"Yes."

"Does that mean I could put my shirt back on?" she inquired.

"Yes, but God, please don't!" he begged, giving her the puppy dog eyes. She knew he wanted to even up the score, but her plan was for him to be naked first instead of her. It might be a little easier for her to get naked if he did first.

Joanne laughed, tossing the card into the discard pile. "I'll behave."

"That's no fun. You could always take something else off."

"I'm good, thank you. Your turn."

"Come on, even things up a little," he said, pointing to her undershirt.

"Only if you get lucky."

When he reached over, she caught a glimpse of his back, which was marred with the same pale skin as the back of his leg. She opened her mouth to ask, but snapped it closed when he turned over another queen. Now it would be her turn to reveal her pale pink scars, and she hoped to God he wouldn't comment on them either. They had faded over the years, like the one on her face, but still very noticeable. The smaller ones, not so much, but she could never get used to the larger ones.

"Well, darling, off with the second shirt."

She did as she was told, revealing her lacy, off-white brassiere. Her breasts weren't as perky as they used to be, so thank goodness for designers who thought of push-up bras. Although she wished like anything she could hide her belly roll, but he didn't appear to be complaining. His eyes had settled on her breasts.

"Much better," he said with appreciation.

Chuckling, Joanne looked over at the remaining 13 cards. Unlucky thirteen. They were getting closer and closer to the devil card, the joker, and it was her turn. Why did she feel like her luck was about to turn?

Nathan reorganized them into three lines—two rows of four and one row of five. The bigger row was closest to her. "Just to let you know. Every time I've played this game, the girl has always gotten the joker in the end."

She wasn't sure which of the two of them she preferred to get the joker. If it was her, then he'd take the reins and do whatever he wanted with her for a minute. If he got it, she'd have a minute to do whatever she wanted to him, but knowing her, she'd probably chicken out and tickle him or something.

Picking up the last card in the row closest to her, Joanne flipped it over and let out a squeak. Taking it, she shoved the card into her pants. There was no way she was letting him see the card.

Chapter Eighteen

Joanne stood up. "I think I'll call it a night," she said, gently patting her mouth, pretending to yawn.

The smirk on his face couldn't get any wider. "You got it, didn't you?"

She took a step back, moving into the doorway. *Oh goodness.* She was in so much trouble. She could already feel his hands on her body, waking her insides even more. Wet heat slipped from her womanhood.

"Don't make me wrestle you to see it."

"You wouldn't."

"Well, if you got the joker, I'm going to remove your clothes one by one anyway. Either way, I win."

"Yep, you win. Good night," she said, taking another step backwards.

But before she realized it, he'd hopped off the bed and grabbed her wrists, drawing her in close to his nearly naked body. Her breasts brushed up against his hard chest, her nipples tightening. She looked up at him, and the fire in his eyes tickled her insides. "Oh dear," she murmured.

Leaning down, he brushed his warm lips lightly against hers. And for a moment, that's how they remained. Neither moving, not even their lips. But then, she felt his oh-so-clever hand sneak down the front of her slacks. He stopped by her womanhood, letting his finger brush against her sensitized bud.

Joanne's head rolled back, and she moaned softly at his gentle administrations. "I think you missed the card."

"But I didn't miss the mark, did I? If you got the joker, I get to do what I want for 1 minute."

"But I didn..." Her words trailed off when his finger rubbed her a little harder. Her nerve endings went into overdrive after having been on a long hiatus. She didn't want him to stop. She couldn't even remember the last time a man had touched her in such an intimate way.

"You didn't what?" he asked, halting his motions.

"Nothing," she murmured as she linked her hands behind his neck, pulling him down for another kiss. His breath was sweet, his scent intoxicating. There was something about it that drew her in. It didn't matter that they didn't really know each other yet. She wanted all of him.

He pulled his hand out and undid her slacks, holding her steady as she stepped out of them. She waited for him to comment on her scars, but like her, he didn't say a word. He reached around and unclipped her bra, letting his fingers trail the sides of her breasts as the bra fell to the floor. She moaned into his mouth. How had she gone this long without a man's touch? She'd forgotten the feel of their palm against her skin, making rivers of passion course through her body. Nathan slid his tongue along her bottom lip, and she opened to him. Two tongues becoming one, learning and tasting.

He turned her around, so she was the one with her back to the bed, and she scooted up to the mattress, eagerly waiting for him to join her. But instead of climbing on the bed, he reached down and searched through her pants for the card. Picking it up, he flipped it over and looked at it.

"Looks like I owe you a spanking."

"I'm lying on the bed almost naked, and you want to spank me?"

His lips curled into a grin. "Oh, very much so," he said, the light above glinting off his shiny teeth. He looked very much like the big bad wolf. Forget about silver foxes. She'd take a silver wolf any day.

Joanne giggled nervously. "I can think of other things we can do."

"Miss Joanne." He climbed onto the bed and trailed butterfly kisses up her body. "Do I need to tie you up to get you to behave?" he asked, before letting his mouth close over her breast, sucking gently.

"God, you're going to kill me," she moaned as she gripped the sheets.

Releasing her breast, he sat on the side of the bed, patting his lap. "Across you go, mi 'lady."

Her eyes widened, and she scrambled up to the head of the bed, her butterflies boxing in her stomach. She didn't think he really wanted to. She thought it was a joke. "You're serious."

"Oh yes. I wanna see how warm and red I can make your ass."

"Are you going to huff and puff, too?" she asked.

"Only if you want me to." He laughed. "Now, up on my lap, hun, or do I have to make you?" A wicked but playful gleam appeared in his eyes again, letting her know he was more than ready to play the game.

Joanne glanced at the door of the bedroom and then back at Nathan, wondering if she could make a run for it. Then she chuckled. Running was something she hadn't been able to do in ages, so she wouldn't get far. He'd probably snag her arm before she got out the door. Her parts tingled as she caught the predatory look in his eyes. The caveman was here to play.

Resigned, but in a hot and bothered way, she climbed off the bed on the other side and slowly made her way to his side with him watching her every step, his smile growing wider the closer she came.

"I can't believe I'm going to do this," she murmured.

"Please take your underwear off," he ordered.

Joanne looked down at her tan cotton undies and hooked her thumbs through it on either side and pulled them down.

With great care, he placed her across his knee, his erection pressing firmly against her side, and it made a delightful shiver ripple through her. She couldn't wait to feel him inside her, and the sooner they got this over with, the sooner she could.

Before he began, he leaned over and whispered, "I wish I could take a picture of this."

"Say what?" She tried to push herself back up, but he held her down securely.

"You aren't going anywhere, darling," he said, running his finger down her spine deliciously so. "Did you know you have dimples?"

But before she had a chance to respond, his fingers slipped between her legs, finding her moist center.

"Oh, sweet mercy," she said breathlessly, biting down on her knuckle. Nathan made a few lazy circles with his finger over her clit. Warmth spread through her as he explored her intimately, dipping one finger, then two inside her. She hadn't realized the pleasure that could come from such a strange angle.

"Do you like that?" he asked.

She murmured incoherently, lost in the sensation of her body rapidly racing toward an orgasm unlike anything she could ever remember. It was like an addiction she had to have. Joanne rocked against his hand, eager to take him inside more deeply, but instead of complying, his fingers slid out of her, and for a moment, he did nothing until...

Slap.

She jumped and let out a cry of shock, her butt feeling the sting of his hand. "Aren't you supposed to like count or something?" Down his hand came again.

Slap.

Electric shocks traveled to the ends of her nerves and back again, her clit pulsating in response. Nathan rubbed her tender butt cheeks, calming the sting, before slipping between her legs again.

"You are so wet."

Not something she'd ever thought she'd hear after being dry for so long. She could barely get wet when she tried to make herself cum. It was nice to know everything still functioned normally. He slipped three fingers inside her this time, and her body vibrated as it raced to the mountain top.

"Oh please, Nathan!" she begged. She had to cum. She needed the release.

He seemed more than happy to oblige by rapidly moving his fingers inside her. Up and down. In and out. Joanne couldn't keep her eyes open any more, her muscles tensing as she dove off the edge of the orgasmic ravine. And when her muscles first clenched around his fingers, he spanked her again and again as she came.

It was like a burst of spicy hot energy filling her. Her entire being trembled with delight, unsure of where her orgasm started and ended. She squeezed her eyes closed so hard fireworks danced behind them, lighting up the darkness.

She went limp on his lap, head down toward the floor. "Holy mackerel," she gasped. He went to help her up, but she held out her hand. "One second. I can't move." She couldn't stop her muscles from trembling long enough to get up.

Appearing to not need her help, he placed his hands on her hips and put her on the bed himself. And somehow, between the time he laid her down, and the time he climbed on top, he'd already removed his underwear. His cock was pressed against her womanhood, ready to make her his.

"Condom?" she asked, breaking the spell momentarily.

Nathan looked down at himself and chuckled. He had been kind of hoping to be naked and free. It had been a while since he's been with anyone, and he wanted to feel her skin against his in the most basic way. But she called him out, and he wanted to respect her. Partially rolling off her, he reached over to his bedside table and opened the drawer. Pulling out a condom, he slipped it on.

"May I?" he asked, hovering over her again.

She reached between them and grabbed a hold of his cock, and it jumped at her touch. Or he did. He wasn't sure which. It took him by surprise but felt damn amazing. She gave him a gentle squeeze, making him press his forehead against the pillow, his face in the crook of her neck as he groaned. His cock hardened even more.

She froze. "I'm sorry, did I hurt you? It's been a while since I..." Her words trailed off as he pushed his hard cock into her sweet, wet heat.

He kissed the side of her neck. "You were perfect," he said, pulling his cock out before pushing into her once more, loving every second of being inside her. He could die a happy man right now. She tilted her hips, guiding him into her as deep as he could go. Nothing else mattered in this moment. No truths. No lies. Just her, the most amazing woman underneath him, giving him a gift no amount of money could ever pay for.

"Harder, please," she begged, bucking against him to get his attention. And he was more than willing to oblige, it was beyond his control now anyway. Faster and faster, they moved, in sync with each other, sweaty skin slapping together in the rising heat. Two hearts raced to cross the finish line together. Her breathing ragged, her nails digging into his scar covered back. Her gray eyes locked on his as they both hit the climax at the same time.

He stiffened, his back arching as he pumped back and forth, her muscles clamping down on him. Hard. She cried out his name, and he cried out hers, certain that the entire camp could hear them. But he didn't care. All he could feel was amazement that she'd allowed him to become one with her. He shivered before his arms gave out, and he lay flush against her.

"You're so good you could kill a man," he exclaimed.

Chapter Nineteen

Nathan knew the moment Joanne's thoughts turned to the unpleasant. She sucked in a breath and turned her head in the opposite direction, pressing lightly against his chest—an indication that this experience was over, and he had ruined it.

He got up and sat on the edge of the bed, facing her, resting his palms on his thighs. "I'm sorry. Poor choice of words." That had been a problem of his, thinking before speaking. The last thing he wanted to do was upset Joanne. He knew this trip was not going to be all fun and games for her, which was why he had asked to take her, to give her that little bit of fun in the meantime and get to know her.

"It's okay," she said. "Can you give me some privacy, please?"

Was she already regretting the choice they had made? He hoped not, because it was hotter than any other experience he'd had in his lifetime. In his younger years, he'd played the card game, but it never ended before he or the other person chose the joker. Not like it did tonight. Then he had to go and open his big fat mouth.

Standing up, he grabbed his underwear off the floor and his phone off the dresser, and then stepped out of the room. He took one last look at her before closing the door. Her expression was a mixture of shock and despair, her eyes glued to his scars.

Nathan cursed under his breath as he stood there naked. For a moment, he'd forgotten all about his disfigured body. A constant reminder of his betrayal, and the reason he could never let himself get serious about anyone. Once a cheater, always a cheater, right? Wasn't that how the saying went? He had heard it more times than he could count. No one in the world believed a cheater could stop, and honestly, he didn't dare put anyone else in that position to find out, especially not a woman as unique and special as Joanne.

Clicking on his phone, he typed in his pin, hoping to see a message from Carter stating he'd started the DNA test, but a picture popped up on his screen instead, distracting him.

"That little tease," he chuckled. She made him wait all this time to see a headshot with her sticking her tongue out at him, wearing a bunny ear filter. It wasn't exactly the picture he was expecting, but it still revved his motor, nonetheless. She had class, unlike some of the other women he'd met.

Hunting around the motorhome, he found some clothes tucked away in a compartment under the seat at the table. It wasn't long before she stepped out of the room, fully clothed with a rather sheepish look on her face, her hair curling in every which direction endearingly. Her cheeks flushed. She folded her hands in front of her. He was speechless. She looked like an angel sent to him from heaven. His heart squeezed a little in his chest. They stood there awkwardly, uncertain of what to say. Him staring at her, and she at him.

"Did we just do that?" she asked, clasping and unclasping her hands. She sounded as surprised as he was.

"I didn't hurt you, did I?"

"Oh no. It was wonderful."

"I mean with what I said at the end."

"No. Not really." She sat on the couch and patted the cushion beside her. He sat down, too, draping his arm over her shoulder and pulling her close.

"Do you want to talk about it?" he asked.

"If I do, you have to promise not to read too much into it."

That intrigued him. It's not like she could say she was a virgin or something. She was a mother and a grandmother. But that made him wonder whether anyone had ever made it to their age and still be a virgin. That would be a Guinness world record.

"The last man I had sex with did die."

"During?" was all he could ask. If that didn't earn a spot on a thousand ways to die, he didn't know what would.

Joanne shook her head and ended up standing up to pace the length of the motorhome. He instantly missed her warmth and the feel of his arm wrapped around her, with her head sitting in the crook of his shoulder.

"I don't even know how to say this," she said, running a hand through her disheveled hair as she looked around the vehicle. "This...all this...it's not me. It's Grace's style." He must have looked confused, so she continued, "She's one of my best friends. Oh gosh, this is embarrassing. I haven't had sex since my husband died."

"Not even a quickie?"

"Most definitely no quickies."

How could a woman go decades with no sex? Did she give herself a helping hand to stave off the urge? That's what he had to do to keep his body from exploding in his sleep. "How'd you manage that?"

"To be honest, I was too busy recovering to give it much thought, and then I was too busy trying to get my family back to care. Once I settled into a life with Alexander's family, I was living a lie. I couldn't bring anyone else into that. And I wasn't one for quickies."

"A lie?" The word flashed like a red neon sign in his mind. That was kind of what he'd been doing since he arrived. He hadn't told anyone about why he was there, aside from being Laryssa's uncle. Maybe she would understand after all.

"I worked as Alexander's nanny and then became his housekeeper. He didn't know I was his mother until he met Laryssa and the story kind of unraveled after that."

"Why didn't he know?"

"At first it was because I couldn't tell him, otherwise his grandparents would have kicked me out and refused to let me see him. And then once I started working for him when he moved away from home, I was afraid he'd hate me for lying to him for so long."

"They wouldn't let you tell him?"

"After my accident, I was in bad shape." She pointed to the scar on her cheek. "I wasn't capable of looking after the boys. My parents and Scott's parents fought to get custody, and they were each given custody of one boy and were told never to let them meet because the families didn't get along. Once I was well enough, I tried to go back and get them, but my dad threatened to institutionalize me. So, I did the only thing I could think of. I went to Scott's family and begged them to take me in at least as his nanny. I told them I wouldn't tell him who I was if they would let me stay. It became one of the conditions of the work agreement."

"I can't imagine he took it too well when he found out."

"He was madder at his grandparents and Laryssa than at me. I think in some strange way he understood my dilemma and saw me as a mother figure already, so we naturally flowed that way."

And that was his problem. If he was Laryssa's father, he was never there as any type of family figure, so he didn't think things would go as smoothly for him. And his reason for not telling the truth wasn't because of any condition. It was more out of guilt than anything. And that's probably why he went on this trip with Joanne. He could delay the inevitable a little longer. Honestly, it's mostly him chickening out. He knew it. However, it also gave him more time to find out the truth.

"That's good. How have things been with your dad?" he asked.

"Non-existent."

"When was the last time you spoke with him?"

"The day that he threatened to send the guys with straight jackets."

He let out a low whistle. She must feel like she's walking into a den of lions. "Have you heard anything about how he's doing?" he asked.

"No. I haven't had any contact with anyone. They made it abundantly clear that they wanted nothing to do with me. What about you? You look like you have a story to tell."

"My scars?"

She nodded.

A whoosh of air escaped through his lips. It wasn't a memory he liked to talk about and certainly didn't want to spill the beans before their trip had finished. "I was in a bad fire. It literally singed the entire backside of my body."

"What happened?"

"I got caught in an explosion. An engine blew. I couldn't get away fast e-enough," he said, biting back the tears that tried to surface.

The pain had been unbearable. But the worst pain was knowing he'd left a kid an orphan and without a family. There wasn't anything he could have done to change that. He was incapable of stepping forward.

"I couldn't even imagine how that felt."

"Honestly, I felt like I was in hell." And not just because of the burns, but because the person he used to be no longer existed. All that remained was a man who had lost all honor and respect. One who killed his brother and deserved to live the rest of his life in exile.

She came and sat down beside him, letting her hand rest on his thigh. "I'm sorry."

He took her hand and brought it to his lips, gently laying a kiss on the back of it. "Thanks for not looking at me like I'm a monster." The sad part was, she would look at him that way eventually, once she knew he was a cheater.

"If you're a monster, then so am I," she said softly, her palm resting against his cheek.

"Far from it."

No reality existed where Joanne could ever be a monster. She was too sweet, too pure. She gave to others more than she ever got in return and does so selflessly. He didn't even deserve to be the one driving her across the country, but he had to. There was something about her that made him want to get to know her better.

"And neither are you. Scars don't make a monster. Scars make a survivor."

Looking away, he wished he could believe her. He'd been called a monster on more than one occasion. Not even those who knew him wanted anything to do with him. His old buddies turned their backs on him when he got tossed in the slammer, except for Carter. He was the one who had encouraged him to come clean about the cheating.

"Hey, look at me." Joanne placed a hand on both of his cheeks and turned him to face her. "You are not a monster."

"You don't even know me," he said, his voice breaking. There was deep pain and sadness in his words. He was carrying a deep burden, much like she had for so long.

"I know what I need to know," Joanne replied with certainty.

If she felt there was anything amiss about him, she would never have agreed to the trip. Sure, he had his secrets, and there was a lot they didn't know about each other, but there was something in his spirit that made her want to do things she hadn't done in ages. He made her come alive.

She liked it when they were playing around in the room because the only thing that existed was the two of them, like their own private fantasy. It was more about primordial instincts than anything else. She felt good letting go for a change. It was rather rejuvenating. Maybe there was still some juice left in her sail after all.

"You are amazing. Do you know that?" he asked, kissing her on the forehead before looking at his watch. "Wow, we better get to bed if we hope to head out by six. Did you want me to make the other bed?"

Joanne glanced between the couch they were sitting on, the bed in the bedroom, and the dejected look in his eyes. She couldn't leave him that way. When they were in bed, it was gone, and he seemed to be at peace. "Enough room for two in there?" she asked.

A smile lit up his face, and the clouds dissipated from his eyes. "You bet!"

He pulled her to her feet and was walking backward with her to the room, removing her clothes along the way, his lips closing over hers as they passed through the doorway.

"Round Two."

"Maybe I should spank you this time," she said cheekily.

"Oh no, mi'lady. I'm the Master, doncha know."

"Not this time," she grinned, pushing him onto the bed.

Joanne turned and closed the door, turning off the lights.

Chapter Twenty

"I hope you enjoyed your stay," the lady at the office counter said as he checked out of the campground.

"More than you'll ever know," Nathan said with a grin. "Have a good day."

He had to admit he slept like a baby after their second pleasure round. And if they wouldn't have overheated themselves, he would have loved to have held her in his arms until they both fell asleep. But he was just thankful she decided to sleep beside him. That was unexpected.

Pushing open the door, he walked outside into the frigid cold air and into the motorhome that was parked not too far away. Joanne was sitting in the front seat, sipping away on her coffee.

"We're ready to go?" she asked.

"Yep," he said, sitting in the driver's seat. She had a radiant glow about her this morning. Her cheeks were rosy, and the look in her eyes told him she was thinking about what they did the night before. That experience was going to be hard to top. He'd have to think long and hard about what he could do to surprise her tonight.

"Where's our next stop?"

"I was hoping to make it to Mount Rushmore today, but it took us longer than I expected yesterday to reach Missoula in the snow, so I think we may have to stop somewhere along the way."

"Any thoughts?" she asked.

He hadn't thought much about it, not while he had Joanne in his arms, but there would be time to do that at lunchtime. "When we stop for lunch, we can go over the map. Maybe see if there's any interesting sights to see along the way."

Honestly, he'd love to prolong their trip for as long as possible, but he knew she needed to get there on time for the reading—if there was actually a reading. He had a feeling her family was going to try something.

He couldn't figure out why her family would treat her the way they did. She was the type of woman you wanted to give the world to and who deserved the sun and the moon. He could see why her husband fell in love with her. It wasn't right that she had been alone since her husband died. She had so much to offer a man.

"Sounds good," she replied with a smile.

Nathan snapped his seatbelt into the clasp and put the motorhome into drive, beginning their exit out of the park. It was a gorgeous area that he would have loved to have stayed another day, especially with her, but it was time to get the show on the road.

"Do you think Yellowstone would be open?" she asked.

"Unfortunately, most of the roads through the park are closed in the winter, so it's probably best to bypass it completely."

She sighed with disappointment. "I guess that's to be expected. I haven't been to Yellowstone before."

"Maybe if all goes well, you and I can go sometime."

"If my son doesn't kill you first," she said.

"Have you heard from him today?" He'd heard her phone chime a few times, but she didn't take it out to look at it.

"I'm kind of afraid to look," she said rather sheepishly.

If it was her son, he was probably getting ready to send the cops after them. "You probably better check." The last thing he wanted was some cop to pull him over and give him the third degree. They were good at asking him about the time he'd spent in jail. His time with her was too precious to ruin with that tidbit of information.

"He's a big boy. I'm sure he can handle not hearing from his mother for a bit."

"We are talking about the same man, right?" he questioned. Alex didn't look like he was a man who could handle being out of the loop. He seemed like someone who had to know exactly what was going on. "Humor me?"

"What if he finds out that we...you know?" she asked, her cheeks suddenly blushing.

"I'm sure he's already figured that out by now and wants to kill me," he said, sending a lopsided grin her way. Her son reminded him of a father who'd be waiting at the door with a shotgun, ready to shoot his ass off the property.

"Oh gosh, I hope not," she said, looking absolutely mortified before covering her face with her hands.

Nathan laughed. Joanne reminded him of a teenager who had been discovered having sex for the first time. He loved her apparent innocence. It turned him on even more. A young woman trapped in an older woman's body. Not that he had any complaints. She was pretty hot.

"Would that be so bad?"

"He's liable to crash the party."

"I guess we'll just have to keep one step ahead of him, eh," Nathan replied as he signaled to turn onto the highway, merging easily with the rest of the traffic. Not too many people were driving around because of the snow, which was falling quite heavily now. Winter was a pretty time of year, but the roads were sketchy at best. Many mountain passes were closed. He'd checked the driving conditions when he woke up that morning, and thankfully, the road they were taking was open.

The tire tracks in the snow made it easier for him to see where to drive without crossing over into the other lane. Snowplows hadn't yet gone through yet, but he wouldn't be surprised if he saw one or two along the way. Right now, it looked like they were driving in a winter wonderland, mystical and surreal. Never did he think he'd travel with another woman sitting beside him, much less one he enjoyed.

"Easier said than done," she commented. "He's a boss for a reason."

He chuckled. "Seems pretty whipped by Laryssa, though."

"Been that way since the day they met."

"Funny how that works, eh?"

Joanne nodded her head, her phone dinging yet again. Reaching into her pocket, she pulled it out, giving a long sigh in the process. She wasn't going to have any type of peace if she didn't respond to him. He would message her every 5 minutes for the rest of the day. There were already ten messages, and they'd barely even gotten onto the road.

>*Where are you?*

>*Are you okay?*

>*Mom, message me when you get this.*

>*Okay, if you don't message me in the next hour, I'm going to call the police.*

One would think he was the parent, and she was the kid. He seemed to forget she could take care of herself and had been doing so for all her life.

>*I appreciate the concern, Alex, but everything is fine. If we get into trouble, I'll call you.*

Just when she was going to put the phone back in her pocket, it chimed again.

>*Why weren't you messaging me?*

>*We were busy getting on the road again, but I assure you I'm okay. Don't worry about me. Go enjoy your family and that gorgeous wife of yours.*

>*Call me tonight? Kids miss you.*

That tugged at her heart. She missed them, too, even though they haven't been gone that long yet. They had a nighttime routine where she sat with the two older kids to read to them, while Alex and Laryssa got the infant bathed and ready for bed. They were growing up so fast. She wasn't sure how time seemed to speed up the older you got. Time was like a speeding train that had no brakes. And if you dared to blink, you'd missed something.

After spending the night with Nathan, she realized exactly how much she had missed companionship. Even while watching Alex with Laryssa, she had started to wish for it. The gentle way he'd wrap his arms around her, pulling her in for a kiss. There were times she wished someone would hold her that way and make her feel special again in a way only a lover could.

Thinking back to last night, she giggled at her antics with Nathan, once again picturing him with wolf ears on his head—her own personal werewolf of sorts—the alpha in their playtime.

"What's so funny?" Nathan asked, glancing her way momentarily before returning his eyes to the road.

"Nothing," she giggled, still unable to believe that he spanked her. It was even harder to believe she actually liked it. Spankings rarely came from anything good, nor end up anywhere as delectable as hers did. Her womanhood tingled at the memory, and it made her cross her legs, stuffing her hands between them. *Oh gosh.* What the heck was going on with her body?

"Thinking about last night?" he asked, with a nod toward her hands.

She removed them quickly, like she'd gotten scorched by a fire, and wrapped her fingers around the armrests. Nathan laughed. That meant he knew exactly what was on her mind. *Oh dear!* How embarrassing. How was she going to survive an entire day of driving with him right beside her? They couldn't seem to avoid that particular conversation. The topic was at the front of both their minds, and she couldn't understand why.

"Just drive," she said, pretending to concentrate on her phone, even though she could sense his eyes on her, feeding her desire. Why couldn't she put a lid on it? It was like her hormones were fighting back with a vengeance after having disappeared on her for years. She'd almost forgotten how hard it was to keep control of yourself when your hormones go wild, reminding her of the television show, "Girls Gone Wild." Last night would certainly have made the cut.

"Want to hear my favorite part?" he asked.

"No," she said, her voice squeaking as her gaze slipped down to the crotch of his pants, vividly remembering his swollen manhood. If he started talking about it, she was liable to tell him to pull over and start round two. Or would that be the fourth? Joanne took a deep breath, trying to compose her body and her thoughts before the train passed the point of no return. She was like a sex-crazed junkie right now, probably from having ignored it for so long.

"Last night really has you tied up in knots, eh?"

"Is it that obvious?"

"Just a little," he said, laughing.

"It's not funny!" she complained.

"You have to admit it is a little."

Joanne tilted her head back and groaned. They never talked about this stuff when she was younger. Her parents always said a woman shouldn't talk about it. They were to do their duty and produce a child, with the right guy of course—one that they picked. She frowned.

"Sorry, I'll let the topic go," he said.

"Thank you," she replied, sending a relieved smile his way. But the moment she spotted his erection pressing against his pants, unmatched hunger filled her core.

"Oh, God. Don't look at me that way," he said, fidgeting in the driver's seat.

She hadn't meant to, but he had a way of bringing out the raw need in her as well, leaving her aching already. Her body should be dead to the world right now. They'd been up half the night making love. She shouldn't want it again so soon. It was like each round fed the beast inside her, leaving her hungry for more.

"If you don't stop, I won't be able to keep driving until we deal with this," he said.

"I'm fine with that."

"We've barely been driving for thirty minutes," he reminded her.

"Oh look, a rest stop," Joanne said, pointing to a sign.

Chapter Twenty-One

The minute he pulled to a stop, she had her seatbelt off and was already working on the zipper of his pants. He turned his seat to face her. Thankful that the motorhome had swivel seats. The rest area was quiet, except for a few semi-trucks on the other end of the lot. They didn't have to worry about peeping toms looking in.

"Should we go somewhere more comfortable?" he asked.

She'd thought about dragging him back to the bed, but she knew they didn't have a lot of time as they had a long drive ahead of them; and, for the first time in her life, she understood the merit of a quickie. And was quite happy to try out the concept. They had spent the night savoring each other bit by bit. This time, she wanted him. Now.

Pleased with her decision to wear a skirt, she slipped off her underwear and straddled his lap, eagerly removing him from his pants. When he was free, she grabbed onto his shoulders, and slowly lowered herself onto his erection, taking him into her body, inch by pleasurable inch, each more glorious than the last.

"You feel so good," he said, gripping her hips, helping her move as she ground her hips against him. Leaning down, she framed his face with her hands and brushed her lips against his.

She didn't want to talk. Talk distracted her. All she wanted to do was feel him inside her. A feeling she never wanted to end. It made her realize her life was far from over, and she could feel very much like a desirable woman. Wave upon wave of intense pleasure crashed into her, traveling through her body with blinding intensity. She couldn't help but close her eyes and savor it, her head rolling back.

They were no longer paying attention to the world around them, such as the parking lot filling with morning travelers as they stopped to either use the washrooms or put chains on their tires.

A little ways back, a trucker had cleared off a spot at a table in front of them and was watching the show with amusement. It was even better than a movie on television, the trucker thought. The man wasn't the least bit embarrassed. Life on the road was lonely, so rest areas became his favorite place to hang. Many enjoyed hitting the trucking food joints, but he liked rest stops. It gave him more of a chance to people watch. When an elderly couple walked by, he tipped his hat to them and lowered his eyes, pretending to look at his phone.

When they left, he once again turned his attention toward their window, unbeknownst to the steamy couple. The man wondered what they were thinking at that moment.

Joanne had leaned back now, her hand gripping the overhead handgrip by the door. She couldn't stop the electrical current zipping through her womanhood, taking her to new heights. His cock hit a good spot, and she couldn't stay quiet any longer either. "Oh, gosh. Yes, like that. Don't stop," she begged.

"As long as you don't," he grunted, barely able to speak English, "I think we're good."

Joanne half chuckled, unable to do much else. Every single cell in her body was screaming at her to let go, her cravings for him growing beyond measure. Not even Scott claimed this much of her, and she'd given up the life she knew for him.

Suddenly, it was like she was racing down the river, going head-first over a waterfall, surrounded by such beauty that nothing else mattered. Frozen in mid-air, like she was flying, she exploded into a million pieces.

Nathan gasped when she clamped down on his cock with such a ferocious intensity. There was no way in hell he could have held himself back. Not even the man with the greatest control in the world could have, nor would they want to. And for a moment, his heart stopped as he came, his senses suddenly jumbled. Unable to see. Unable to hear anything except the pounding of blood in his ear. He sucked in a breath, his body shuddering.

She buried her face against his neck, and they sat there a moment. Too exhausted to move and too disoriented to try. What the heck was happening? Did someone transport them to another universe where only love and pleasure existed? If they had, he'd happily stay here for the rest of his life.

After a few minutes, he managed to open his eyes, and as his vision cleared, he saw the guy sitting at the table on the grass part of the rest area. "Hun, you might want to move."

"Why?" She sat up and looked around, glossing over the individual sitting at the table. Too dazed to comprehend what she was seeing.

"We have an audience."

"What where?" she asked as she looked around more carefully this time. The man at the table grinned and saluted them for the show. Joanne dove sideways, falling off his lap. "Oh my gosh."

Nathan laughed. "That's what we get for being impatient."

"How can you be so nonchalant about this? Did you know he was watching?" she asked, covering her face with her hands.

"No, but I doubt he could really see anything."

Apparently too embarrassed to get up, Joanne crawled on the floor to the bathroom, her skirt still up to her hips, giving him a glimpse of her glistening folds where he'd been buried momentarily before. And he couldn't help but want to take her again, just like that.

Doggy style. But he chose to respect her and stayed put as she disappeared into the bathroom. She would be too unnerved to do another round so soon, but God, she looked so good.

Reaching over, he grabbed a few tissues off the dash and quickly cleaned himself up before rearranging himself so he could stand up without showing anyone anything and went back to his room for a change of clothes.

He couldn't remember the last time it felt so good, especially riding free without a rubber between them. That didn't happen often, and he was kind of surprised that he forgot about it. Not that he had anything to worry about with her, though. he hadn't had sex with anyone, and she couldn't get pregnant, so there were none of the usual worries. And he knew he was clean.

She was still in the bathroom when he came out of the room. "Are you okay, Joanne?"

"Is he gone?" she whispered.

Nathan glanced over and found the table still occupied by the gentleman. "Yes," he said, just to get her out of the washroom. When she stepped out, she immediately saw the guy still sitting there.

"You lied!" she cried, trying to step back inside, but he pulled her into his arms.

"Hun, don't be embarrassed. It's a guy you'll never see again."

"What if he filmed us?" she asked, covering her face. "Oh gosh, Alex is going to kill me."

"Do you want me to go ask him?"

"No," she said, her voice raising an octave as she gripped his forearms. "Can we get out of here, please?"

"You'll have to let me go first." He had a feeling her fingers were going to leave marks on his arm. The poor woman was spooked out of her mind.

Releasing him, she walked over to her seat and sat down, looking everywhere but at the table outside or him. She slumped in her seat so low her head barely reached the dash. "Now, please!"

It was quite comical, really. He didn't care so much about being seen. It wasn't his first public indiscretion, but it was the most exciting. They were right when they said who you're with makes all the difference. He didn't think he'd ever find someone like that before he died. And what sucked was, he was dying. He knew he shouldn't bring anyone into that bubble of misery, but he couldn't give her up yet. There was something about her that sucked him in. And he wanted all of her.

Settling back into the driver's seat, he started the motorhome once again. Eager to see what the rest of the day would bring and break himself out of the horrible reminder of his upcoming doom.

"Alex, you need to relax," Laryssa said, watching her husband hit the punching bag for the hundredth time in succession.

"How can I relax? That man is taking advantage of my mother."

"You don't know that."

He did a roundhouse kick, knocking the bag into tomorrow. "I'm a guy. I know how guys think."

Laryssa sighed. There was no getting through to her husband. She'd had to hold him back when he wanted to go after them, reminding him that his mother was a grown woman who could make her own choices. Of course, they didn't learn much about Nathan in the time he was there, but he didn't seem like a bad guy, just a very close-to-chest person.

"You mean the same guy who took me into his house when I was in danger?"

"That's different. You were having my brother's babies."

"Yes, but you didn't know that at the time, remember? We didn't even know each other."

Alex punched the bag numerous times before looking over at her. "Why are you sticking up for him and not supporting me?"

She opened her mouth to respond when she realized she had no answer. Was that what she was doing? Honestly, she was thinking more about Joanne than Nathan. Laryssa knew her mother-in-law hadn't had a relationship with anyone in a long time, and she could feel that instant spark the minute Nathan showed up on their doorstep. Who was she to get in the way of that? Joanne didn't get in their way. She only supported Laryssa's decisions, even got mad at Alex when he didn't treat her right.

"If your mother had any concerns, she wouldn't have gone with him."

"She's been out of the game for a while."

When he stopped jumping around so much, Laryssa wandered over to him and wrapped her arms around his waist. "Ya, but that doesn't mean she's stupid. She helped us, didn't she?"

He turned around and wrapped his arms around her, too. "I just worry about her."

"I know you do. Come on. Let's go take your mind off it."

"What about the kids?"

"I've shipped them off to Melissa's house for a bit."

That seemed to perk him up a bit, a slow grin spreading across his face. "You mean we're in an empty house?"

"Yep," Laryssa said, backing away from him so they were no longer touching. "Gotta catch me first." And off she ran, with him hot on her heels. Maybe for once, Joanne was having fun, too.

Joanne sat in the front seat, unusually quiet, unable to look at him. All she could see was the man sitting at the table, grinning at her. She wasn't an exhibitionist. Yes, she had had sex in public places before when she was younger, but secretly though, and no one ever found out. Once, they had almost been caught when she and Scott were hiding in a secluded cove. They were behind some tall grass, and someone walked about five feet away from them. She'd put her hand over Scott's mouth to stop his moans from being heard, trying hard not to giggle when he dug his fingers into her side.

Oh, how she missed him. Missed the way he laughed. Missed the way he smiled. The way his touch drove her wild. He was never too far away from her heart, especially when she looked at Alex. The boys were her ultimate gift from Scott. But what bugged her currently was that she couldn't remember having this kind of burning need for him. The drop everything, forget everyone, got to have sex now need—one that was so strong she forgot her sensibilities.

"Don't let it bother you," Nathan said, glancing over at her as she bit her nails. "He's probably already found someone else to spy on."

"That doesn't help."

"Never been caught with your pants down before?"

Joanne cringed at his word usage. "I'm a private person in case you didn't notice."

"I was caught with an old girlfriend once. Her parents walked in. Needless to say, I didn't stick around for her mom's paddle to hit me on the ass. She chased me down the driveway while I was butt ass naked."

"You're lying," Joanne said, eyeing him.

Nathan laughed, his cheeks turning red. "I wish."

"Oh, dear heavens, I would have died."

That's one thing she refused to do. Have sex in her parents' house. They weren't the forgiving type. Her dad would have killed Scott, not just chased him off with a paddle. When you had a lot of money, you had a habit of thinking you could do whatever you wanted and get away with it.

The idea of going back kind of scared her, especially without her mother there. Her mother had been the buffer between Joanne and her father, even if she had bowed to him most of her life. It still hurt that her mom hadn't stuck up for her when Joanne's father stole her life from her. She felt like she'd fallen into hell and there was no way out.

Now they were back on their way to meet the devil himself.

Chapter Twenty-Two

Joanne pulled her jacket closed and wrapped her arms around herself as wind and snow whipped all around her, barely letting her see five feet in front of her. Nathan was kneeling beside a flat tire, trying to hook up a jack to raise the vehicle, and was apparently failing miserably based on his constant trail of swear words.

"Can I do anything to help?" she asked.

He blew on his reddening hands. "Could you, by any chance, run inside and grab my gloves off the table?" he asked. The temperature had dipped big time. And now they were stranded on the side of the road halfway to Billings. They ran over a piece of wood that was half hidden under the snow, which had a nail sticking upright. And now the rusted jack Nathan had taken from a compartment on the side of the motorhome wasn't working. It had seen better days.

Thankfully, they were able to pull over to the side without spinning out, but it was a little eerie being in the middle of nowhere. Joanne looked one way and then the other. No signs of life anywhere. No car headlights. No stores. Nothing. Even their phones didn't work in the mountain pass.

Stepping into the motorhome, she quickly grabbed his gloves off the table and took them outside. Nathan was standing up with his hands on his hips, staring down at the stubborn machinery.

"No luck?" she asked.

He shook his head. "I should have checked the damn thing before we left."

"Why don't we go inside for a bit and warm up, then try again? I could make some hot cocoa," she offered, placing her hand on his arm. "Maybe the snow will let up soon." It wasn't much fun working outside when snow slipped down your collar and into your shirt. Joanne shivered a snowflake did just that.

"As enticing as that sounds, I have to get this thing working. We don't want to get stuck here for too long with the way the snow is coming down. I know this motorhome can make it through almost anything, but snow like this gathers quickly."

"Okay, well, I'll go boil water and have it ready for you when you come inside."

Life certainly had a way of keeping you on your toes. The laws of nature ensure that you never have it too easy, lest you take it for granted. The bad times, though, help you appreciate the good times when they come, and those were what she lived for. Her family. Her kids. Grandkids. Now Nathan. She never expected to find someone to be with again. And while she didn't know where their relationship would go after this, she was going to enjoy it while she had it. She knew how easily things could be ripped away, so she learned early to treasure every moment.

Joanne walked inside and went over to the stove to put on the camping kettle, then pulled the hot chocolate from the cupboard. She smiled when she saw marshmallows on the cover. *Oh, the little joys.* It might put her into a coma after drinking it, as warm milk always seemed to, but she could live with that. There wasn't much to see on the drive, and her body was sore from all the activity it had seen in the last twenty-four hours.

She chuckled. It was more activity than she'd seen since Scott. Had they ever done it that much in twenty-four hours? The most they'd had sex was twice in one day. But she had to admit, he never left her wanting either. He made sure that she'd come a time or two before he even started round two. What would Scott think of Nathan? Was he looking down on them, happy that she'd found someone to enjoy life with again? Or was he trying to convince God to strike them down?

Reaching up, Joanne touched the rings on the end of her gold-plated necklace. Their wedding bands were together forever, as she wished the two of them would have been. The hardest part of losing Scott was not being able to say goodbye. He was gone before she even regained consciousness.

They'd ripped her babies from her womb, and she had been unable to see them. No matter how hard she had begged. Joanne closed her hand around her rings, fighting a tear that threatened to breach the corner of her eye. Her dad's actions stole her chance to see her children's first step, their first word, and the first tooth cutting through their gums.

Taking her hot chocolate, she went and sat down on the couch. There was so much she received in the end, though, that she shouldn't be complaining. Just by being with Alex and sticking with him, even after he grew up, allowed her the chance to meet the woman who gave birth to Aidan's daughters. And, in some way, she was with both her children again. That gave her a peace she hadn't realized she needed. Seeing Alex happily married and becoming a father fulfilled her heart's desire for him.

She couldn't imagine how different her life would be if the accident wouldn't have happened. Would she have had more kids with Scott? Would she have had a girl? A little smile played on Joanne's lips. She imagined they would have been a lot like Laryssa's little girls.

A sudden deep scream pierced the air and then the door slammed open, breaking her from her reverie. Nathan dove into the room, pulling the door closed behind him. "Holy fudge knockers."

She would have laughed at his attempt not to swear if it were not for the look of fear in his eyes and the blood dripping down his arm. Joanne looked around frantically, trying to find a towel to wrap around his arm when something banged against the door of the motorhome. "What the heck is that?"

"Cougar. Stupid thing jumped me. I didn't see it until it was almost too late," he said quickly as he grabbed the cloth off the fridge door, pressing it on the gaping wound in his right arm. "That damn thing was big."

"Where's the first aid kit?"

"Under the sink," he said, pressing his hand on the gaping wound on his right arm. With having been outside, one would expect Nathan's face to be red, bitten by the cold, but it was pale.

Dropping to her knees in front of the sink, she opened the cupboard and pulled out the kit. "He didn't snag you anywhere else, did he?"

Nathan got up, legs wobbling, and sat down at the table, blood staining the dark blue rug. "No, just my arm. But I don't even know how I got away. I think he slipped on ice or something."

"Thank the blessed Lord for that," she replied, joining him at the table. Unzipping the kit, she pulled out a non-stick pad, some gauze, and a few other odds and ends. "I'm sorry that I didn't stay outside. Maybe the two of us would have kept him away."

"You can't blame yourself, hun," he said, grimacing when she cleaned the wound with saline solution, air hissing softly as it passed between his teeth. "Damn, that stings."

Joanne pulled her hand back and blew on the wound gently, glancing up at him. She paused for a moment, taken aback by the desire evident in his eyes and the color that flooded his cheeks, making him look like a healthy man again.

"Is that better?"

He nodded. "Took the pain right out of my mind, but I think I could do with some Advil."

"Let me just get this wrapped and I'll grab you some. Did you, by any chance, get the tire changed?"

Nathan shook his head. "I was working on the jack when the cat came out of nowhere."

"What are we going to do? You need a doctor, and we're stuck." Joanne pulled the curtain back and glanced outside, the snowstorm blocking her view. It kind of reminded her of an avalanche. Most of the time, being inside and watching the snow would make her feel warm and cozy, but cozy wasn't how she felt right now.

"I'll be fine, but we need to figure out how to get the tire changed. Otherwise, we have to flag someone down."

"How can we do that without getting attacked again?"

"I think if we wait a bit, he might move on. Maybe smell another animal."

"But we can't let you keep bleeding," she said, her adrenaline spiking. If they couldn't get him to a doctor and stop the bleeding, he would bleed out, and she didn't want to lose him.

"It's really not that bad. It's already calming down," he said, trying to reassure her, but his sweaty forehead and pale skin told her another story. Joanne examined the wound. It's like the cougar scraped his claws over his arm from one side to the other and across the back of it, leaving three cuts that appeared deeper than a quarter of an inch. It hadn't nicked an artery, not that she could tell, but it was still bleeding more than she'd liked.

Standing up, she moved to the front of the vehicle and hit the four-way flashes, not that anyone was going to see them if the storm didn't let up. She didn't like their odds. They had a few choices, but none of them were optimal.

They could wait for help. A cop should drive by eventually and get mad at them for stopping in a no stopping zone. She could try fixing the tire herself, but that beast was still out there and has had a taste of human blood.

The other option was to drive the rig slowly and carefully to the closest town and hope there was a mechanic. But she knew doing that could ruin the vehicle completely, and by the sounds of it, he lived in the motorhome.

"We need to keep driving to get you to a doctor."

"I'm good. Let's wait it out and then fix the tire."

"Hun, you're seeing a doctor and that's final," Joanne said, wagging her finger at him. Why did men have to be so picky about seeing the doctor? Their arm could literally be falling off, and they'd still refuse to go. Her son, Alex, never set foot in a hospital for years until Laryssa came around. "You did get insurance for yourself, right?"

Nathan chuckled sheepishly, refusing to answer. To be honest, he wasn't sure how to answer. No insurance company would dare give him travel insurance, knowing he was sick. Who would have thought that the one time he took a trip into the states, he would get hurt. The plan was to go through the states to the East Coast and then return home through Canada to lower the possibility.

"Oh my gosh, don't tell me you didn't?"

"It's a little complicated."

"What the heck are we supposed to do now? You have to get stitches and a rabies shot."

He shook his head. "Oh, hell no. Ain't no one sticking a needle in my ass."

Joanne chuckled. "They don't do it that way anymore."

He sighed in relief, but he still didn't want a needle. "It's winter, and he was probably hungry. Not easy to find food these days. I'm sure he didn't have rabies."

"I'll call Alex and borrow some money to take you to a hospital here."

He adamantly refused the help. The last thing he wanted was to owe her son money. What type of man would he think Nathan was? Incompetent? Alex would probably fly in a helicopter or something just to come down and rescue his mom from Nathan's carelessness.

"Fine. What else do you suggest?"

"Let's continue with our trip. I'll be fine."

Joanne muttered something under her breath that he didn't quite catch, but he was certain it matched the newly lit fire in her eyes. "I'm calling Alex."

"No. Please don't. If you want me to see someone that badly, we'll head to the north and cross back into Canada. Chinook Regional Hospital is to the North in Alberta, but it's at least a six-hour drive."

That meant they wouldn't be able to see Mount Rushmore, and now he felt like an utter heel for getting hurt. This was supposed to be a fun and enjoyable trip for Joanne, and it was up until now. He couldn't blame the animal as it was only following his instinct, but man, how could he have been so stupid? They were near Chestnut Mountain, so it shouldn't have come as a surprise. Cougars didn't hibernate like bears did. He'd given himself a false sense of security.

Nathan looked down at Joanne's decent wrapping job. The woman knew how to wrap a cut. She had tightened the gauze enough that it created the pressure needed to stop the bleeding, but, man, it hurt worse than getting stung by a murder hornet.

"I guess we can try going north as long as you don't get any worse," she said, giving his arm one last glance before standing up. "I'm going to go fix the tire."

He grabbed her arm. "I can't let you go out there."

"I don't think we have much choice, do you?"

Nathan growled. If she went out there and got hurt, he'd be up the creek without a paddle, and it would be Alex using the paddle to push him toward the waterfall.

"Okay, we'll both go." There was an ax hidden in the compartment under the cushions they were sitting on at the table. If the animal came back, they'd be able to defend themselves. As he stood up, his vision blurred, and it made him sit back down. The room spun, even without alcohol in his system.

She stood up and patted him on the arm. "You aren't in any condition to help. Just sit here and relax."

"You can't do it alone. That thing is hungry and dangerous. And the weather is so bad that you can't even see it coming." His throat squeezed close, and his chest tightened, worry filling him.

"What help are you going to be? You can't even stand up."

"If I don't go, you don't go," he said adamantly. At least if he was out there, it dropped the chances of her getting attacked to 50/50...either him or her. But if she was the only one out there, she'd be the target.

"If you die on me..."

He interrupted her words by pulling her down with his good arm for a kiss. Oh, God. It was like chocolate heaven, which made him remember she was making hot chocolate before this happened. Maybe chocolate being an aphrodisiac would help him with the pain.

"I don't plan to," he said as he slowly stood up this time, being careful not to make his blood completely drain from his head this time. "Let's go."

Chapter Twenty-Three

Joanne was ecstatic when they finally pulled into the hospital parking lot eleven hours later. The snow had made it difficult to move any faster. Today was the first time she'd ever driven anything larger than a car, and she couldn't say she enjoyed it. Back when they were trying to fix the tire, a cop drove by and stopped to see if they needed help. It was basically the only vehicle that drove by them during that whole time. She felt like they were caught in an apocalypse of sorts—where there were very few living beings around.

Her road trip companion was asleep in the passenger seat. Nathan had wanted to lie down in the bed, but it was better having him up front, where she could see him. His temperature had gone up, and she hoped the wound hadn't become infected. She had done her best to clean it, but one never really knew for sure.

When she parked the big rig in the far back, away from all the other vehicles, she put the vehicle in park and pulled on the emergency brake as she turned it off the engine. "Rise and Shine, Nathan. We're here."

"Huh, what?" he asked groggily.

"Do you think you can walk, or should I get a wheelchair?" she asked.

"I don't need a wheelchair."

Yep, stubbornness and the need not to look weak must be a genetic trait in the male species, and it was not exactly a flattering one. They'd rather end up dead than accept help. It made her want to slap them up the side of the head sometimes. Joanne opened the door and stepped down to the ground, then turned to help him.

"I'm fine. It's okay," he said, giving her a weary smile. As he stepped down the two steps to the ground, he grimaced in pain and grabbed his wounded arm. The painkillers must have worn off. "I think I liked it better when I was sleeping."

"Hopefully it won't be too busy inside, and they can give you something else to help with the pain."

Stepping in through the automatic doors, there was a blast of heat. She shivered. It was still dreadfully cold outside. Something her ancient bones didn't like. She looked around the room. It was virtually empty, except for three people sitting in the row of seats off to her right, and one man standing at the check-in window.

"Looks like we lucked out," Joanne said, stepping into the lineup behind the gentleman. They were likely going to have to camp here for the night now because it was already seven in the evening, and she didn't want to drive any further in the dark. She didn't trust herself or like how the big vehicle handled even though she'd been behind the wheel for hours already. The lack of visibility with no rearview mirror made her nerves kick up a notch, especially when she had to change lanes.

Soon the man ahead of them was finished, and they stepped up to the window. "What seems to be the problem?" a lady with dark brown hair and light brown skin asked as she sat back down in the chair after passing off the paperwork that had been in her hand.

"He had a run-in with a cougar. It cut his arm up pretty bad," she said as she handed over his care card.

171

"How long ago did it happen?"

"About eight hours ago?" she said. "Oh, sorry, I should be letting him answer." She was so used to answering for everyone because they never stopped her.

"How'd it happen?"

"I was outside repairing a flat tire when it lunged at me," he answered.

"Is the wound on your arm the only injury? Did you hit your head?"

Nathan shook his head.

"I'm afraid it might be getting infected," Joanne chimed in again.

After finishing the array of different questions, they went into the back to a small square triage room where a medical professional took his blood pressure and asked more questions. She half tuned them out until Nathan froze when the nurse asked him if he had any other medical conditions.

"I...uh..." He glanced up at her with a pained expression. Joanne wasn't sure if it was from the pain or from what he was about to say, and it made her adrenaline spike. "I have cancer."

After he'd been stitched up and given a rabies shot, they found their way to a campground on the East side of Lethbridge. He taught her how to hook up the motorhome as his arm was in a sling. Once they finished everything, the pain killers knocked Nathan out, while she remained awake.

She never had the chance to ask him about his revelation in the hospital, but it had been stuck in her mind. She had the poor guy running a marathon all last night. That couldn't be healthy for someone who was sick. But he seemed healthy before, full of energy, so she couldn't have known.

Now, all she could see was how hollow his cheeks appeared to be, and how his collarbone protruded from the neckline of his shirt. She could swear he hadn't looked that way the other day, or maybe she wasn't looking for things like that specifically? Hopefully, it was only her imagination going into overdrive from having such a long day.

She wanted to lay beside him, but after what he'd been through, she didn't have the heart to disturb him and pulled the couch out into a bed instead. There'd been a few options, but that seemed to be the easiest. He needed his rest, and she intended to give it to him. Now that they were back in texting range again, she questioned whether to tell her son what had happened.

Earlier, while Nathan was getting his arm stitched, Alex had texted her asking how things were, then he'd followed that with five other texts. He seemed to forget she was a grown woman.

>*Are you still out of range?*

>*We had some vehicle trouble, but we're settled into a camp-ground now.*

>*Where did you guys stop for the night?*

Joanne brought up the edge of the phone to her lips in contemplation. Why was it so hard to tell him the truth? It's not like she wanted to hide things, but the nervous feeling inside her made her feel like she had no other choice. Something felt off in her life somehow, and what bothered her most was that she didn't feel that way before they left. Maybe it was the fact she was about to see her father, but her mother would no longer be with him. The two of them had moved over from the United Kingdom a few years after her accident, taking Aidan with them. Her father made sure that she knew they were leaving and leaving without her in their life. Her heart broke that day, never fully repairing.

>*We decided to head into Alberta and stop in Lethbridge.*

>*That's quite the detour.*

>**shrugs**

>*What aren't you telling me, Mom?*

>*I'm going to bed, Alex. I'll fill you in soon.*

Fine was her son's reply. Joanne placed her phone on the counter and lay back on the bed, trying to ease her racing heart. They had a long trip ahead of them, and Nathan would not likely be up for steering this big lug of a vehicle. She wondered if maybe she should let him rest here and take a flight the rest of the way.

He didn't deserve to get lost in her mess of a life anyway. Yet, she didn't want to leave him. She liked having him around. He added more sunshine to her day and made the trip to see her father bearable, otherwise, she likely would have told them to send her an email instead. She honestly wanted nothing from her parents. Anything she got would be a solemn reminder of what they took from her.

Closing her eyes, she tried to envision better times, but all she could see was the fire in her father's eyes when she came home and told him she wanted to marry Scott and that they'd been dating. That was the first time she got a full-on beating for going against his wishes. She couldn't remember much about it, but her back certainly remembered the sting of the belt.

She'd had some misguided notion that if they could see how much she loved him, then maybe they would accept him and not judge him based on the past actions of his family. That wasn't the case, though. They turned their back on her instead.

His family took her in when her family kicked her out. They weren't anything like what her father described. His reactions were biased and full of prejudice. They believed if one was bad, then all were bad—a narrow-minded viewpoint in her eyes.

Joanne pulled up the crisp blue sheets to her chin and tucked her shoulders under the fleece throw, rolling onto her side trying to get comfortable. She'd never been a back sleeper. It was either her side or her stomach. That was what made it so easy to tuck into Nathan's arms when they'd slept together.

She kind of felt like they'd been together forever, so much so, that it was weird to be on the couch without him. It was almost like they had had a fight or something, and she was in the doghouse. She knew that wasn't the case as it was her decision to sleep out here. But she figured if she didn't, she'd wake him up because her thoughts were going a hundred miles a minute.

As much as she didn't want to, she'd tell him in the morning that she'd be going the rest of the way alone so he could recuperate. All she could hope for was that he'd understand.

But if she thought he would, she had another thing coming...

Chapter Twenty-Four

"Why didn't you come to bed last night? Was it because of my cancer revelation?" Nathan asked after remaining quiet while they ate breakfast. She'd made him bacon and eggs after popping into the convenience store while he was still sleeping. He'd been out like a log until nine.

"You were so tired. I didn't want to disturb you."

"And that's why you want to take off without me?"

"You've already gone out of your way to help me and look what happened. I'm not going to be the reason you've put off chemo either. I heard what you told the doctor."

"I'm not doing chemo," he said softly.

"But you heard the doctor. The recovery rate on yours is high when caught early."

"I've lived a long miserable life, hun. I'm ready to see what's on the other side."

"Oh, pish tosh. You couldn't have had any more of a miserable life than I've had. You don't see me giving up."

He put the fork back on his plate and leaned back in his seat, pain squeezing his heart. "You don't know what I've done."

"Then tell me."

"I can't," he said, agony lacing his tone. "I'm not the person you think I am."

"Did you lie about being Laryssa's uncle?"

He didn't even know how to answer that question because even he didn't know the direct answer to it yet. He could be or he could be her father. "No." Not as far as he knew anyway. Man, he wished life came with an instruction manual. Something that told you what you should do, where you should go, who you are, and what you should say. No one would live their entire life questioning who they were or who they were meant to be.

His time in jail was a real eye-opener. Not everyone in there was a bad person. They'd simply made a single bad decision that was bad enough that someone threw the book at them. In his case, it was what happened on the boat.

"How do you think Laryssa will feel if you don't fight? You're all she has from her family's side."

Once he told the truth, it wasn't like she was going to want him in her life anyway. "Maybe you're right."

Joanne reached across the table, with concern etched into her features, and genuine goodness emanating from her eyes. "Not maybe. You owe it to her to fight, and you owe it to me after convincing me to go on this trip with you."

"Then why are you trying to run away from me?" he asked, his voice deep and full of hurt. He'd had no intention of sounding like someone was taking away his favorite toy. But he hadn't realized how much he'd come to enjoy her company. And he didn't want to lose that time with her yet. He'd been expecting to spend the entire week with her before losing her.

"My life is cursed, doncha know?" she said with a wry grin as she pointed to his arm.

He raised his arm. "This? It could have happened to anyone."

She tilted her head and gave him an 'oh really' look, which made him chuckle. Not too many people could say a cougar attacked them, but he doubted it was her luck that brought the thing his way. "It wasn't you, Jo. Honest. It's that time of year when they go beyond their usual territory to look for food because it's scarce."

"Are you an animal expert now?"

"Animal instinct," he said, wiggling his eyebrows at her suggestively.

She laughed. "Something you speak fluently, I'm sure?"

He leaned forward and turned her palm over in his hand, tracing the lifeline. "Maybe we need another reminder,"

"I need to get going if I'm going to catch my flight," she reminded him, shivering deliciously when his finger created little circles on her wrist. He wanted to march her right back to his bed, but she was right. They'd taken quite the detour and had to get back on track.

"Don't be silly. I'm not an invalid. I can make the trip. And I'm not letting you go yet either. My plan is to pleasure you in ways you could only dream of."

"You've already done that."

"Then let me do it some more, please," he begged, pleading with puppy dog eyes.

He wanted to have as much fun as possible before he couldn't anymore, even despite his arm being wrapped. 'You're using her to distract yourself,' his conscious hounded. "No, I'm not," he muttered under his breath.

"What was that?"

"Nothing. Come on, let's get packed up." He wasn't giving her another chance to take off on him.

"You'll drop me off at the airport?"

"I'm still capable of driving. It's lifting that's the problem."

"Are you sure? I don't want you to get hurt because of me," she said. "And I can't guarantee what my dad will do when we get there."

"I don't care. You're stuck with me."

She gave him a weak smile. "Okay."

❧

178

Joanne was thrilled when they pulled into the next campground that evening. They had pushed hard, taking turns driving, and she was exhausted. She drove whenever his arm needed a break. Thankfully, the drive was uneventful and relaxing. Sometimes they talked. Sometimes she read a book. Sometimes she got lost in thought and was grateful for the silence as she sorted through them.

So far, her nightmares, which had occurred for a few days after they heard from the family's lawyer, hadn't hit again. That surprised her as she had been wondering and worrying about what was in store for her, wondering what other way her dad could destroy her life. Or would he be different now? She laughed. That was an unlikely scenario. What man changed in his old age? They are creatures of habit by then.

She'd gone beyond hoping that things would get better. It was the only way she had survived all those years. She basically refused to think about it or him, but now she had no choice. She was heading back into the lion's den, so to speak. The lawyer never said her father would be involved in any way, but she had to assume so because it was his wife, her mother, who had passed away. He would do whatever it took to keep the inheritance from her if she had one coming.

"You're awfully quiet tonight?" Nathan said, brushing Joanne's hair from her eyes as she sat cuddled beside him. "You've been staring at a blank screen for a while."

"It's hard to believe that my mom is gone. I wish I knew what happened."

Her mother had been in her mid eighties but didn't have any health complications that Joanne was aware of. But then again, who would contact her about them anyway? She'd been disowned, so it's not like anyone would care to keep her apprised. There were times she'd tried to contact her mom, despite everything, but her dad was quick to disconnect the call if he knew.

"Maybe the lawyer knows?"

That was doubtful, unless her dad went into detail about the circumstances surrounding her mother's death, and that was unlikely. Her dad was more of a silent man until he gave an order, then everyone heard him. His eyes hard and unyielding. A man buried under his own hatred for the world. That's probably why Aidan turned out the way he did. Thankfully, her in-laws were wonderful people, for the most part. They did make a bad choice to hide her identity, but under the direst of circumstances. They were afraid of the power of Joanne's parents. Scott's family only had half the amount of money they did. A little pull and power, but not enough.

"Hopefully," she said, resting her head against his shoulder. She was sitting on his left to not jostle his sore arm. Nathan turned and kissed the top of her head. Lifting her head, his lips found hers in a gentle sweet caress. Not demanding or overpowering, but rather, treating her like a delicate flower deserving to be cherished.

It surprised her how close they'd grown in the short time they'd been together. She felt like she'd known him her whole life. There was a comfortability there that made her love their time together. They could chat. Be silent. It didn't matter. Even though she didn't know his past, she felt safe and cared for. He was a good man. Now he was hurt because she accepted his help.

"Is your arm feeling okay tonight?" she asked.

"The pain killers are still working. Did you have something in mind?"

"Not really, just concerned. We should check it and change your bandages."

He scrunched up his nose. "What if the bandage sticks?"

"I'm a mom and a grandma. You'll be fine," she said, kissing him on the cheek before standing up. "I'll go grab the antibiotics, too. I don't think you've had them today yet."

As she was walking away, he slapped her on the butt, and when she turned back around to give him the evil eye, he was grinning and squinting in pain at the same time. The action must have jarred his arm.

She stuck her tongue out at him. "Serves you right."

"The pain's worth it," he said unapologetically. "It was too tempting."

Joanne shook her head as she gathered the items she needed. "Come into my parlor..."

"Said the spider to the fly..." he murmured.

All she did in response to his words was pat the table, her eyes sparkling with unspoken laughter. If that didn't freak Nathan out a little, he didn't know what would.

"What are you planning, lady?" he asked, sitting down and crossing his legs in the process to hide his jewels.

That made her laugh out loud. "I'll be good, I promise. The light is better over here," she said, holding up a pair of scissors.

Her attitude been fairly serious for most of the evening, so he was glad to see her smiling. He loved it when her eyes lit up. She looked so beautiful. There was something about her spirit, her heart, which made her sexier than any model could ever be.

He watched as she concentrated on his arm, cutting her way through the gauze with deft precision. Much to his surprise, the bandage was exactly as it stated on the package, non-stick, although one stitch got caught in it when she removed it.

Joanne carefully washed around the wound, careful not to get it wet as they were told to wait forty-eight hours. The edge around each scratch was red, but they'd said that would be a normal reaction to his wound. It was good to see that there was no infection festering yet, and he hoped his luck would continue. They were back in the states now and couldn't afford another detour back to Canada.

"It's looking good," she said, smiling with relief.

"Does that mean I can play again?" he asked, his lips pulling to one side in a grin.

"We're going to behave, so we don't hurt your arm."

"But I don't wanna," he whined.

Joanne ripped open the package of a non-stick bandage and gently laid it over the wound. "Don't worry, big boy. You'll survive."

"I might, but he won't," he said, pointing to his irritating erection.

It happened anytime she touched him, which was proving a little frustrating. Had he become a sex addict or something? He closed his eyes, wishing away his hard-on. She was obviously not interested in him right now, which wasn't surprising at all. She just learned he was dying.

"I'm going to let you rest whether you want to or not. We've had a long day, and you need your sleep."

"Well, will you help a guy with a problem?" He pouted playfully. His member was pressing against his briefs uncomfortably, stuck partially pointing downwards. He reached down and rectified the problem.

Joanne leaned back against the seat and then, a second later, he jumped when her foot pressed against him. She slid her foot up to the head and back down. He murmured something even he didn't understand. He wasn't even sure if he used words.

"Help you by doing this, you mean?" she asked, making slow circular motions with the ball of her foot against the tip, pressing it against his lower stomach, causing wonderful breath-freezing friction. He wasn't sure what about the action that was so arousing, whether it was being able to look and see the heat in her eyes, or if he was developing some type of foot fetish, but, man, it felt good. Nathan leaned his head back and closed his eyes, unable to focus. And then, as suddenly as she started, she stopped.

Chapter Twenty-Five

"Hey," Nathan complained, raising his head to look at her.

He sat up immediately. Agony and pain had diluted the joy that had been in her eyes. She was staring at her phone, her handshaking. Her foot dropped to the ground with a thump.

"Joanne?" he inquired. "What's wrong?"

When the tears started spilling down her cheeks, he knew she was far from all right. Immediately, he rushed to her side and took her in his arms, holding her tight. "What is it?"

She handed over her phone, and he noticed that she'd received a text from an unknown number.

>*Be careful. He's going to kill you.*

"Who would even send you a message like that?"

"I don't know. They shouldn't have my phone number," she cried, hiccupping.

Nathan reached behind him and picked up the tissue box on the counter. "We better call the police."

"How will that help? They'll just tell us to contact the police at our destination."

He hated to admit she was right. They were passing through

North Dakota. It would be better for them to head to the police once they reached Toronto. If they tried to talk to anyone here, they'd likely say it wasn't their responsibility, as it wasn't within their district.

He came over and sat beside her. "Do you think it's from your father?"

"I don't want to believe that he'd stoop that low to keep my inheritance, but..."

"You think that's what this might be about?"

"I don't know what else it could be," she said, shivering.

He rubbed his hand up and down her back, trying to provide her with what comfort he could. "Do you know of anyone else that might not want you to come back to Toronto?"

"No. I don't really know anyone else there."

"Do you want to go home?" he asked.

Joanne shook her head. "No. I have to see this through. I need to face my demons."

"You're a strong woman, you know that, Ann?"

She sucked in a breath and wiped at the tears falling down her cheeks. "No one's called me Ann since Scott."

He pulled her into a bear hug. Joanne buried her face in the crook of his shoulder, and Nathan held her tight as she cried. It seemed to be a mixture of sad and happy tears. Remaining quiet, he comforted her in the silence of their motorhome, realizing exactly what a rare gem she was. She needed to be treated like a queen.

She never deserved her father turning on her and making her life a living nightmare by taking her kids away. The fact she faced that and still had the courage to go to Toronto, and possibly see the man that behaved so horribly toward her, showed a strength inside her nothing could compare to.

She was more incredible than he could have ever imagined. And it made him begin to question his life choices. If she could face her demons, then maybe he could, too. Maybe he could even find true love despite his own experiences. He wasn't sure whether this was love yet, but she was making him wonder if such a future with someone like her was possible. He certainly didn't feel worthy of it, though, and didn't feel worthy of finding a woman as wonderful as Joanne.

He'd often leave a relationship before they found out about his past, because it was easier that way. Deep relationships had been out of the question. It was easier to keep the pain buried and deny anyone the chance to turn their back on him.

"I'm here for you," he whispered into her hair as she clung to him. The way she shook in his arms made him never want to leave, and it made him want to beat up the one causing her pain. He wished he knew what crawled up her father's ass that made him into the prick he was.

"Why am I so hard to love?" she whimpered, barely audible.

"Oh, hun, I can say with 100% certainty that this isn't about whether you're lovable or not. This is all him and his issues. Nothing to do with you."

"I look at my kids and my grandkids, and I couldn't ever imagine hurting them this way. Why? Why does he do it?"

That he had no answer to. "I don't know, Ann. Some people just aren't in a good frame of mind to be parents, and they learn that too late."

"Or never at all," Joanne said, sniffling.

Her dad was not the loving type. He acted like a stinking military general, and he wasn't even in the army. There were no hugs or kisses. No loving embraces, not even when she'd run over and hug his leg as a toddler. He'd just shake her off. Once, she had hit her head on the coffee table, and he didn't offer any kind words or empathy as she sat there crying.

Those were her oldest memories. She could remember promising herself and Scott that she'd be different. That she'd be a better parent than her father ever was, but he robbed her of that chance. She could care for Alexander but couldn't be as close to him as a mother could be without causing waves with Ruth and Mitch, even though they were incredibly understanding. That's why it meant the world to her that she was around for her grandkids as their grandmother and not a nanny.

Hearing the word Nana from their lips was almost enough to make her cry every time because she loved them so much. It was the best feeling in the world, especially when Justin took to calling her Banana, which always made her laugh. He could never understand why she was laughing, but gosh, it was so precious.

And just like that, her crying spell was broken. Little by little, she stopped shaking and the tears stopped falling.

"Feeling better," he said, giving her another kiss on the top of her head.

"Yes. Thanks for coming with me, Nathan. I don't think I could do this without you."

"Baloney, you have more strength than you realize. But I'm glad I could help. And speaking of help, I better help you get to bed because we have an early start tomorrow, and it's already nearing midnight."

"Wow, really?" Joanne flipped her phone over and glanced at the time, eleven forty-five at night.

"And I demand that you sleep in my bed."

She quirked an eyebrow at him. "You demand, do ya?"

"Yes. Doctor's orders."

"We're playing doctor now?" The words were out of her mouth before she could stop them.

Heat flared in his eyes. "I'm game if you are."

Joanne glanced down at his arm resting gingerly on his lap, wrapped with gauze. She'd love to play around but didn't want to do anything that caused him more pain. "We better wait until you can use your arm."

"I can still use it," he said, and as if to prove it, he tried to pull her onto his lap and then yelped in the process.

"Serves you right, you dingbat," she said affectionately, with a quick kiss on his cheek.

Nathan chuckled. "I guess rough play is out of the question."

"Yep, unless you want another emergency room visit before this trip is over."

"That's no fun," he said with a good-natured pout.

"Come on, let's go to bed." She bumped his hip to get him to scoot out of the table bench.

After he stood up, he held his good hand out to help her up and pulled her close. "You're an amazing woman, my dear."

"You're not half bad yourself," she said, linking her hands behind his neck as she stared up into his lovely brown eyes, which were swimming with emotion, like he'd go to the ends of the earth for her. Nathan leaned down and stopped a fraction of an inch from her lips, letting her close the distance.

When their lips touched, it was like fireworks blazing in the night sky, making her insides smolder with fresh desire, connecting them in ways that shouldn't be possible. People always said that the romance scenes in books or tv shows were all fake, that no one felt the burning desire to rip one's clothes off and become like animals, but she was beginning to see that with the right person anything was possible. The foot popping kiss, ripping the buttons off the shirt, unable to wait any longer to become one with them. A treasure so many took for granted in their day and age.

When his tongue traced her bottom lip, she opened to him, letting him take all she had to offer. She didn't want to let him go, didn't want to send him to bed without tasting every inch of him. But when his bandage came to rest against her arm, it made her pull away for fear of hurting him. She knew he needed his rest.

"Oh, no you don't," he said, trying to pull her back, but then he winced when he applied too much pressure, trying to keep her in place.

That settled it for her. "We'll have to wait until another day," she said, giving him one final kiss.

"But, but..." he tried to protest, but she shook her head.

The woman in her felt mighty powerful, though, as his cock pressed into her belly. She couldn't help but feel bad for turning him down, but he'd been through enough for now, and even she was tired. They'd had a long few days and could do with a good night's sleep.

Joanne turned and walked toward the bathroom to get ready for bed, but then turned to glance at him before heading inside. "Don't worry, darling. I'm not done with you yet."

Chapter Twenty-Six

The next few days were uneventful. They took turns driving and this time the motorhome mostly behaved. Thankfully, she had finally gotten accustomed to driving it. But she'd be glad when she didn't have to back the big hunk of junk into a camping stall.

That night they were settling into Grand Rapids, nearing the end of the journey, and she couldn't help but feel a little bummed. She wished their trip would last forever and end on a happier note. But they were both feeling nervous as they neared Toronto. The mystery person never messaged her again, and no one tried calling her, except for Alex.

She eventually told Alex that Nathan had been injured, but that they had decided to continue their trip. He hadn't been too impressed. She couldn't imagine what he would have done had she told him about the nasty text message. One that she was certain was from her dad, trying to scare her off.

She hadn't called her father at all over the years, so he technically shouldn't have her number, but she had given it to her mom. Why she'd given it to her mom, she didn't know; it's not like they ever spoke. Maybe there was a part of her that hoped her mother would eventually escape from her father's clutches, but that didn't happen until now.

A woman shouldn't have to die to escape a bad relationship. It broke her heart that her mom never realized her worth and stuck with her father under the mistaken belief that since she married him, she had to put up with it all. Why couldn't her mom have found a backbone? She was very timid and could barely look him in the eye, and he relished it all. Joanne couldn't recall a time when her mom defied her father. However, she herself had done that enough for them both.

"Hey, the steaks are almost done," Nathan said from outside the motorhome. After she finished adding hot cocoa mix to her water, she grabbed the fleece blanket with the picture of a killer whale and carefully made her way down the steps to the patch of gravel below, lightly covered in snow. He'd already used the shovel to clear a nice patch around the fire pit and had a sweet fire going. Two plastic white chairs were placed around it. He was sitting in one and was leaning toward the fire, turning two steaks on a spit.

"We could have always used the grill inside," she said, settling into the chair with the blanket wrapped tightly around her.

"It's a nice evening out here, despite the chill."

He was right about that. The moon was high, and the stars twinkled like diamonds in the sky. There was a bright one beneath the moon. "Hey, I think we can see Venus," Joanne said, pointing up to the sky.

"Oh, that's Aldebaran, I believe."

"Alde who?"

"Aldebaran. It's also known as the Eye of Taurus."

"Makes you wonder how they came up with all the names."

"That's a good question. It has something to do with Zeus changing into a bull and winning the heart of a princess. Not quite sure why he chose a bull, or why she found a bull compelling, but I guess anything goes with some people," he said, shrugging his shoulders.

"Maybe he wanted to disguise himself because he didn't think she would accept him for who he really was."

Nathan remained silent at that, poking at the fire with a stick while turning the steaks with the other, appearing to ponder her words. She knew everyone hid a part of themselves from others. The more vulnerable side—the side with secrets. Sometimes the secrets came out unexpectedly, and sometimes they were revealed when trust was earned.

"It can't be easy being that close to the fire," she commented cautiously, knowing he might not like her barging into his horror story.

"There was a time that seeing one reminded me of what happened because all I could see were their faces in the flames.

"Other people were with you when it happened?"

Nathan let the spit go and sat back against his seat, his eyes losing themselves in the flames. He rubbed his chest, trying to get rid of the tightness that threatened to take over. This was a conversation he didn't exactly want to have. A lump formed in his throat, making it hard to speak. He hadn't meant to blurt out what he did, but now he'd let the cat out of the bag.

"We were going on our annual fishing trip. Something my brother and I had done since we were sixteen."

Joanne's eyes widened as though she were just catching on now, but she didn't say a word, allowing him to continue. Not that he wanted to. Talking about it brought up a world of hurt he tried to keep buried.

"This time, though, he wanted to bring Catherine along. He said he wanted to teach her to fish, so they left Laryssa with a babysitter, and we headed out. I should have said no, should have told her to stay home."

"You couldn't have known what was going to happen."

He had an inkling. The storm cloud brewing in his brother's eyes told him something was off. He could barely contain himself. Within minutes of leaving the dock, Joel turned on them and said he knew everything.

"I should have clued in."

"How? You couldn't have known the engine would blow."

"Before we left, I accidentally spilled gas on the deck and didn't realize it must have leaked into the engine bay, too. I thought I cleaned it all, but I didn't. I killed them, Joanne." Nathan leaned forward and placed his head in his hands. "I made her an orphan."

Joanne threw the blanket off her shoulders and went over to him, dropping to her knees. And ever so gently, she pulled his hands away, cradling his face with her palms, tears in her eyes. "No, it wasn't you."

"Yes, it was," he said, his voice cracking. He's the one who picked up the ax when Joel came at him with a harpoon. He raised it over his shoulder to ward him off and it fell down into the engine bay. It must have created a spark when it hit the metal and the gas ignited. He pulled her hands away and stood up, moving away from her.

"You don't understand, Joanne." Nathan ran his hands through his hair, his gut spinning. "Oh, God." He didn't want to tell her yet, didn't want to ruin what they had.

She struggled to stand up, and he temporarily went over to help her up before returning to his position on the other side of the fire. She looked so beautiful in the light of the fire, her hair glowing like specks of gold. An angel sent in his hour of need.

"You can tell me anything," she whispered into the silence of the night. All the other campers had toddled off to bed, so that eased his stress. No one else had to overhear his confession. It was almost like he was in a confessional at a catholic church.

"Forgive me, mother, for I have sinned," he tried to joke, but it came out like a cat that was suffering, scratching away at his peace with its claws as pure agony bubbled inside him. He looked at Joanne, tears forming in his eyes as his confession turned into the most genuine one he'd ever given in his life. "I slept with Catherine."

Joanne sat down on the chair and didn't say a word, but her

expression was one of compassion and not judgement. That gave him the strength to continue.

"My brother found out, and he was pissed. He attacked me, and I tried to scare him off by raising an axe over my shoulder. In the process, I accidentally dropped it into the engine bay. It must have hit some metal, creating a spark, igniting the gas. We never realized it started a fire as we were too busy fighting. Catherine tried to warn us, but it was too late. The engine quickly exploded after that."

"Is that why you never came to see Laryssa?" she asked.

"Partly, I mean who would want to see the man that killed their parents?"

"But you didn't kill them."

"Then you are the only person who thinks that way." He gripped the back of his neck, struggling to hold back the cry bubbling up inside him. It was his fault. "I was in jail, Joanne. My fingerprints were on the axe and the gasoline can."

He should have disappeared after his indiscretion and never returned, but he stuck around because Catherine announced she was pregnant. She was adamant it wasn't his baby, but he wasn't so sure. Laryssa had his eyes and his smile, but that could also be because they were related.

"They charged you?" Joanne asked.

"Yes."

"How long?"

"Six years until the charges were overturned."

"That had to have been hard," she said softly.

He nodded. Hard didn't even begin to cover the experience, but it was easier than what he still had to face once the truth came out to Laryssa.

Joanne templed her fingers and held her index fingers against her lips, quietly processing the newly released information.

"At first, I didn't try to fight what happened. I felt like I deserved to be in jail. I made a little girl an orphan, but my girlfriend at the time was rich, and she fought for me despite my telling her to drop it. She thought it would get me to propose to her, I guess."

"You didn't?"

"I did, but it didn't work out. I wasn't up for a serious relationship at the time, especially knowing that I was a *cheater*. A woman deserves more than that."

"You do realize that one mistake doesn't determine who you are, right?"

"How can you even say that? You don't even know what caused me to cheat or how often I did."

"You don't strike me as the once a cheater, always a cheater type."

"How can you say that? You don't even know me."

"I have a sixth sense about these things," she said, shivering. "Why don't we finish cooking the steaks and head inside? It's too cold to sit out here, and you can tell me more of what happened if you feel comfortable."

Nathan bent down and examined the steaks on the spit, spinning it around a few times. There was something about Joanne that made him comfortable, like he could be his true self with her. That was something he hadn't felt in his life, ever.

"It's not really much of a story. Our families grew up together. We all knew each other since we were kids, Catherine, her brother, myself, and Joel. Catherine and I ended up having a quick fling. A friends with benefits kind of thing, before she got together with my brother. Nothing serious. Later, she married my brother, and all seemed to be going well until they had a fight. She showed up at her brother's place where I was living and asked to stay because she needed a break.

"We ended up drinking too much and one thing led to another," he said bitterly, standing up with the spit in hand. "But I'll spare you the sordid details of my transgression."

"I take it that's one of the reasons you no longer drink?"

He nodded. Between that and the boat accident, where he'd had a few, he quickly learned drinking wasn't for him. Some people could handle their booze and not make stupid decisions, but not him. "When I'm not drinking, my head is clear. I may be alone, but I can at least be happy with my choices."

"Are you though?" she asked, trailing up the motorhome steps behind him.

"What?"

"Happy?"

Nathan grabbed a plate and removed the steaks from the spit, placing them on the counter, contemplating what he should answer. Sometimes he was happy, other times he felt lonely. Although, he hadn't realized exactly how lonely until this trip started. Sharing his day with Joanne had quickly turned into a bright spot in his life.

Turning to face her, he pulled her into his arms. "Right now, I am," he replied. He'd felt lighter than he'd had in years. Whenever Joanne was in the room, the demons he struggled with faded away.

Her palms came to rest on his chest as she looked up at him. "Thanks for trusting me with your story. That couldn't have been easy to talk about."

"I think it has something to do with the company," he said, resting his forehead against hers. "Has anyone told you how wonderful you are?"

Sliding her hands up, she linked them behind his neck. "Careful, one might think you are trying to woo me into bed."

"And miss the chance to eat my steaks?" he asked, grinning. "What kind of man do you think I am?"

"I suppose I'll let you eat just one," she said, playing with the hair on the nape of his neck.

"You'll let me, eh?"

"For being a good boy."

"Did you come with me because I'm a good boy or because I bring out your naughty side?"

She tilted her head and stared over his shoulder, pulling her lips to one side as she thought about it, her eyes sparkling. "I'm quite enjoying the naughty side."

"Oh, screw the steaks," he said as he started to back her up to the bedroom. His body quickly getting to the point of no return.

"Okay," she said, taking a step around him to go back to the kitchen.

He grabbed her hand and pulled her back to the foot of the bed. "Funny, funny."

Joanne chuckled. "I thought so. But what about your hand?"

"Screw the hand."

She opened her mouth to speak, but he covered it with his hand. "Don't say it."

Joanne grabbed his shirt and spun him around so that he fell back on the bed, his hand falling from her mouth. "Just shut up and kiss me."

"Wait, I thought I was the boss."

"I let you think that," she said, climbing on top.

"I think we might need to have a talk here," he protested.

But when she cupped his cock with her hand and gave it a gentle squeeze, all the words fled from his mind. The sweet sensation boggled his mind as she moved her hand up and down his length. Joanne watched it leap against his pants, seemingly mesmerized.

"Please," he begged. "Let the poor guy out before he loses circulation."

She giggled. "Oh, sorry."

That's when they realized they were both still fully clothed with their outdoor clothes, winter coats and all. "We wouldn't have gotten very far, would we?" she said giggling as she stood up. He followed suit. As they removed all their winter attire, Nathan's stomach growled like a bear.

"Maybe we better eat the steaks before your stomach eats you," Joanne said.

"It will give me strength I need before I ravish your delectable body."

"Delectable?" she snorted. "I wish."

"I could show you right now how delicious I find you," he said, ignoring the loud growl from his stomach again.

"Just go eat your food," she said, pushing him toward the bedroom door.

"Are you coming?"

"Right behind you."

"I'd rather it be me behind you," he said, with a cheeky grin.

Joanne chuckled. "Men!"

"Women!" he mimicked with a grin, and she gave him another light shove toward the food.

"Just move."

He chuckled. "I love you and your sense of humor."

Chapter Twenty-Seven

They both froze in place upon hearing his words, unsure who should break the silence first. It was Nathan's turn to look like a deer caught in the headlights.

"I...uh..." he stammered, running a hand through his silver hair, utterly shocked, although not entirely dismayed. "God! I don't think I've ever said those words before."

"We can pretend you didn't if that helps?" she suggested softly. Her own feelings were a puddle of mush, unable to sort them in her own head. She hadn't had much time to think about what their relationship was evolving into, beyond having fun with him on the trip. But if he wasn't going to get his cancer treated, did she really want to get deeply involved with him?

"Do you want me to?" he asked, his voice unsteady and a little dejected.

Joanne took his hand and led him to the couch to sit down. Their food forgotten. With all the butterflies setting her stomach blaze, she'd lost her appetite anyway. The last time she'd heard someone say those words, aside from her son and his family, was on the day Scott died. But if there was one thing she knew, it was that life was short, and you don't look a gift horse in the mouth, especially one as incredible as Nathan.

"Everything is moving so fast," she said.

"We can slow down if you want?" he suggested, even though his face begged her to say the opposite.

Joanne stared at their joined hands that were resting on his lap. "I've always been taught to take things slow, that you can't really know someone in such a short time, but I feel like I've known you forever."

"That's a good thing, right?"

"Honestly, I didn't go into this trip expecting a relationship by the end of it. I thought it was going to be like a fling. My friend Grace has them all the time."

"I take it I have her to thank for you agreeing to go on this trip?"

"Yes."

"Remind me to thank her when we get back."

Joanne ran her thumb over the back of his hand as she thought about what he was saying. She kind of thought he'd drop her off and then continue his trip wherever he wanted to go, and she'd take the plane home. But apparently, their plans were changing.

"I didn't mean to get all heavy on you," he said.

"No. No. It's good. It's not like we're twenty anymore and have our entire lives ahead of us to figure things out."

"We could still have a good twenty or more years left."

"Or we could only have today," she whispered almost inaudibly. As much as she cared for Nathan and maybe was even falling in love with him, she didn't want to get seriously involved with someone who thought death was his only escape. She came on this trip to finally live again, to feel like a woman again, with a man whose company she enjoyed.

"Is that all you want?"

"What do you want?" she asked, hoping to turn the tide of his questioning and find out what was going on in his mind.

"You in my life."

"But for how long? I already lost one husband, Nathan, and that wasn't even his choice."

Nathan cast his eyes downward. "It's my cancer, isn't it?"

"It's not so much about that. It's the fact you think there isn't anything worth living for to even consider fighting for a future for yourself."

He didn't say anything for a moment, just squeezed her hand a little tighter. A flit of emotion passed over his features as he appeared to ponder her words. She wished she could read minds so she could find out what was going through his head. Was he considering getting help? Would he do that for Laryssa? For her? *Wait.* She back tracked their conversation to when he brought up that they could have twenty or more years left. And it filled her with hope.

"Have you changed your mind?" she asked.

"If it means having you in my life, I'll do anything."

"As much as I'd love to see you do it for me, you have to want to do it for yourself. I know how hard chemo is. I've watched a friend of mine go through it, and I don't want you to come to resent me because of it. Your will to live needs to come from you and you alone."

Nathan knew she was right. But his will to live had died when his brother did. All he'd been doing was surviving from day to day. Waiting for that inevitable moment when his heart gave out and death took him away. Or, in this case, waiting until the cancer kicked his butt. Then he could fly away and never have to feel guilty or mess anything up ever again.

But feeling Joanne's warm hand in his gave him a renewed vigor for life, not just to have her in it, but to actually want to live again. And for the first time in a long time, he could see the light, knowing things could get better. All the philosophers were right when they said nothing stays the same forever. He hadn't expected it would be Laryssa's mother-in-law who opened his eyes to the truth.

And there lay his conundrum. He loved her, but what would her family say when they found out the entire truth? Would they be as kind and generous as Joanne? Somehow, he couldn't see it. Alex would probably toss his ass back in jail, especially for stealing Laryssa's DNA with the hair sample. They had already been put through the ringer with family secrets.

But Joanne showed him he could enjoy himself even after what happened. That happiness could still exist in his life. His problem was that he hadn't felt like he deserved it, and he was still questioning that. But if she could look past his heinous crimes and still be able to touch him without flinching and run her fingers along his skin, looking at him with a smile, then maybe there was hope yet.

"You're right. I need to choose it for me, and I am. You've given me so much, Joanne. More than I deserve," he said. "And for the first time in my life, I actually want to see what the future has in store for me."

Her eyes were gentle and soft as they studied him. A sweet smile broke across her face, which was as sweet as the look in her eyes. Honestly, he was in awe that she could look at him with such tenderness, like an angel sent from heaven giving him a second chance.

She reached up with her free hand and placed her palm against his cheek. "That means the world to me," she said as she pulled him closer to kiss his cheek.

At the last second, he turned his head, and his lips meet hers instead. He didn't care about dinner. Didn't care about food. Just her. As long as he was holding her, touching her, everything was right in his world. He nibbled at her bottom lip, trying to get her to open for him. She did so willingly, allowing him to deepen the kiss. Her taste was unique, like an aphrodisiac on his senses, hitting all five at once. Sight. Smell. Touch. Taste. Hearing. Her gentle moans wrapped around his ear drums, drawing his heart in even further.

He could stay like this forever, in this place with her—their own cocoon. Away from the nastiness of the world, and no one to interrupt them. It honestly felt like a dream. With one final moan, Joanne pulled back and looked up at him, eyes burning with desire. "As much as I like doing that with you, we really should eat," she reminded him.

"I'm more than fine with your lips as my dinner."

She gave a half-grin. "I'm not exactly nutritious."

"Nope, you're like a bag of Doritos, where you can't have just one."

"I'm a chip?"

"No, you're my sweet addiction."

"I like the sound of that," she said, standing up.

As she walked by him, he slapped her on the butt and said, "Me too."

Joanne rolled her eyes and laughed, proceeding to dish out their food.

Later, while in bed, she lay with her head against his chest in bed. The room silent. They'd had another wonderful, amazing round of sex. It was hard to believe her body still worked right after all these years. She was floating on cloud nine. His words from earlier echoed in her mind. He had said he loved her, and she knew she felt the same way, but wasn't quite ready to say the words yet. They were words that didn't come easily to her, not even to her own family. It was always easier to show how she felt than to say it.

He didn't seem too bothered by the fact she hadn't said it back. When someone you love lets you down, you tend to hold the words closer to your chest. Maybe it's because they had the power to heal and the power to destroy. So many people say it far too easily, making you wonder if it meant anything to them. But then you have people like her father who never cared enough to say it at all. Not even to her mom.

"I didn't spook you, did I?" he asked, breaking an hour long, mostly comfortable, silence.

She tilted her head to look at him, smiling. "Nope, just a lot on my mind, really."

"I can't imagine it's getting any easier the closer we get to Toronto."

"I can't help but wonder what it's all about."

"You think there's a trick up his sleeve?"

"There always is." She suddenly wished she would have allowed a security team to go with her, like Alex had suggested. But she had wanted to have fun and have some alone time with Nathan, and a security detail would have got in the way of that.

Was her dad going to try something? She couldn't help but hope he'd grown as a person since she'd seen him last. There were a lot of unknowns in the air right now, and she didn't like unknowns.

"Shall I show you a magic trick?"

"Hmmm?" she murmured in response.

Nathan reached under her pillow and pulled out the joker.

She buried her face in his shoulder and laughed. "And here I thought I'd hidden it well."

"Nope," he said. "I've just been biding my time. We never did finish the game, you know."

"The game?" she asked innocently.

"As if you've forgo—" He froze, utterly mesmerized, when she sat up and the sheets fell away from her body, revealing her naked breasts. He licked his lips unconsciously.

Joanne plucked the card from his hand. "Nope, I just wanted to distract you so I could get the card."

"And here I thought, since I had the card, I'd let you do whatever you wanted to me," he said. "But since you have the card now, it's my turn to do whatever I want to you. Game rules."

Oh. Crap. She forgot that part. She thought if she had the card, she could do whatever she wanted to him. Maybe she could fudge the rules a little. "Nope. My card equals my rules."

"Wait a second. I thought I was the boss in bed."

"Equal opportunity, remember?" she exclaimed as she threw the sheets off the bed, revealing his hot naked body, his cock rising to the occasion.

"So, what does my queen want?"

"That," she said, pointing to his erection.

He chuckled. "It's kinda mine."

"That's the point," she said, wrapping her fingers around his length.

Nathan tensed wonderfully at her touch, his eyes drifting closed. When she reached the base, her one hand cupped his balls, while the other retraced the steps up his cock and back down. His member hardened even more.

She loved being able to watch his expressions and his body language. The way his eyes scrunched up in concentration as he tried hard not to come. The knowledge of his excitement made her womanhood ache with need.

Her plan had been to make him come and show him how much she valued his needs and desires, to give what she could when the words wouldn't come, but she needed him inside her, and needed him inside her now. Shifting, she straddled him and quickly dropped herself on his length, burying him deep inside her. His eyes shot open with a look of surprise.

"I loved what you were doing before, but this," he said, resting his hands on her hips, "is much better."

She giggled. "I thought so, too."

He moaned. "Do you know I can feel it when you laugh?"

"Really?"

"Ya, the walls of your pussy vibrate."

"I'm a vibrator?" she asked as another bubble of laughter grew inside her, making her collapse against his chest in a laughing fit. All while he was still inside her.

"God, girl, you're going to make me come by doing that," he said, trying to hold her body still.

He failed miserably because she couldn't stop laughing. In one quick swoop, he had her on her back and he was on top. Yet, somehow, he magically stayed inside her. Nathan grabbed her hands and held them above her head. "Are you going to stop?" he asked. "I don't want it over yet."

She pressed her lips closed, trying to swallow her laughter, but she couldn't, and it ended up coming out the other end in a fart. "Oh geez," she murmured, pulling her hands away from him so she could cover her face.

Chapter Twenty-Eight

"Well, that sounded juicy," he commented, his face going red as he tried to hold back his own chuckle.

"Please, tell me you didn't just say that?" she said, peeking through her fingers. "I think I better go to the washroom. Old lady troubles." The downside of getting older was that certain parts of her body took on a mind of their own.

Nathan glanced between them and shrugged. "You look fine to me. Besides, we have some unfinished business," he said, rocking against her gently, reminding her that he was still very much inside her.

All she wanted to do was hide. She'd never farted during sex before, and now she was afraid she would do it again. Taking her hands, Nathan held them above her head again. She tried to wrestle them away, but he had a firm grip on them. Leaning down, he kissed the tender spot below her ear as he pulled out and pushed back in again. The warmth of his breath sent a shiver down her spine.

Joanne tilted her head back, giving him better access. She couldn't help but give all of herself. He deserved that and more. He deserved to know he was a man worth loving. A man worth having.

No matter the mistakes he'd made in his life. She'd lived long enough to know they all made mistakes. No one was perfect.

Lifting her knees, she dug her feet into the bed to meet him thrust for thrust. She loved the feel of him deep inside her, claiming her body, soul, and spirit. Every time they came together, a little bit more of her heart was lost.

His breathing grew ragged, and his eyes closed, but she couldn't close hers. They were locked on his face, watching every squint and every expression. She wanted to reach out and touch him, but he wouldn't relinquish her hands.

"I want to touch you," Joanne murmured huskily. She almost shouted with glee when he finally released them. Immediately, she traced the contour of the scars on his back and lifted her head to kiss the edge of one on his shoulder.

He froze for a moment. She cupped his cheeks with her palms and pulled his lips to hers. "Beautiful," she whispered.

"Liar," he responded with a chuckle as he started moving again.

Her own response disappeared as she allowed herself to get lost in the sensations, and soon all she could think of was her body racing toward her orgasm. Every nerve on high alert, ready to explode when given the command. What it was about him, she didn't know. Kindred spirits. Soulmates. Mates...hmm, being in his arms felt like being in heaven.

He moved faster and faster, and she matched his speed. And as she reached the brink, she held her breath, waiting for him to share in her fate. He didn't disappoint. His body stiffened.

"Oh god! I love you, Joanne," he cried as he emptied himself into her.

She kissed him hard, burying his cries of passion with her own as her body joined him in the wonderful orgasmic fray, flying into the sky on a cloud that flew higher than any other.

As they floated back down, she shivered with delight and said, "I love you, too."

It took a minute or two before Nathan found the energy to roll off her, kicking the covers completely off the end of the bed, his body glistening with sweat. "It doesn't get much better than that," he said.

Reaching down, Joanne entwined her fingers with his and squeezed his hand. "Incredible."

"I didn't think it could be like that."

"Do you think we should be doing that if you..."

"Sick?" he finished. "I may be sick, but I'm definitely not dead."

"Good, cause I'm not into necrophilia," she said, laughing, then a strange thought came into her mind. "Do you think having sex with a vampire would be considered necrophilia?"

"Oh god," he said, laughing. "I'm never going to be bored with our conversations, am I?"

"Happy to please," she replied with her own chuckle.

Nathan could honestly say he's never met anyone like her before, and he doubted he ever would again. Things were moving quickly for them in the relationship department, but he was quite happy that it was. With time feeling like it was speeding up as he got older, every second was a precious commodity, and who you choose to spend your moments with became even more important. He couldn't afford to waste time when he wasn't getting any younger.

"Could you imagine never getting old, though, like a vampire? To always be youthful and in the best shape ever," she said, continuing to ponder her thoughts.

"In my eyes, your shape is perfect, and after what we just did, I'd say it's very youthful." He was rewarded with a blush that crept up her neck into her cheeks. "But I could always bite you and see what happens."

She gently slapped him on the shoulder before curling into the crook of his arm. He couldn't think of any place he'd rather be. The wind was howling outside, and the snow was gathering on the ground, but he was warm and cozy with the woman of his dreams. He pulled her close and held her tight, praying and hoping that a new future was beginning for him, for them.

But that was be contingent on whether her family could accept him. He'd hate to lose her once all this was over if they gave him the boot. He couldn't bear the thought, but he knew it was a possibility. However, maybe the two of them would get so close during this trip she'd convince her family to give him a chance.

But he wasn't exactly a good luck magnet. All he could hope for was to somehow redeem himself in their eyes. But what that was going to look like, he had no idea. With that thought rambling through his head, he closed his eyes and fell asleep.

He was up and awake before she even stirred. The snow had piled up overnight and was surrounding his motorhome in a winter wonderland. Nathan glanced at his arm and then at the shovel. There was no way he'd be able to clear the road in front of them. After their rigorous activity last night, his injury and back hurt like hell. He hated not being able to do his usual morning workout to get the kinks out of his back. Walking toward the front of the vehicle, he grabbed the window cover and gave it a tug to pull it off. Thankfully, all the snow came with it.

He unhooked the hoses and stored them in the side compartment of the motorhome and then removed the blocks tucked under the wheels. Joanne was still sound asleep, and he didn't have the heart to wake her. She'd likely sleep for another hour or so, as it was only six in the morning. His plan was to reach their next destination by nightfall. The only blip in the plan would be a closed road due to snow or ice, but there didn't appear to be any road closures at the moment.

Nathan walked to the door of the bedroom and glanced inside. Joanne was on her side, sheets curled under her chin, her brownish-gray hair flowing behind her. The light shone in the window, creating a halo around her head. She couldn't look more like an angel if she tried. Sliding the bedroom door closed, he walked through the motorhome to the driver's seat. They were ready to head out.

One thing he liked about the West Coast was that it didn't get a lot of snow, at least not very often. Every once in a blue moon, snow would accumulate, but nothing like the East Coast. He thought it was pretty to look at, but very awkward to get anything accomplished in. Slipping the keys into the ignition, he listened to the roar of the engine as he turned it on. This was his baby, and it usually behaved beautifully. Although now that he'd said that, he had probably jinxed himself.

Nathan laughed as he put the vehicle into drive and inched his way forward through the snow, avoiding potholes as he drove out of the park. As they made their way toward their next destination, he couldn't help but wonder what was ahead for Joanne. The death threat always sat in the back of his mind. Or, rather, more like at the forefront. Was he driving her to her doom? Man, that didn't sit well with him. He'd prefer to drive back the other way to keep her safe.

After a good hour of driving, the door to the bedroom slid open, and she wandered out. When he looked over his shoulder, he gave her a warm smile. She had slipped back into the clothes she'd worn yesterday, her hair going every which direction.

"You look lovely this morning," he said.

Joanne thanked him before slipping into the washroom. That man really needed to get his eyes checked. Her hair was a mess, and her day-old mascara made her eyes look like a raccoon. She'd forgotten to remove it before they went to bed. More and more lately, she was getting tired of putting on a face. Her skin was okay exactly the way it was, and not spending time in front of the mirror was much easier on her leg, which had been aching more with the cold weather lately. The motorhome was warm enough, but her body seemed to know it was winter and didn't want to play nice.

Although, this morning, she had a secondary ache coursing through her, too, making her want to grab Nathan and drag him back to bed.

Had she turned into a sex fiend? Her grandmother would have flipped had she tried something like this when she was younger. *Oh, Grandma Clara, why did you have to leave us so soon?* She was the only one who had a handle on Seth. She had kept him on the straight and narrow, but the minute she left the world, her father had become worse than he'd ever been.

Joanne's night had been restless, probably because they were getting closer to Toronto. Dreams of the beatings she had received at the hand of her father hit her whenever she fell asleep. She couldn't help who she had fallen in love with, and she wasn't going to let some hundred-year-old feud destroy her chance at happiness. Why couldn't he have changed after they got married and figured out how to live with it?

Grabbing the cloth off the hanger on the door, she rinsed it with water and gave her face a wash and refocused her thoughts to Nathan, and with that, warmth spread through her body.

"Much better," she murmured. Her cheeks had a touch of pink in them, making it look like she had put blush on. Joanne couldn't help but run her fingers along her cheek, tracing the color as she grinned. Standing up, she quickly did an assessment of the rest of herself.

Her hair, thankfully, still looked okay, so she didn't need a shower, but she'd need one by tonight before they did anything that might require the use of her parts. Maybe they could rent a hotel room that had a large bath/shower, and they could shower together. She wouldn't mind running the soap down his body as far as she could reach and back up again, and watch his manhood rise to the occasion. Something she never tired of.

Eventually, she left the washroom and joined him upfront. She stared out the front window, her jaw-dropping at the amount of snow they were trudging their way through. "Wow, it hit hard, didn't it?"

Nathan nodded. "Almost too deep to drive."

The snowplows hadn't come through yet and not too many cars were on the road, so he was forging his own path. She had no idea how he knew where to drive because the road blended in with the shoulder. No yellow or white lines could be seen.

"Are you okay to drive? How's your arm?" she asked, noting it was resting on his lap.

He lifted it and turned it this way and that. "It's sore, but I'll survive."

"We probably shouldn't have done anything last night," she said.

"It was worth the pain, so think nothing of it," he replied.

"Do you want me to drive?" she asked hesitantly. Her anxiety was kicking up a notch thinking about it, but she didn't want him to drive if it was hurting him.

"I'm good, but I'll let you back the rig in when we get there."

"Yippy," she groaned.

"I'll pay you after."

"How so?"

He gave her a look that heated her instantly. She didn't have to ask again because she knew exactly what he was thinking.

"How long do you think it will take us to get there?" she asked.

"Seven hours, give or take."

That gave her something to look forward to instead of the dread that threatened to overtake her. Nathan made the trip bearable. She'd been able to forget about the threat she was walking into whenever she focused on him.

"I look forward to it," she said, sending her own spicy look back and was rewarded by heat flaring in his eyes.

"I might need to pull over," he said.

"I have an idea."

"What?"

"Let's rent a hotel room. My treat."

"Tired of my little home already?" he asked with curiosity and absolutely no animosity.

"No. I just want us to enjoy a nice big bathroom."

"I like the way you think," he said, giving her a wink, making him press down on the gas pedal a little more to speed up their trip.

"I'll book the room."

Chapter Twenty-Nine

Joanne sat on the bed and looked around the hotel room. She was grateful they didn't have to hook up the motorhome for once, and they could both spend the evening relaxing. Although, by the look on Nathan's face, he was already worried about something.

"I'll be right back. I'm gonna make sure the motorhome is locked up tight for the night. I think I forgot to lock the window."

"Okay. I need to call Alex and let him know we made it safe and sound."

After the door secured behind Nathan, she dialed her son's number. "Hi, Alex."

"Mom, I was getting worried," Alex's voice boomed. "I've been trying to reach you all day."

Something in his tone made her sit up straight. "What's wrong?"

"I just got a text message that told me to say goodbye to you. What's that all about?"

Her chest tightened. How had they managed to get their hands on her son's number? She'd never given it to them, not even to her mom, because her dad could have found it too easily.

"I honestly have no idea."

"Is something going on that I don't know about?"

She hesitated to tell him about the message she had received, because she wasn't even entirely sure what it was about, whether it was meant for her or whether it was a wrong number. Her heart said it was from her dad, but she still couldn't help but hope it wasn't.

Groaning, she said, "I received a death threat a few days ago. I'm sure it was—"

"What the hell, Mom? How could you keep that from me?"

"Don't take that tone with me," she said, wagging her finger in the air even though he couldn't see it. "I'm sure it's nothing."

"A death threat is not nothing."

"We're contacting the police in the morning. We haven't reported it yet because we were on the road."

"What hotel are you staying at? I'm sending a security detail."

Joanne sighed. She knew at this point it would be futile to argue with him. Alex was already worried about her father and what he would do. She gave him the name of the hotel. It was on the outskirts of Toronto. It wasn't the fanciest, but she figured her dad wouldn't look for her out here.

"Let me make a few calls. I'm glad you're in a hotel and not the motorhome now, though. That makes me feel a little more comfortable."

Even though his worrying attitude frustrated her, she was incredibly proud of the man he'd become. He went through a lot and still had a tender heart.

"I love you, son," she said with a fond smile. She wished she could have met her other son, Aidan, before he died, but in a way, he lived on in Alex…minus the bad attitude and behavior that Aidan got from her father.

"Love you, too. Talk to you soon," he replied before hanging up.

As she dropped her phone on the bed beside her, Nathan strolled into the room. "Everything okay?" he asked.

"I told my son about the threat," she said. "He's sending a security detail."

"That's probably a good idea until we can find out what's going on. Did you want to contact the police tonight, or did you want to wait until the morning?"

"We should probably contact them tonight, but I don't feel like waiting for hours for them to show up over a text message."

"Then shall we have our shower?" he suggested, holding out his hand.

"I'm up for that."

"Aren't I the one that's usually up?"

Joanne laughed and shook her head, her tight chest easing. "That's so corny."

He took her by the hand and led her into the bathroom.

Later, they lay on the bed, cuddling as she created lazy circles with her finger on his chest. Something she found herself doing every night. "How do you do that?" she asked.

"What?"

"Wake my body up so easily?"

"You aren't in the grave yet, my dear."

She couldn't help but wonder if she would ever stop wanting him. Every time he looked at her, her motor revved. Making love to him happened so easily. They occasionally needed lube, but not very often. And she loved that fact, sincerely enjoying being turned on again.

"There's just something about you, Nathan Mitchell."

He turned his head and kissed her forehead. "I feel the same way about you."

"Do you think that..." She paused for a moment before continuing, "You might want to stick around after our trip?"

"Do you want me to?"

Joanne nodded. Did he want to stay with her? Did he want a future with her? Her stomach danced like crazy as though all the butterflies in the world were congregating there.

Nathan stared at the ceiling, his fingers lightly stroking her shoulder. "Your family might not want me to stay."

"They'll come to love you like I have."

"I'm not sure it will be that simple, sweetheart."

"Then let's do it here and not give them a chance." She propped herself up on her elbow and looked at him.

"Do what?"

"Get married."

As she spoke the words, Nathan swallowed and his saliva went down the wrong way, making him cough. He hit his chest, her face falling in the process.

She went to get up, looking extremely embarrassed, but he grabbed her arm. "Sorry, you shocked me. I just figured I'd be the one doing the proposing."

Joanne shrugged. "It's the twenty-first century. I figured I might as well grow with the times."

"You sure know how to surprise a man."

She pouted and flopped back on the bed. Disappointment fluttered across her face as she pulled her hands away from him. "Sorry, I just thought…"

He turned onto his side, propping himself up on his elbow as he pressed two fingers to her lips. "I'd love to, but I know your son would have a fit if I did things without his blessing."

And after everything he'd done in the past, it was only right that he followed proper etiquette here.

"He's going to have a fit anyway," she grumbled.

"I can handle a grown son." *Maybe.* "When that time comes, I will ask for your hand." Hopefully, Alex respected his mom enough to want her to be happy. He might still be given the boot, and Alex might lock her in the tower, like Rapunzel.

"He's not my father, Nate." At the mention of the word father, her eyes grew sad and misty.

"Don't," he said.

"What?"

"Don't let that man get you down. He's not worth it."

"It's hard not to. He's supposed to be a father. My father, damn it." Joanne slapped her hands across her mouth. "Sorry."

"Hey, what are you apologizing for? I think your father deserves stronger words than that even."

"I don't like saying stuff like that. I try hard not to, especially because of my grandkids," she said, dropping her hands to the bed.

He couldn't imagine ever treating his kids the way her dad treated her. Nathan wanted to wring his neck, swinging him back and forth like a rubber chicken against the concrete. If Seth tried anything, he'd have no mercy for the man. No one touched his woman! Seth was a worthless piece of trash, in his opinion.

Mind you, he wasn't one to talk. If Laryssa was his, he had stayed away like a worthless piece of junk, too. And even if she wasn't, he could have tried to adopt her, but his chances of being awarded custody after what happened weren't very high. Man, he hoped his friend would contact him soon. The uncertainty was weighing heavily on his mind. Was he, or wasn't he, her father?

"I think you are still absolutely wonderful, even when your words are filthy," he said, giving her a wink. "In fact," he continued, slipping his hands under the covers, "we should practice talking dirty. Tell me what you want."

"Don't you think we should wait till we're married now?" she asked innocently, but he knew she was joking by the twinkle in her eye.

"Is that what you want?" he asked, slipping a finger inside her.

"Oh geez," she gasped. "Your mouth. I want your mouth."

He chuckled as he threw back the sheets. "Much better." Nathan moved down to the foot of the bed while she moved up toward the head of it a little bit more, giving him extra room to lie comfortably on the bed, his head situated between the apex of her thighs. She smelled like a sweet candy.

Joanne moaned and shuddered when his tongue licked her clit, making delightful shocks vibrate through her body. Each motion sent another jolt to the ends of her fingertips. She struggled to keep her body relaxed by releasing her fists, so she could find the peak more slowly. But Nathan picked up the pace and slipped a finger inside her. One, then two, and she welcomed him inside by tilting her hips. And that's when he hit it. The sweet spot that made her eyes roll back as she cried out his name, her fingers clenching the sheets with no hope in heck of releasing them. Her body cried out for more.

"Please, Nate, I want you inside me."

"I am inside you."

"Your hard cock. I want it. Now!" she demanded.

He moved up over her, resting on his forearms, his erection poised at her entrance. "Who am I to refuse a lady?"

Joanne wrapped her legs around his waist, coaxing him inside with a kick to his behind. Nathan laughed but happily obliged. He filled her to the brim in every way. Suddenly tears formed in her eyes as they lay there in each other's arms as close as two humans could get. She didn't even know why.

He glanced up at her and froze. "Wow, are you okay? I didn't hurt you, did I?" he asked as he started to pull out. She tightened the hold she had on him with her legs.

"Don't you dare," she warned. "I'm just happy."

"And that makes you cry?" he asked hesitantly.

"I thought this trip was going to be horribly unbearable."

"Gee, thanks," he said wryly.

She bopped him on the good shoulder. "Not you. Seeing my..." Joanne let her words trail off. She wasn't going to ruin a good moment by talking about her father. Nathan was a wonderful man who was doing amazing things to her body—his cock fitting as snug as a bug in a rug inside her. The thought made her giggle.

"From crying to giggling, I don't think I'll ever figure you women out," he said, shaking his head as he glanced between them to watch his cock pull out of her and push back in again. He loved watching himself disappear inside her, loved the feel of her warmth surrounding him. There was no place like home. The one place a man was naturally built to go. She was his perfect fit. His soulmate. Something he never believed in until now.

Soon, all thoughts fled from his mind, and all he could focus on was the feeling of her closing around him. He moved faster and faster, his breathing in sync with his pace. Joanne cried out as she came, her muscles tightening around him.

"Oh, god!" he moaned as all his energy was ready to explode into a great supernova in the pit of his belly. He tried to open his eyes to watch her, but he had no hope in heck of doing so, as a fireworks display took over with each wave of his orgasm. His body was no longer in his control. He couldn't stop pumping into her again and again as it continued.

Wave after wave of emotion ricocheted through him. And he was more certain now than ever that he loved her and wanted to spend eternity with her. Whatever happened at the end of all this, he was going to make sure that happened. No one could chase him away now.

Joanne lay panting beneath him, a sexy smile playing on her face. "We sure aren't getting much else done, are we?" she said.

"If we could do this all day, I wouldn't complain." He went to push himself up, but then winced. "Although, I think my arm would protest."

Worry filled her delicate features. "Oh, I'm sorry. Do you need your pain meds?"

"I think I could do with them now, yes," he said, gingerly sitting up, careful not to put any more pressure on it.

"You need to tell me when it hurts."

"Men don't complain."

Joanne quirked an eyebrow. "Since when?" Nathan dug his fingers into her side and tickled her. She tried to squirm out of his reach but didn't succeed. "Mercy!" she cried, giggling.

Just then, there was a knock at the door.

Chapter Thirty

"Just a minute," Joanne yells.

Sitting up, they slip their clothes on, and Nathan went over to open the door.

Joanne leaned forward to look around the wall and saw two cops standing there, a woman and a man in blue. Okay, technically they're wearing black, but the nickname still stuck in her head.

"Is Joanne here?"

Nathan waved them inside.

"Joanne Richards?"

"That's me." Why were the police at the door? She hadn't called them.

"I'm Constable Jamieson, and this is Constable Sierra," the tall, slender male cop said. "Your son, Alex, called us to let us know that you received a death threat the other day?"

Of course, he would call them and make them check on her tonight. "Yes. I got a text message from an unknown number."

"Can we see it?" the woman asked.

All she wanted was to be left alone for the night. Get a good sleep before she had to face all this crap, but it looks like her son brought it their way tonight.

"Hang on." Joanne wandered over in her bare feet to the chair in the corner of the room where her jacket was sitting and pulled her cellphone out of the pocket. She held it out to them. "Here."

Constable Jamieson took the phone and frowned. "Do you know who might have sent this to you?" he asked before giving it to his partner to look at.

Joanne was so glad she wasn't the type of person to have anything embarrassing on her phone. No racy pictures or text messages. The thought made her giggle when she remembered the silly picture she had sent Nathan a few nights ago.

Nathan came over and put his arm around her. "I'm betting 100 percent that it was her father."

"Your father?" Constable Sierra glanced at her curiously.

Great. Did she have to tell everyone her sordid story? "My mother just passed away, and I'm here to meet with the estate lawyer. He's probably trying to scare me away."

"You don't have a good relationship with him?" Constable Sierra asked, handing Joanne back the cellphone.

"Let's just say he hates my guts."

The woman raised her eyebrows at that. "Care to elaborate?"

"It's a wee bit of a long story," Joanne replied.

"Is he the type of man who would do something like this?" Constable Jamieson asked.

One wouldn't think a father could stoop so low, but there wasn't anything her father wouldn't do, which was why she no longer had contact with him. If he knew where she was, she'd probably be dead by now for polluting the family line.

"He stole my kids, so yes," Joanne said bitterly. She hadn't realized how much resentment she still had for the man and hated the guilt that often came with it. God wanted people to forgive each other, even when they didn't deserve it, but she was finding that difficult to do.

"Is there any way to check the number?" Nathan asked hopefully.

"If you do *69 right after a call, that's a possibility, but not if you've had other calls since then. We can make a request to the phone company to release the records, but that could take a while. If you want, we can pay your father a visit, but I think until we know for sure, it's probably best not to. When do you meet with your lawyer?"

"Two more days."

"I'd recommend trying to get the meeting out of the way as soon as possible and then head home. Your son says his place is pretty secure."

"I won't be a prisoner in my own home or a prisoner of my father's. He should be in jail for everything he's done for me, but no," Joanne snapped. "He's too well connected for that."

Nathan gave her shoulder a squeeze. "Uttering threats is a crime, right?"

"Yes, however, we need to make sure it came from him first," Constable Sierra said.

"He's not stupid enough to do it from any of his phones. If it was him, he'll have used a friend's phone or stolen one," Joanne said.

"Mind if I take a picture?" Constable Sierra asked.

Joanne waved her hand. "Go ahead." Moments like this made her hate technology and the internet. She loved when you could just drop off the face of the planet back in the day, and no one knew how to find you. She missed the simpler days, although she couldn't say she'd had any simple days. Everything in the world seemed to rally against her.

Nathan kissed the top of her head, making her nerves settle a little. It was nice having him around.

After Constable Sierra was done with her phone, she handed it back. "We'll do what we can to look into this. We'll call you if we find anything. In the meantime, be careful. Your son mentioned that he'd be sending security?"

Joanne nodded.

"Good," Constable Jameson said. "Call us if anything changes."

"Thank you," Nathan said as he walked with them to the hotel room door.

Joanne flopped back on the bed the minute they left and let out a loud sigh. Would her life ever be normal? All she wanted was a quiet life where she got to do what she wanted, go where she wanted, and never have to worry about a thing. Maybe that's why Nathan lived in a motorhome. If you got tired of one place, you could easily pack up and go somewhere else.

"How are you doing?" he asked, sitting on the edge of the bed.

"I wish I could snap my fingers and have all this business over with so I could get on with my life."

"I don't blame you there. But I'm here for you, and we'll get through this."

Holding out her hand, Joanne wiggled her fingers, hinting that she wanted him to lay down beside her. She wanted to get lost in his touch, in the feel of his arms around her. Her body might not be up for another round of sex right now, but she needed to be held, cuddled, and made to feel like nothing else on earth mattered but her.

And Nathan seemed to sense that because he propped himself up at the head of the bed and gestured for her to come to him, his eyes full of pain and concern for her. "Come here, hun."

It was midnight now, but her heart was pumping too fast to sleep. She cuddled up next to him, resting her head against his chest. He pulled her in close. And more than anything else, she felt safe in his world and in his arms. It's where she wanted to spend the rest of her life. Moaning softly, Joanne focused on her breathing to slow her palpitating heart, which wanted to go off in all sorts of directions.

Nathan reached over and turned off the lamp beside the bed, flooding the room in darkness. It allowed her mind to focus on the sound of his soothing heartbeat and the slow rise and fall of his chest.

"Thank you," she whispered, resting her palm against his chest.

"It's my pleasure."

And it was in that position, she fell asleep.

Nathan woke to his arm going numb. He was still propped up at the head of the bed with Joanne in his arms. He hated that he couldn't do anything to make this easier for her. If he had his way, he'd go see her father and put him in the place he belonged. If Seth was threatening Joanne, the man deserved to be in jail, and he was going to make sure that happened.

Reaching over, he pulled his phone off the nightstand and glanced at the time. He couldn't see the clock on the table without moving, and he didn't want to disturb her. She looked so restful, peaceful, and that's what she deserved to be.

As he lay there debating on what to do, another knock sounded at the door. For some reason, they had become rather popular. Easing his arm out from behind Joanne, he carefully lowered her head to the pillow. She stirred and let out a soft sigh but continued sleeping. Poor woman was exhausted.

Nathan walked over to the door and opened it, and a tornado of a brunette rushed by him and into the room.

The woman gasped and covered her mouth as she stood at the foot of the bed. "Oh my gosh, it is her." Her thick hair flowed halfway down her back, and she was wearing ripped blue jeans and a plain pink t-shirt. Her eyes were a sparkling hazel color.

Joanne stirred and opened her eyes, letting out a shriek of surprise. "Nathan!" she cried, looking around for him. He hadn't quite recovered yet and was still standing at the door with his hand on the handle.

Shaking his head and gathering his wits about him, he placed himself between Joanne and the woman. "Who are you?" he asked.

"I can't believe it. I can't believe this is actually happening," the woman continued, waving her hands in front of her face, tears gathering in her eyes. "You, you're Joanne right. Please tell me I have the right room?"

"First, tell us who you are?" Nathan said, who was more awake than Joanne was. She was staring blankly at the woman, her mouth opening and closing.

"Oh, right. Sorry, I'm Amber." She said it like it was supposed to mean something, but Joanne didn't appear to recognize her.

"I think we need more information than that," Nathan said, taking charge. "Otherwise, I'm going to call the cops."

"Oh, please don't. He'll find out that I came here."

"Seth?" Joanne asked.

The woman's eyes darted to the door before returning to Joanne. "Ya. He doesn't know I'm here, and if you call the police, he'll know."

"What are you doing here? And who are you?" Nathan asked, watching Joanne grow paler by the minute. He wished the young brunette would stop bouncing around long enough to keep eye contact. Something didn't smell right about her.

"I'm your daughter," she said. "I'm not supposed to know, but I do."

"But I only had two boys," Joanne replied, her voice wavering with uncertainty. There was much she didn't remember because of her head injury, but the ultrasound techs only said she was having twins.

Amber pulled a letter out of her pocket and held it out to Joanne. "That's what Seth—Grandpa told you, but it's not true. I found Grandma's will after she died. It was hidden in a vase in the corner of the living room."

Could it be true? That *was* her mother's favorite place to hide things. She always thought no one knew, but Joanne did. In fact, she'd found a Christmas present or two in there before.

"How old are you?" Joanne asked, her stomach queasy. It would be so like her father to keep a third child a secret. And she knew that a hidden child was not impossible in a multi-birth pregnancy. Oh goodness, was it true? Did she have another child?

"I'm thirty-six."

"Birthday?"

"Come on, Mom, you know when my birthday is."

"Humor her," Nathan said, crossing his arms.

Amber rolled her eyes before catching herself and said, "Fine. It's April twenty-fifth."

Joanne gasped. It couldn't be. The woman couldn't be her daughter. There was no way the hospital could have messed up so badly with her birth records. Wait. Had she ever seen the birth records from the hospital? She narrowed her eyes and scrunched up her nose as she tried to think back to the early days.

Oh god. Having been in a coma, anything could have happened. Lies told. Stories made up. She didn't want to think it could happen in a professional establishment, but crooked people worked in every environment and could be bought with money. Had they snuck a kid out of the maternity ward somehow?

"Do you think we could go somewhere and talk privately?" Amber asked.

"Wherever she goes, I go," Nathan replied.

"Please, I want to get to know my mom. Just her and I. We don't have to go far. There's a coffee shop on the corner," Amber suggested. "I'd really love it, please."

Joanne looked up at Nathan, who was silently shaking his head behind Amber's back. He was going to be mad, but she needed to know the truth. "I don't suppose there is any harm in it," she said. "It's just down the road, Nathan."

Amber did a little jump and clapped her hands as though she was a little kid who got her wish. "Goodie."

Nathan frowned. He didn't like this. Not a single bit.

Chapter Thirty-One

Joanne and Amber left Nathan behind in the hotel room, much to his reluctance. It was broad daylight. The hotel and streets below were busy. There wasn't any reason to think anything would happen. There was concern in his eyes, though, and she loved him for it.

"Who's the guy?" Amber asked curiously, her hands wringing together in front of her as they walked, her eyes darting this way and that.

"My daughter-in-law's uncle. But enough about me. I want to hear about you."

"Well, I was raised by Grandpa's sister and honestly didn't know anything until about ago. I went over to his place to help him clean, as he can't get around very well anymore, and happened to find Grandma's will."

"What did it say?"

"It tells of everything that happened when we were born, and how she wanted the truth to be revealed. She left everything to you and us kids. Grandpa gets nothing."

Oh, that probably tickled him raw. Is that why he was threatening her?

"He doesn't know about the reading of the official will on Thursday. He thinks they are going to read the old one he found. That's why I had to meet with you first. I didn't know what you had planned, and whether you were going to see him or not," Amber said.

"I had only planned on attending the reading." Joanne glanced down at girl's left hand and noticed a ring. "Are you married?" Could she possibly have another entire family waiting to meet her?

"Not quite, but hopefully soon. We haven't picked a date yet because there were some complications, so I'm okay with waiting." Amber opened the door to the small café, and they both walked inside. A painted mural of a tropical destination with an orangey red sunset covered the wall, blending into the dark yellow floor and ceiling. The tables were a deep red color. Joanne almost felt like she'd walked into the Caribbean. They even had music to match. She loved it immediately. Maybe she and Nathan could come in here later for dinner.

"So, no kids?" Joanne asked.

Amber blushed. "Actually, I'm eight weeks pregnant."

"No way?" Joanne squealed. If everything the woman said was true, she was about to become a grandmother again, and that was exciting, to say the least. She knew Alex was going to want to get a DNA test, but the girl looked a little like Joanne did at her age, before her brownish gray hair and saggy skin joined the picture.

"I have to go to my ultrasound in an hour. You're welcome to join me?"

"I think Nathan would have my hide if I did. Could he come?"

"Sadly, I'm only allowed to bring one person."

"The father doesn't want to go?"

"He can't. He's at work," Amber replied, waving over the waitress dressed in a yellow romper with a white apron to their little table tucked in the corner, away from the window. "I'll have a cream cheese bagel. Mom?"

Joanne shivered, a full head to toe shiver. It suddenly felt like she'd entered the twilight zone, and she had no idea why. Could the full impact of the revelation finally be hitting her? Was she in shock?

"I'll have a breakfast sandwich with bacon," Joanne said, giving her head a shake.

"Mom, are you okay?" Amber asked. "You're looking pale."

Joanne nodded. "I guess you could say that I'm just a bit mind blown."

"You can imagine how I felt," Amber said with a nervous chuckle. "One minute I'm an only child, next I have two brothers."

"How are you feeling about it all?"

"I haven't talked to Grandpa yet. I don't know what to say. My goal was to get you out here first so we could talk."

Amber calling Seth Grandpa sounded funny to Joanne. Wouldn't it be Uncle Seth if Amber had been raised by Seth's sister, Leanna. Man, she hadn't talked to anyone on his side of the family for a long time. They all seemed to be in cahoots with each other. Who would willingly take another woman's baby? Aunt Leanna didn't seem overly terrible, but if a woman could be bought to live a lie, then maybe she had misread her. Joanne sighed. She chose to live a lie, too, hadn't she? But hers was forced. Had Leanna been forced to, as well?

It wouldn't surprise her in the slightest. Her father had that particular way about him. He'd do whatever it took to get what he wanted. She felt so happy that Scott's parents had raised Alex. They'd done an impeccable job with both kids. Scott was kind, caring, thoughtful, and always stood up for what was right.

"I wasn't sure you'd come, though," Amber said.

"In all honesty, I didn't want to, but I knew for my mom's sake I had to. I..." Joanne stopped talking for a moment. She stared at Amber, still trying to process who she might be. They appeared to have the same nose and smile, but that could just be her wishing it to be so. "I can't believe I have a daughter." She still wasn't sure she believed it. It seemed too good to be true.

Amber dropped her hands to her stomach. "And I can't believe

I'm going to have a kid myself. Do you think I'll have twins or triplets, too?"

The thought that the woman was pregnant floored her and worried her. What was her father going to pull on this poor girl? Would her father snatch Amber's baby, too? It wouldn't surprise her in the slightest.

"Is that why they are doing an ultrasound so early?"

The girl's mouth opened, but she closed it right away, her lips pressing into a firm line. That made Joanne really curious. Amber continued her silence for a bit longer until the waitress placed their food on the table. Then, she seemed to find her footing again.

"I'm a bit high risk, I guess you could say."

"How so?"

"Do you mind if we don't talk about it? It's too public here."

Joanne nodded and went silent while they both munched on their food. After taking about five bites, Amber threw her hands to her mouth and jumped up, making a mad dash for the bathroom. Joanne struggled between protecting their food and drink or checking on the girl. But if it was morning sickness, Joanne doubted Amber would come back and eat the rest anyway. Morning sickness had been super bad for her, too.

But motherly concern had her getting up and going anyway, and she tapped the nearby waitress. "Can you keep an eye on our food for a few minutes? My...uh...my daughter isn't feeling well." Gosh, that sounded weird even to her own ears.

The waitress shrugged her shoulders, and said, "Sure."

Joanne hobbled her way to the bathroom and pushed open the door. Inside were three stalls, one of which was closed, and Amber was gagging up a storm.

"Do you need any help, hun?" Joanne asked, standing at the door to the stall.

"One sec," she replied, with another full-on heave.

Joanne glanced around the washroom. The floor tiles were cracked, and the paint had begin peeling on the walls. However, the one thing the room had going for it, though, was that it was clean, except for a few pieces of paper towel on the floor around the garbage can.

Lots of public washrooms were a disaster, and it drove her crazy. She was a wee bit of a neat freak. Grabbing a piece of paper towel, she leaned down and picked up the stray pieces, tossing them in the garbage can. As Joanne was washing her hands, Amber came out of the stall, her face rosy.

"Morning sickness sucks," she responded.

"That was always my least favorite thing about being pregnant."

"Would you mind helping me get home?" Amber asked. "I know your guy at the hotel probably won't like it, but I don't want to be alone right now."

"Didn't you say you had an ultrasound to go to?" she asked.

Her daughter mumbled something Joanne didn't catch under her breath before saying, "Oh right. Sorry. Pregnancy brain. I think I'm going to cancel. I'm not feeling up to it."

"I know you aren't feeling so hot right now, but it's best to get it done to make sure everything is okay."

"I suppose. Does that mean you'll come?" Amber asked, hope filling her eyes.

Joanne wasn't sure how. She didn't have a car, and she'd rather not have to drag the motorhome anywhere. "Do you have your own car?"

"Yes. It's just down the road," Amber answered.

"I just need to let Nathan know before—"

"No," Amber said quickly, almost a little too sharply for Joanne's liking. "Sorry. I'm running out of time and need to change my clothes before the appointment. I got some puke on my shirt. Could you drive? I'm still feeling a little off."

Joanne glanced at the tiny wet stain on Amber's pink t-shirt and figured it didn't look that bad. But if that's what she wanted to do, then who was Joanne to say otherwise? "Let me call—"

Amber did a quick heave and covered her mouth, eyes panicking. "Please, Mom, can we just go before I get sick again?"

Joanne glanced back toward the hotel, frantically trying to decide what to do. Being pushed to make a split-second decision didn't sit well with her. If she didn't tell Nathan and she disappeared, he would contact Alex, then all hell would break loose.

"How far?" she asked Amber.

"Ten minutes, fifteen at the most."

That wasn't too bad. She could be there and back in a jiffy. Much to her hesitation and dislike of the circumstances, she reluctantly agreed to go. "Come on," Joanne said, climbing into Amber's car.

Being guided by her daughter, they drove to a small two-floor house with gray brick siding. Nothing looked overly suspicious about it. Certainly nothing her father would own.

"Is this your place?" Joanne asked.

Amber nodded. "Been here for a few years now."

"By yourself?"

"More or less," was her cryptic response.

Joanne thought she caught a smirk on the corner of the woman's lips, but it quickly disappeared, and she couldn't help but wonder if she had imagined it. They stepped out of the vehicle, and Joanne went around to her Amber's side to help her. "I'll wait here for you."

"Aw, don't you want to check out my house? I promise it won't take long."

"I better not. I'm already going to get in trouble by just being here."

But Amber refused her answer and instead grabbed her arm, pulling her toward the door. "I promise we'll be in and out before you know it."

As Amber was dragging her toward the house, Joanne's phone rang. She tried to grab her phone, but it was in the same pocket as the arm that was currently in Amber's possession.

Unable to do anything but go along for the ride or risk falling over, she hobbled her way toward the door. "Careful, please. I have a bad leg."

"Oh, right. Seth—I mean Grandpa told me about that, sorry."

Amber didn't seem to have anymore disdain in her voice when she spoke about her grandfather. Joanne couldn't understand why she could speak about him so casually now when she couldn't at the hotel. When they reached the door, her phone rang again, and she could answer it this time. It was Alex.

"Hello?" she asked as Amber pulled her inside and closed the door.

"Mom, Nathan said you went off with some stranger?" Alex asked, his voice an octave lower than normal, indicating his frustration and worry.

"Oh, it's fine. I'll tell you all about it later. Turns out you have a—" Her words were eaten when something hard rammed into the back of her skull, dropping her to the ground. Everything went dark.

Chapter Thirty-Two

"You let her do what?" Alex shouted into the phone.

Nathan had to hold it away from his ear, so he wouldn't blow out his ear drum. "I didn't exactly let it happen."

"A woman shows up claiming to be her daughter, and neither of you thought it fishy?"

"What about you? You didn't even send a security detail like you said you would," Nathan snapped as he paced back and forth in his hotel room. After she didn't return to the hotel as quickly as he had hoped, he went to the café they had went to. That's when he saw them getting into a car, which flipped his panic switch. And now that Alex told him Joanne was in trouble, his insides were twisting into a pretzel.

"I thought you'd keep her safe long enough for it to be organized. They were going to be there by tonight."

"How was I to know something was going to happen? They were just going to the damn café."

"Uh, in case you haven't noticed, my mother hasn't been making the smartest of choices lately," Alex growled, his tone hard and unrelenting.

He figured if the man could reach through the phone and ring his neck, he would. Nathan couldn't blame him. How could he have been so stupid?

"Let me guess. You didn't get anything helpful?" Alex snapped.

"I'm not that useless. I got the license and make of the car." Nathan gave him the information. What had he been thinking, letting her go to the café alone? He should have insisted, but like the dolt he was, he hung back, thinking that mother and daughter deserved time alone to talk and connect. Being Joanne's daughter must have been a ruse.

God!

Someone else was going get hurt because he was an idiot. His stomach rolled as acid rose in his throat. If something happened to her because of him, he'd never be able to live himself. They entrusted him with her safety.

"I'll get my people on this, but damn it, call the police. Let them know that I think my grandfather has her, and he's a dangerous man."

For a grandson to say that, Nathan knew the man wasn't fooling. And for the first time in his life, he was sincerely afraid for Joanne. People often exaggerated what their family was like, but he knew this was not one of those times. As soon as they hung up, Nathan called the police and told them everything he knew, which sadly wasn't as much as it should have been.

The police wouldn't give him any information on how to track her down. They told him to leave it to them, but he didn't want to sit around and wait for an update, not during a time like this. Hell, no. He was going to get his woman back before anything happened to her.

Heading back down to the café, he stopped in to speak with the waitress. Someone had to know something. Pushing open the door, he made a direct beeline to the counter for a waitress dressed in yellow. "Hi Ma'am, I need to ask you about two women you saw in here this morning. One was wearing a pink t-shirt, and she was with an older woman."

"What about them?"

"Have you ever seen the young one before?"

The lady shook her head. "No, it was the first time having her in our café, and I've been here for years."

"Damn."

"Is everything okay?"

"You don't, by any chance, have any video cameras set up? The police may need to look at them."

She pointed to the corner of the ceiling by the outer window. "Right there. If you think they need it, they need to come in and speak with our manager."

"Thank you," he said and then turned around to leave. That didn't really get him anywhere. He'd been hoping someone in there would know her. Shoving the door open, he stepped into the frigid air, with the snow up to his knees. Why the heck would she drive away with someone she barely knew.

Nathan smacked his forehead. It was all his fault. She did, after all, go away with him before she even knew what he'd done. Nathan leaned his head back and groaned. Her son was right. She wasn't thinking straight about stranger danger. He had to find her, even if he had to drive up and down every God damn street in the neighborhood.

Returning to their room, he searched through her belongings. She had to have something that had her dad's address on it. Even the letter should give him a little bit more info to go on, like the lawyer's name. Eventually he found the letter in the side pocket of her suitcase.

"Bingo!" There was a phone number for the lawyer in the top left corner of the page. Snatching his phone out of his pocket, he called the number and asked to speak to the one in charge, stating it was a matter of life and death.

"What's it pertaining to, sir?" the receptionist asked.

"I believe Joanne Richards is in danger. I need to speak with him immediately."

"Give me a moment." Elevator music began playing much to his frustration. He tapped his foot on the ground while he waited for the lady to return. Normally he didn't mind waiting, but times like this, he'd rather cut out the middleman and go straight to the source. But it's not like he had time to go across town and barge into their office. She might not have that long.

"Hello, how can I help you?" a man's voice answered.

"Hi, yes, I know you don't know me, sir, but I'm a friend of Joanne's," he said rather quickly.

Appearing to sense his urgency, the man asked, "Is everything okay?"

"No, it isn't. I have reason to believe that Joanne has been kidnapped by her father. Is there anything you can tell me that might help? Like his address or something?"

"I'm afraid I can't give out that information because your name isn't on the file, but I'll contact the police and give it to them if they need it."

"Damn it! This is a matter of life and death. I need to help her."

"My heart goes out to you. It really it does, but I'm bound by confidentiality laws," the lawyer said, his voice sounding a little too uppity. Was the lawyer in on it? Could the whole thing have been a lie, and there was no will at all?

"Please," he said to the man. "You have to help."

"I'll do what I can, but I can only give his information to the police."

"Fine!" Nathan growled. "Contact them."

It irked him that the letter didn't have her mother's address on it, only the address of the lawyer's office. The only other thing he could do was canvas the neighborhood and hope they didn't go too far. Here it was, a week before Christmas, and it felt like his early Christmas present got ripped out of his hands.

He had to find her. Leaving his hotel room, he made his way back to the street again. His motorhome wasn't going to do the trick for looking around. He'd have to rent a car. When he stepped outside and onto the sidewalk, he noted a rent-a-car place conveniently on the other side of the road as if it had been put there for him.

After about thirty minutes and his patience wearing thin, he got into a small gray Honda. The guy inside wanted to talk his ear off and often stopped typing so he could use his hands to gesture. He finally had to tell the guy it was a matter of life and death, and he needed that car. And he had needed it yesterday.

Carefully pulling out of the lot, he went in the direction of the white Porsche that they'd gotten into. He still couldn't believe he'd let the woman dupe him, and for Joanne to get in the car, she had to have been duped pretty bad, too. If he could kick himself in the butt, he would. He knew finding her would be a long shot, but he had to try.

It was still broad daylight, so that made things a little easier. The area was densely populated, but the car should stand out if he saw it. There weren't too many Porsche cars around. He canvassed the area, block by block. Slowly but surely, he worked his way in one direction, while still trying to contact Joanne. The call was going through, but she wasn't answering.

Sharp pains radiated in his chest. He couldn't lose her. Not now. Not when things were getting good between them. And he couldn't be the one response for her getting hurt either. It was hard enough to lose his brother and his wife, but to lose the next person he allowed to get close to him would break him into a million pieces.

Nathan scanned the driveway and roadside. There was parking on both sides of the road. Pulling up to a red light, he came to a stop, tapping his fingers impatiently on the wheel. When the light turned green, his phone started ringing, but he couldn't answer the damn thing. As soon as he found a parking spot, he pulled over and picked up the phone off the seat beside him.

"Hello?" he answered.

"My guys are at the hotel. Can you head back?" Alex said.

"Let me just finish this last block, and then I'll go and meet up with them."

"Thank you. And by the way, do me a favor," the man said, his voice slightly clippy. "After we find my mom, leave."

Nathan's airway tightened, and the pains in his chest grew. Did Alex find out the truth? That was the only explanation. "Don't you think that's for your mom to decide?"

"If you like her, you'll do what's best for her. She doesn't need her heart broken again."

"We should be worrying about finding her, not worrying about my relationship with her, which, by the way, is none of your business. She's a grown woman who deserves to be loved."

"Yes, but not by you."

"What if that's not what she thinks?" He was beginning to take a strong dislike to her overbearing son. Was Alex the reason Joanne was still single? He couldn't imagine any other reason why a man hadn't snatched her up yet. The man cared for his mom, Nathan knew that, but it almost seemed a little too much.

"She's not going to want to upset my wife by keeping you around. I know everything, Nathan."

Nathan coughed and pounded his fist against his chest, trying to open his suddenly clogged airway again. "How?" Did he know he was testing Laryssa's DNA for paternity? He didn't want to ask in case he didn't know.

"I have my sources. And you aren't going to breathe a word of this to Laryssa. When my mother is home safe and sound, you are going to disappear. Got it?"

Nathan hit his head a couple times against the headrest, frustrated silly. "So, you really are judge, jury, and executioner, aren't you?

"Just do what needs to be done," Alex ordered, and then the phone line went dead.

He tightened his grip on the steering wheel, fighting with the pressure rising inside him. It would appear that bad luck had continued to follow him. As soon as people found out about him, they backed away and wanted nothing to do with him. And he couldn't blame them. Why should this surprise him at all? It's why he was a hermit. He very rarely came out of hiding to interact with people.

Nathan pulled the vehicle to a stop at a stop sign, pondering which way to turn. Finally, he settled on turning right. He could finish this block and then double his way back to the hotel. Glancing right and left, he drove slowly, trying hard not to miss anything. And that's when he saw it.

A sweet white Porsche with the matching license plate of the one he saw.

"Bingo!"

Chapter Thirty-Three

Joanne groaned and tried pressing her palm against the back of her aching skull, but she couldn't move her hands. What the heck happened? When she tried to open her eyes, another sharp pain hit her hard.

"Welcome back to the land of the living," said a voice that immediately grated on her nerves—one she recognized with ease despite not having heard it in years.

"Hi, Dad," she mumbled. The sound of her voice bounced around inside her head, making her squeeze her eyes closed as tight as they could go. So much for hoping he'd changed over the years. When the pain settled, she tried to open her eyes and look around the room.

She noticed, even with her blurry vision, that Amber and her dad sat hand in hand on the tan-colored couch, with his other arm around her shoulders. They both had wicked smirks on their lousy faces.

"See, I told you she'd believe it!" Amber said, laughing.

Joanne's heart fell. "You aren't my daughter, are you, Amber?"

"Hell, no, I'm your stepmom. See." The woman held up her ring finger and on it sat a sparkly diamond ring. "Oh, and my name's Ebony."

Joanne's mind spun like a hurricane, her stomach following. Of course, he'd do something like this. It wasn't like he cared for her mom anyway. "Mom hasn't even been dead for a month."

Ebony hackled. "I was seeing him long before that. Remember, I told you I was eight weeks pregnant. I'm going to be giving birth to your sister or brother."

"I knew you were low, Dad, but to cheat on mom?"

Her dad shrugged. "It's not like she was giving me what I want."

"Enough about her mom," Ebony snapped. "Make her do it!"

"Do what?" Joanne asked.

"Sign the papers."

"What papers? I don't know what you're talking about." Joanne looked around the room. They appeared to be in the basement. There were stairs off to the side and a big screen television hung on the wall behind her. She was sitting on a wooden chair in the middle of the room with her feet tied.

"Turns out your mother—that bitch—made you the only bene-factor of her will. She put money in an account for you, unbeknownst to Seth, for years. We want it for our baby," Ebony snarled.

Joanne rolled her eyes. Why did it always have to be about money? "Dad has plenty to give you and your kid a good life. You don't need mine."

"Judith had no right to give you anything. You were disowned a long time ago," Seth said with a low growl. "You are going to sign the papers, or I'm going to make your life an even worse living hell."

Joanne glared at him. "Don't threaten me!"

"In case you haven't noticed, I'm in the exact position to make threats," he said, gesturing to her position in the chair.

"Isn't it enough that you took my sons from me?"

"No, it'll never be enough. You broke my heart when you married Scott."

"I broke your heart? You don't have a heart," she spat.

Ebony lurched forward and slapped Joanne across the face. Her head whipped to the side, her cheek stinging. "Don't speak to him that way."

"Man, you two really belong together. You finally found a woman exactly like you, haven't you, Dad?"

It was a match made in the bed of hell. Why couldn't she have used her head and followed her gut? She knew it couldn't be true. Never in all her years had the idea ever pop into her mind. Only her two sons were ever in her heart. She would have known if she had another kid out there.

"Darling, I'm getting hungry. Let's leave her to think about it and go get me some peanut butter ice cream."

Her dad squeezed the woman's shoulder before standing up. "I can't wait to have a kid that actually listens to me."

All she ever did was listen to him until it came to matters of the heart. Those decisions were hers and hers alone to make. She yanked at the ties binding her hands to the chair. "Let me go before I scream."

Ebony laughed. "No one's going to hear you. It's pretty much soundproof down here."

"You can't do this! It's kidnapping!" Joanne begged.

Her father leaned down, near the side of her face, and said, "Funny thing is, I can do anything I want."

Joanne pressed her lips closed, preventing herself from spitting in his face, which she so desperately wanted to do. She was normally a peaceful, gentle woman, but if there was ever anyone she wanted to hit or hurt, it was him. All the pain he'd caused her started to rise to the surface, bubbling inside her like a witch's cauldron.

"There's one thing you don't realize," she said. "I know someone with more money than you now." She wouldn't normally use Alex's money as leverage, but there was no way she was going to let her father get away with this. Never again would he get the upper hand on her.

"Do you now?" her father sneered. "Then he'll pay handsomely to get you back if you don't sign the money over to us. Either way, I win. Again!" She looked up at him. His eyes held no warmth for her. No love. The only thing that existed was the eyes of a maniac. One bent on getting money and making her pay the price for his anger.

"I don't understand. What made you become like this?"

"You!"

"Come on, babe, let's let her stew for a while," Ebony said, placing a hand on his shoulder.

Seth's eyes softened slightly as he turned to look at her. "Right, sorry. You wanted ice cream."

And with that, they left her alone in the dark, with only a tiny window to provide any light at all. They hadn't realized that they had left it open a crack. She wasn't sure which side of the house she was on, but she hoped to God that the window faced the street. The downside was that it was a good twenty-five feet away, and they had tied her feet to the chair. She couldn't hobble her way over without falling over, and if she yelled too loudly, they would hear her.

Joanne listened to the sounds around her, hoping to hear the front door close or anything to indicate that no one else was in the house. She wasn't sure if her dad and Ebony went on the ice cream hunt together, or if he left her behind. With the type of personality Ebony appeared to have, she couldn't imagine the woman letting her father go without her. She'd have to be there to pick out the exact one she wanted.

After waiting a few more minutes, Joanne let out the loudest scream she could muster.

Nathan parked across the street from the house and watched to see whether anyone would appear in the window. The curtains were pulled back, giving him an unbashful view of their living room. He couldn't see Joanne, but she had to be in there. There wasn't anywhere else she could be in such a short timeframe.

Pulling out his phone, he called nine-one-one. He wasn't going to, but after talking to Alex, he knew something bad was going on. After informing them of the situation, and letting Alex know where he was, he went to step out of his car.

But he yanked his door closed and ducked when the front of the house opened and out walked Ebony and a man. Nathan watched them climb into the Porsche. Where was Joanne? Did they stash her somewhere else, or was she in the house? Where were they going? Why wasn't she going with them? Had they already killed her?

God, please don't be dead!

He hated not knowing what was going on. "Get moving already," he snapped when all they did was sit there in the car. He needed to get into that house.

After a few more minutes, they finally drove away. When they disappeared down the street and out of his line of sight, Nathan threw open the door and jumped out. There was no way of knowing how long they would be, or how long the police would take to get there, so he had to act fast.

He slammed the door shut and raced across the road just in time to hear a loud scream. Her voice was unmistakable.

"Joanne," he cried, his voice hoarse.

Fear clogged his throat, and his heart hammered in his chest, as he ran toward the front door. The front door was solid wood with no window to break. Nathan tried the doorknob, but found it locked.

Stepping back, he glanced around and saw a small window down near the ground on his left. Nathan hopped down off the landing and dropped to his knees in front of it. And there she was, sitting in the middle of the room.

"Joanne!"

Her head snapped up. "Nathan?"

"I'm here. I'm going to get you out."

"No. They aren't going to be gone long. Please go get help. Don't get yourself dragged into my mess," she begged.

"I'm not leaving you."

There had to be a way inside. Nathan walked over to the side of the house and saw a gate leading into the backyard. After making sure no one was watching, he pushed it open and stepped through it. The back had a small red shed in the corner and very tall, unkempt grass. Man, for being made of money, one would think they'd make things look a little classier, even when their insides were nasty.

Along the wall, there was a short set of stairs leading up to a porch, and much to his surprise, a window was wide open as though forgotten about. Not the smartest people on the block. Quickly looking to the left and then to the right, he leaned forward and pushed it open as far as it could go. He climbed through it, ending up with his feet in a sink full of water.

"Great!" he grumbled, stepping down to the floor. His shoes squeaked as he made his way across the green flowered tiles and over to a door off to the right. He wasn't sure if it was going to be the kitchen pantry or the stairs that led downstairs. Hopefully, it was the latter.

Grabbed the door handle, he turned and opened it carefully. Hopefully, they hadn't left anyone guarding her. He didn't think so, but anything was possible. He let out a sigh of relief when he saw stairs leading down. So far, he was on a roll.

"Joanne?"

"Down here!" she cried.

Flicking on the light switch, he rushed down the stairs and into a large open room with her sitting in the middle. He went over and dropped to his knees in front of her, turning her head this way and that, checking her for any obvious injuries. "Are you okay?" he asked.

"I'm fine, but please hurry. They won't be long."

Nathan glanced at the zip-ties on her reddening wrists and ankles, frowning. Why couldn't it be ropes—something he could untie? Looking around the room, he spotted a tool chest in the corner. It couldn't be that simple, could it?

"One second," he said, kissing her cheek. He rushed over and threw open the chest, looking for scissors or anything that could cut the ties. But after going through the contents, he grabbed a screw-driver and threw it against the wall, imbedding it. The only thing he could do was go upstairs and see if there were any scissors in the kitchen, his anxiety growing. "I'll be back."

"Promise me that if you don't find anything, you'll run. I don't want you here when they get back. They'll kill you. Just call the police and let them do their job."

"I already called them." But if his instincts had any say on the matter, he'd say the man had the police in his back pocket; otherwise, they'd already be here. That was probably why Alex was bringing in his own men, but as of right now, he was Joanne's best hope. And he wasn't going to leave until she was safe. That was a promise.

He took the stairs two at a time and then pulled out every drawer in the kitchen, looking for something that could help. Opening the last drawer, he saw it was full of junk and a pair of scissors resting right on top. "Gotcha!"

Chapter Thirty-Four

Joanne's mind raced at the possibility of Nathan getting caught and ending up in the same boat she was in. She didn't want him dragged into her mess. And the one thing she knew was her life was always going to be a mess while her father was alive. The worst part of it was that even if Nathan freed her, her father would try to spin it and make her look like the psycho one. But thankfully, she had Alex and his entire legal team at her disposal if she needed it.

She couldn't understand why her father wouldn't put aside his pettiness and just move on. It made no sense to her. But now she knew one thing for sure. He would never change. She could only hope like heck the ministry would remove the baby from their home for the child's safety.

It was so like him to find someone as twisted as he was. Joanne couldn't believe he'd cheated on her mom. Even after all her mom did for him, he still dishonored her. It's no wonder she didn't leave any money to him. This must be her mother's way of making things up to her, and she did it at such a time that her father couldn't hurt her anymore.

There was a sudden clunk on the stairs, followed by a storm of curse words as Nathan slipped down the seven stairs leading to the basement, landing flat on his butt.

"Nathan, are you okay?" she asked in a panic when he didn't move right away.

"Anyone get the number of that bus?" he groaned as he sat up, rubbing the back of his head that had hit the second step from the bottom on the way down. It wasn't until he tried to get up and look for the scissors that he wobbled slightly and dropped to the ground again. This time she saw the scissors sticking into his leg, and he sat staring at the blood covering his hand.

"Nathan!" she cried. Her memories went back to when a stalker had captured Laryssa, and Alex had been shot while trying to rescue her. "Nathan, please, get up."

Crawling over to her, while holding a hand against his thigh, he grabbed the arm of Joanne's chair, pulling himself into a kneeling position. They both stared at the scissors in his side, knowing that if he removed them, he could bleed to death if it hit the artery.

"Don't remove them," she begged him. "Go get help."

"We don't have time," he said, his voice barely above a whisper. With both his hands surrounding the end of the scissors, he tugged hard. He screamed in pain, his cries echoing off the walls of the room as it came out. His face turned ashen as blood pooled to the floor. He didn't pay attention to himself, though. He used the scissors and cut her free before dropping to the floor again.

She grabbed his arm and tried to help him up, but he pushed her away. "Go, get yourself out of here."

"I'm not leaving without you."

"I'm as good as dead, Joanne. Go!"

"Not as long as I'm alive. Now, move it!" she ordered as she put an arm around him, slipping it under his armpit to hold him up. He grunted but got up as instructed, holding his injured side gingerly.

"You aren't going to be able to get me up the stairs," he said hoarsely.

"We're going to do it even if we have to crawl." She may have a bad leg, but she wasn't an invalid. This was a matter of life and death. They would make it out if it was the last thing she ever did. Their lives depended on it.

Nathan held his thigh as they hobbled to the stairs. Joanne's back gave out under his weight as nerve pain shot down her leg. He was right. She had no idea how they were going to get up the stairs. She couldn't carry him. Her body wasn't designed for lifting anymore.

"You aren't going to get me up the stairs," he said again, grunting with pain as she pulled him toward them.

"It's not over till the fat lady sings," Joanne said. "And you aren't going to wimp out on me. We're going to get up the stairs one way or another."

They stopped at the bottom of the steps, and she looked up. Maybe if she stepped up with her good leg, she stood a chance. But could her other leg support both their weights without collapsing? Only one way to find out.

"Hold on to me," she ordered as she grabbed the railing with her free hand and hoisted herself up to the first step. Nathan struggled to lift his shaking leg, and after a loud grunt, he succeeded.

"Only a few more to go," Joanne encouraged him, trying not to watch the drops of blood landing on the tan carpeted stairs. Her gut clenched. He was badly injured. Stepping up to the next step, her body shook awkwardly, her leg straining. *Please, let me do this!*

"Where are the police?" Nathan croaked. "I called them."

"My dad has his hand in the police force. I doubt anyone's coming, so it's up to us."

"Does your dad have his hand down everyone's pants?"

"Nate, you have no idea!" She still couldn't believe he had been having an affair with a girl that was more than half his age, and one as awful as Ebony. But then again, awful does attract awful.

They made it halfway up the short staircase before her leg gave out, and they collapsed. Nat hit his thigh on the edge of the stairs and cried out loud in pain.

"I'm so sorry," she said, guilt lacing every syllable.

Joanne forced her body to move and stood back up, putting her arm around Nathan again to help him up. His face whiter than before. His eyes barely open. "Come on, hun, please," she begged as both their bodies shook under the strain.

After a few more tries, they made it to the top and into the kitchen. She took him to the kitchen chair while she tried to find a cloth. Anything to press against the wound to stop the bleeding. They'd taken her phone so she couldn't even call for an ambulance.

"Is your motorhome outside?" she asked.

"Huh?" he asked with a dazed look in his eye.

"Your motorhome. Is it outside?"

Nathan shook his head and almost fell off the chair when doing so. "I rented a car."

After finding a dishtowel, she hurried over to him and told him to hold this against his thigh. She tried to help him stand up, but his body was like a noodle. "Come on, we have to go."

"I can't."

Her chest tightened as tears of worry filled her eyes. Fear festered like a bullet ricocheting inside her. "I'm not leaving here without you, so move that butt!" she ordered, pulling his arm.

"Just go without me," he said, giving her a light shove toward the living room. "There is a small gray Honda across the street."

"No!" she refused adamantly. "Get up before I knock you up the side of the head."

"Damn it. Go, Joanne!" he said. Anger flickered like a flame in his eyes, blood dripping off the seat beside him. "I won't let you die for me. Get out of here! They'll be back any moment."

"We got all the way up here. We can get out to the car," she said, refusing to give up.

"I'm as good as dead anyway," he said between short sharp breaths, squinting with each painful word. "Get out of here. Now!"

She tried once again to put her arm round him, but he wouldn't let her, and her stomach dropped into the bottomless sea, taking her heart with it. "I won't let you give up. We have a life to live together."

"No, we don't," Nathan said bluntly, his voice void of feeling, like he'd turned into a robot. "Even if I were to get out of here, I can't stay with you, Joanne. It's not in the cards for me."

"I'm getting you out of here even if I have to drag you."

"Stop being stubborn. We don't have time to discuss this."

"That's right. We need to go. You came here for me, and I'm not leaving without you."

"That's what's going to happen anyway. You know it, and so do I."

As they sat there arguing, two car doors slammed out front, and she heard her dad's loud voice mixed with Ebony's. They appeared to be arguing about something. The store probably didn't have the ice cream she wanted.

She glanced back at Nathan, her eyes wide. "Please, Nate. Don't do this to me."

"I am, and I will. You need to live. I don't. It's the only way."

"No, it isn't!"

"Well, it's my way. Now go."

Joanne plunked herself down in the seat beside him. "If you don't go, I'm not either."

Nathan slammed his hand on the table and then winced horribly. "I'm making a decision."

"Well, so am I!"

Nathan struggled to stand up. "Damn you!"

"Damn me all you want. We're both going or we both don't. I reckon we have a few minutes before they come into the house."

He couldn't understand why she was being so stubborn. He was trying to save her life so she could go on living and spend the rest of her life with her family. But she wasn't having it. Either they both made it out or none of them did. Groaning, he held out his hand, and she took it with a smile. He wasn't going to be the reason she died today.

"We'll have to go out the back," he said, pointing to the door beside them. The downside was that the back door had a clear view of the front door and as soon as they stepped outside, the front door opened. The two of them made a mad stumbling dash toward the back gate, knowing that going around to the front would be impossible now.

"Shit! Ebony, go around the side and head them off," Seth roared. "I'll grab the gun."

"Hurry!" Joanne cried, struggling to support his weight while they crossed the yard.

"I'm trying."

But as soon as they reached the back gate, a gunshot sounded, and they both dropped to the ground like a rock. Joanne lay there underneath Nathan, neither moving. Either too afraid to find out what happened or unable to move. Had he got hit? Did she? Did she want to know? She stayed motionless, unsure of what to expect next. Was he going to shoot again?

When nothing else happened, she lifted her head and tried to twist to look at him. "Nathan?" she said with bated breath.

"Hey, guys, they are over here!" a new voice sounded. "Are you guys hurt?"

"Check him. Please, check him!" Joanne cried. "I'm okay. I think."

It didn't take long before the newcomers rolled an unconscious Nathan off her body, examining him for more wounds.

"He has a deep wound on his thigh," she blurted. "I think it hit an artery."

A young woman wearing swat clothing helped her stand up. Joanne glanced back at the house and saw her father sprawled out on the porch. A guy was beside him, checking his pulse. Ebony was on her knees with her hands behind her head along the side path.

"Is he..." she started to ask, nodding her head toward her father.

"Dead."

She waited for the pain to come, but her insides were too numb to feel anything for him. He'd made her life a living hell, and now he couldn't hurt her anymore.

"You." The one man who rolled Nathan off her pointed to the woman who helped her. "Go to the front and wave down the paramedics when they get here." He waved at the man over who was tending to her father. "Peter, give mouth to mouth. I'm going to start chest compressions.

Joanne collapsed to the ground as the men clamored around Nathan. He didn't appear to have been shot. "No. No. No!" she cried, clasping her hands and bringing them to her mouth as she tried to hold back a loud sob. She should have used his belt to stop the bleeding, but she forgot. She forgot.

He had to be okay. She couldn't lose him now. They did round after round of compressions, still to no avail. She had no idea who the men were, but she was grateful for their help. "Please, Nathan, breathe."

Her chest was tight. Her body cold and shivering as she kneeled there in the snow, watching the next love of her life struggle for his. It was another five minutes before the paramedics arrived with two ambulances, one for her and one for him.

"No, I'm going with him," she argued as they carried him quickly to the vehicle. She wasn't going to be separated from him. Not now. Not after all they'd been through.

"Please, ma'am, we have to do an assessment on you."

"I'm fine. I'm not injured," she said stubbornly.

The woman who'd helped her earlier walked over and squeezed her shoulder. "Hi Joanne, I'm Claire, Alex sent me. He's getting on the next flight and will see you at the hospital," she said, before glaring at the paramedics. "Let her into the damn ambulance, or there will be hell to pay."

By this time, the police had arrived on the scene and were taping off the crime scene to start their investigation. One officer, named Larson, walked over to her and began asking questions, but Claire stepped in front. "Any questions you have can be continued at the hospital. My clients need to be transported now."

Joanne sent a grateful look her way and climbed inside the

waiting ambulance. She took the seat behind the driver's seat and watched as the paramedics tried to revive Nathan. And just as the doors closed, his heart started again, and it was in that moment the flood gates opened, and she couldn't stop the tears flowing from inside her.

He was alive, and the man who had caused her unending grief was dead. The man who had stolen her children from her and made her life miserable was gone. He wouldn't be able to hurt her anymore. And Ebony, his newest partner, would be going to jail for a long time for aiding and abetting a crime.

She had a mixture of elation and sadness inside her—a very odd combination. How could she be sad and happy about her father's death at the same time? Did that make her some type of sociopath? Leaning back in her side seat, Joanne closed her eyes. She couldn't understand why her father couldn't love her. Was she so unworthy of love?

That's what hurt the most. She'd never know what it was like to have a father who loved her, who would throw his arms around her and tell her everything would be okay. That he'd always be there for her through thick and thin. But she'd lived her life this long without him. And she knew that she'd live the rest of it just fine, too.

As long as she had Nathan.

Chapter Thirty-Five

Joanne had fallen asleep leaning forward in the chair next to Nathan's bed, her head resting on the pillow beside his when his phone dinged, waking her up. He hadn't opened his eyes since his surgery, nor had he really responded to stimuli. The doctors were suspecting a brain injury from the lack of oxygen, but she still had hope he would recover.

Picking up his phone, she glanced at the screen. There was a message that said the DNA test results were in, and he wasn't Laryssa's father.

"Holy crap!" she said, sitting up straight.

That must have been Laryssa's hair she found in the motorhome at the beginning of their trip. But why hadn't he mentioned anything? He'd had every opportunity, especially after she told him her own story. Did he think she wouldn't understand?

Oh gosh. What if all this was a rouse while he waited for the results to come in? The thought made her sick to her stomach. Had she been deceived? Her emotions spun in circles with the newfound revelation. Maybe he really didn't love her, and she had pushed him into saying it.

No, she argued with herself. He'd said it first. That wouldn't have happened if he didn't have feelings for her. Maybe he hadn't worked up the courage to tell her yet. But he had told her that he slept with Laryssa's mom, so that would have been the perfect time to admit his suspicions. And how the heck hadn't she considered the possibility? Was she really that oblivious? He came out of the blue, trying to make amends. Was he just wanting to find out the truth before he died? If so, she had to admit there was honor in that, even if it was done deceptively.

The only thing she didn't like was the fact that he'd given up on her again in the house. Was that his pattern—to give up when the road got tough? If so, she wasn't sure she had the strength to fight every time he decided to give up. She thought he'd changed when he said he wanted them to be together, but during their next hard moment, he wanted her to leave him. And as he lay in the hospital bed, that same energy emanated from him.

"Fight, Nathan, fight. I need to know you want this. I need to hear the truth from your own lips."

He fluttered his eyelashes, but that was the only response she received. Exhausted, Joanne sat back in her barely padded hospital seat and let out a loud yawn when she heard a sound at the door. Turning her head, she saw Alex leaning on the door frame. His body stiff, reminding her he still hated hospitals.

"Mom," he said, his voice shaky, "are you okay?"

She held out her hand to him, encouraging him to come to her. Her body was too tired to get up and move. She had barely slept all night. Alex took a deep breath and strolled into the room, his face growing whiter with each step.

"Don't forget to breathe," she said softly as he took a seat on the other chair beside her. Even though he'd overcome a lot, losing his daughter had made him hate hospitals. And she couldn't blame him for that.

Putting his arm around Joanne, he asked, "How's he doing?"

She leaned against him, and he kissed the top of her head, which eased her pain a little. "They are worried that he may have brain damage from a lack of oxygen."

"Is he responsive?"

Joanne shook her head. "Other than an eye flutter, not yet."

"Are you cold, Mom? You're shaking."

"It's a mixture of things, I think. Tired. Stressed. Worried."

"Why don't you go get some sleep? I'll watch over you both and let you know if anything changes."

"No. I can't leave him," she said, refusing adamantly. If she wasn't in the room and he died alone, she'd never forgive herself. He was in here because of her, because he had to be the hero and rescue her.

"You need to sleep."

"I have slept," she argued. "Right here."

"You need to sleep in a bed. I could have the nurse bring you something."

"No! I'm not leaving his side. He never left me. I won't leave him."

Alex looked between her and Nathan, a new understanding dawning in his eyes; although, by the way he glared at Nathan, he hated the thought. "You really like him, don't you?"

"I do," she said as she reached out and wrapped her hand around Nathan's, his skin pale compared to hers.

"I'm guessing he hasn't told you anything then."

Her head whipped in his direction. "What's that supposed to mean?"

"He killed Laryssa's parents."

"He did no such thing—you know what, never mind," she said. "This isn't the place to be having this discussion. The doctor said he might still be able to hear." She refused to bring any negative energy into the room that could hamper his recovery.

"But..."

She turned dagger eyes toward him, and thankfully he snapped his lips closed. Alex had no idea what he was talking about. Her son had the resources to find out anything on anyone and could rival even the greatest detectives, but he had lousy timing. They would have to discuss things, but now was not the time. Anything could be discovered with the right intel, but the deeper truths of the circumstances don't always get revealed. And she had a feeling her son only had half the story.

"Fine, but you really do need to get some sleep. You'll be no good to him half dead on your feet, too."

"He's got nobody else."

"Mom, do I need to get a nurse to make you?"

Her breath hissed between her teeth as she tried desperately not to snap at him. Her son only wanted what was best for her, she knew that, but he was being so irritatingly pushy. "I love you, son, and I know you are just trying to help, but I'll be fine."

"You took a big bump to the head. Sleep is your best bet right now."

"Oh, pish tosh. I'll sleep when I need to sleep." Okay, that was probably a lie. She hadn't climbed into a bed in about twenty-four hours now, so she probably looked like death warmed over. But Nathan needed her more than a bed did.

Alex stood up, towering over her. He could have been intimidating, but she knew he wouldn't hurt a fly. "Okay, you're making me pull my hand."

"Do what you must and so shall I." That included getting them both put in the same room if she had to. He had forgotten who he'd inherited his stubborn streak from. It's the only way she'd managed to keep living her life after what had happened. She wouldn't have been able to cope with the tragedy if she'd been an emotional push over.

"Oh, I booked a room at the same hotel."

"Okay," Joanne murmured. The doctors figured if her symptoms weren't any worse by tomorrow, they would release her; but she hoped they'd let her stay for Nathan's sake. Being close by helped her heart.

Her son left the room, his dress shoes clacking on the tiled floor, which made her migraine pulse viciously. She'd been refusing pain meds because they made her sleepy, and she couldn't afford to close her eyes. The doctors had said that the first forty-eight hours were critical. The longer he stayed unconscious, the worse his odds were.

Tears pricked the corners of her eyes. Was this her fate? Why did it seem like everyone she got involved with on an intimate level was doomed to die? Or did her dad's death finally break that curse?

Joanne sat back in her seat and rubbed her hands down her face. The battle with her family was finally over. She didn't have to sit in the shadows anymore, worrying and waiting to see what would happen next. It felt like a huge weight had been removed from her shoulders. On one hand, thinking that way made her feel like a horrible person, but on the other, it was like a heavy burden had fallen off her back.

There was a sliver of pain inside her at the loss of her mom Her mom was a woman who had lived in her dad's shadow—a timid, quiet lady who never opposed him in any way. So, it was strange that she had put money aside for her...if that part was true. The reading of the will was only a day away, and Joanne couldn't help but wonder what was waiting for her.

The lawyer had agreed to come to the hospital if she wasn't released yet. Joanne could have put it off until after, but she wanted to proceed according to plan so she could be back at the house for Christmas. She wanted to be there with the family, hopefully with Nathan by her side.

Christmas was a time for miracles, right? As she sat there beside the bed, Joanne crossed her fingers and made a wish to be home for Christmas. A minute later, a nurse came in with orders for her to go to bed. Begrudgingly, she obeyed and disappeared into her room.

Nathan groaned, his voice sounding distant, like there was a barrier between his mouth and his ears. His mouth was unbearably dry, and something hard was stuck between his teeth and going down his throat.

There was a distant sound of clacking, and he struggled to open his heavy-lidded eyes. They only partially opened. Everything had this white hazy mist, like he was in a different world. He tried to shift his body and let out a howl when pain accosted him.

"H-elp," he tried to say, but he couldn't move his tongue. Reaching up, he attempted to pull at the device in his mouth, but something soft came to rest on his hands preventing him from doing so.

"Easy there, Nate," came her sweet melodious voice. It was like music to his ears. "I'm going to go get the doctors."

As he waited, his noticed a gradual improvement in his vision, but he remained trapped in a hazy world.

It wasn't long before a nurse came into the room. "Welcome back, Nathan. I'm Jenny, your nurse. The doctor is on his way."

He only managed to stay awake for a few minutes before he faded back out from sheer exhaustion.

"He was awake. She saw it," Joanne said, pointing to the nurse when the doctor came in.

Doctor Jacobs smiled. "That's a good sign. Let's get the tube out."

Joanne stood back as they unhooked the intubation tube, her heart racing. This was the first time he'd actually opened his eyes and attempted to talk. Before that, it was brief responses, like squeezing her hand, a groan, or eyes fluttering. And she was elated. That told her he was going to be okay.

Christmas was only a few days away now, but she hadn't wanted to return home until she knew he was going to be okay. Her family had been begging her to come home, but they had each other for Christmas. Nathan had no one. No visitors. No friends. And he was in a strange place. There was no one to watch his motorhome, which she had eventually parked at a campground.

The doctors removed the tube that had helped him breathe to see if he could breathe on his own, and thankfully he could. Joanne breathed a sigh of relief when his chest rose and fell of its own accord.

"He'll likely be in and out for a bit, but things are looking good," the doctor said.

Nothing had ever made her feel so relieved, with the exception of when they said her son was going to be okay after he was shot. They said bad things came in threes. So, hopefully, this was the worst of it, and things would start to look up from here. No one's luck could be all bad, right?

Taking a seat in the chair beside his bed, she leaned back and closed her eyes. They finally brought in a reclining chair as opposed to the hardback one from before, which allowed her to get some shut-eye. However, even the hospital was making her leave more often now to make sure that she got some proper rest, but that didn't happen often. Everything back at the motorhome made her miss him. It didn't feel right to be there without him.

As Joanne sat there beside his bed, she dozed off, but was later jarred awake when somebody touched her shoulder. Opening her eyes, the first thing she noticed was that the sun had gone down and sky was dark. Boy, the day had gone by fast.

"Hi, Joanne," the nurse, Jenny, said with a tender smile. "How are things?"

Joanne's lips turned down. "He hasn't woken up again."

"It's hard to watch, isn't it?" she said. "This happened to my son when his bike was hit by a car."

"Is that why you became a nurse?"

The woman nodded. "I'd thought about becoming a doctor, but another ten years of school at my age was not my idea of a good time," she said, chuckling.

"Your age? You couldn't be more than thirty."

"Ha, I wish. I'm forty-two."

"That's still young enough to go after a dream."

"Nah, I'm good. This is enough for me," she said as she checked Nathan's wound and applied a new dressing. "Sadly, though, as much as I'd like to let you stay, you need to go get some sleep. He'll still be here in the morning unless he gets legs and walks away."

"I hate leaving him."

She said the same words every time she was told to leave. It's not like she slept much when she did. She slept better in the reclining chair. It felt right to stay by his side. Waking up in a strange place, with no one you recognize, could be a traumatic experience.

"I know, but hospital policy states that unless you are a family member, we have to adhere to visiting hours."

"He's the uncle of my daughter-in-law doesn't that count?" she asked hopefully. "I'm also going to marry this man."

"I'm sorry, dear. You need to head home and get some rest. He'd want you to stay healthy."

Leaning over, she kissed him on the head and then left the hospital to go back to the motorhome. It didn't take long to get back and the minute she got inside, she plunked herself in the front seat, holding a copy of her mother's will. She couldn't believe that her mother had left her with her Faberge Egg collection and everything else from her estate, leaving her father with nothing. She'd apparently learned of his affair and didn't want any possessions to go to the young sleazy woman he'd hooked up with. It turned out that Ebony had threatened her mom's life, and her dad had done nothing.

In a way, she wished she would have convinced her mom leave her father, but her mother had been taught to be faithful to the bitter end, and she was. But surely God would have understood if had she left? No one had to put up with abuse. Joanne was certain God wouldn't have wanted that for her. Her mother had poured her soul into the letter she'd left Joanne, apologizing for all the actions they'd taken against her, and that she'd saved up money right from that very moment under her father's nose. She wrote that if she couldn't leave him, at least she could leave Joanne with something that showed she never stopped loving her or thinking about her.

No wonder her dad and Ebony were furious about it. That made Joanne feel somewhat vindicated in a way. The eggs were set to be delivered next week to Alex's house in Vancouver. The money had to go through some hoops and hurdles, but it shouldn't take long to be sent to her bank account. Now she wouldn't have to rely so much on Alex.

Maybe tomorrow, if the weather was warm enough, she could stop by her mother's grave and somewhat thank her in person. The sad part was that their reconciliation happened after she had already passed away and not before.

Joanne let out a sigh before standing up. "Mother, I hope you're at peace now."

A warm breeze fluttered through the closed motorhome and landed almost like a hand on her shoulder, leaving her with peace in her soul knowing her mother had just visited her. She smiled. Life was getting better and better. She couldn't wait to see Nathan in the morning.

Maybe they could finally start their life together now that he was waking up. She could even have a minister stop by the room if they had a chance to talk about it a little more.

She couldn't wait to marry him, providing he wanted that, too. With that, she went to sleep with wedding bells in her head.

It was early in the morning on the day before Christmas, and Joanne stepped into the lobby of the hospital as she had done every day for the last while. She couldn't wait to see Nathan. He'd been more and more awake each day. Yesterday, he'd been awake for almost the entire day until dinner time, so she'd gone back to the motorhome to give him a break.

She knew their visits exhausted him, and she'd begun feeling bad about it. He even tried to convince her to go back to her family to be with them for Christmas. They deserved her presence during such a special time, way more than he needed it, he'd said. Even her son had grown frustrated with her for wanting to stay. It was almost like he was jealous. He's never had to share her with anyone before.

Taking the elevator up to the third floor, she opened it and stepped into the crisp clean hallway. He'd been moved out of Intensive Care and into a regular hospital room. They were even talking about releasing him because he was steadily improving. She wanted to be there for Nathan when he got out and be a help to him while he healed. Surely, her family could understand that.

"Hi, Nate," she said, her face beaming as she walked into the room. He was on his feet and standing next to the window looking out. A grim expression on his face, making him look ten years older than he'd look the day before. It made her pause in the middle of the room. "What's wrong?"

Nathan turned to look at her, his eyes hollow and forlorn. Yet somehow, he appeared to be begging at the same time. "Joanne, you've been a life saver, really. You've done more than I deserve, but you need to go home."

"We talked about this. I'm not leaving. We have to talk about our plans for when you get out."

His gaze diverted to the floor while he fiddled with a string on his hospital gown. "You mean your plans," he said, his voice almost a croaky whisper as though he didn't want to say the words.

That threw her for a loop, and she didn't know quite what to say. "But you wanted them as much as I did."

"I was humoring you."

She stood rooted in her spot, the floor opening beneath her. He couldn't be saying what it sounded like. He had an entirely different demeanor than the one from their entire trip and even the last few days.

"But this whole trip was to buy time until I got my answer," he answered.

"You mean about Laryssa?"

"How'd you know about that?"

"I saw your text from your friend."

"Oh."

"So, was that all I was to you? A passing affair?"

He nodded his head and then turned away from her, but not before she saw the war in his eyes. They bounced between being full of pain and being cold as ice as though he couldn't decide which to be.

This may have started out as an affair, but she thought they grew beyond that. They talked about a future together, hadn't they? Or was that all an act to get his way with her? She studied him from behind, his shoulders slumped, his head low. They were more than an affair. She could sense it in her heart.

"No! I refuse to believe that," she said, taking a step toward him.

As though he sensed her approach, he turned around and put his hands up to ward her off. "Please, Joanne, don't make this any harder than it already is."

"I don't understand. You didn't act like this yesterday or the day before. You never said a darn word."

He shrugged his shoulders. "I didn't know what to say or how to say it."

"I stayed and took care of you. How could you do this?"

"I didn't ask you to."

"I love you," she said, desperately trying to get him to stop pushing her away.

Nathan pressed his lips into a firm line, his eyes full of pain. His hands tightening on the reclining chair by the window.

"I can see it in your eyes. You love me to," she argued, "So why are you doing this?"

"Just go, Joanne, please. I don't want to fight."

"Tough luck. I'm not going anywhere."

"Damn it, woman. I want you to go all right! *Get the hell out of here.*" He enunciated each word fully and completely, shooting them at her like darts as he rubbed his chest. "Sorry, I don't mean to be rude, but I don't want you here anymore."

She balled her fists, nails digging into her palms, refusing to listen to his rejection. "This isn't you."

"Maybe it is me, and you don't want to see it," he snapped. "I am a murderer after all, remember?"

"Give me a reason."

"I don't love you."

Her entire body went numb, and she didn't know what to think or feel anymore. It was like someone else was writing her story and playing with her life all over again, and she didn't have a say in what was happening.

Was he telling the truth? Did he really not love her just like her father hadn't? Her legs shook as all her emotion gathered in her throat, bursting out of her mouth in a sob.

"I don't believe that." She shook her head viciously.

"Tough beans, babe. I don't know how I can make myself any clearer. Please, don't make me bring the nurse in to kick you out," Nathan said, turning his back on her again.

"I-I..." She fought with what to say. "I wish you the best, Nate. Merry Christmas," she whispered before turning and leaving with tears rolling down her cheeks.

Chapter Thirty-Six

By Christmas day, she was celebrating back in Vancouver, but Joanne couldn't find it in her spirit to be jolly. She tried to keep the season magical for the kids' sake, but her heart remained back in Toronto—the trip had turned out to be the worst ever in her life.

"Nana, look." Ashley held out her new baby doll. "Look, I can feed it, too."

Joanne pulled the young girl into her arms and gave her a much-needed bear hug for her own sanity. "A beautiful doll for a beautiful girl."

Ashley allowed her to hug her for a moment before she scrambled off her lap to open more gifts. Alex and Laryssa were sitting on the couch across from her, and Sarah, the nanny, was in the recliner with Justin. In a way, her family didn't need her as much as they used to. She missed how busy she used to be with the kids and the house.

Laryssa opened her gift from Alex, and it turned out to be a gold charm necklace that had tiny pictures of her kids in the locket, and a small picture of themselves as well. The perfect family unit. "It's beautiful," she gasped, holding it up to her chest before turning and giving him a great big kiss.

What should have been a golden moment, seeing her son's family so happy, left her feeling empty inside. She missed Nate's arms wrapped around her, and how he used to whisper sweet words in her ear as his hands trailed over her body. Even the thought of it awoke the beast within her, and it made her all the more depressed.

Laryssa glanced over at her, compassion etched into her features. She was just the sweetest thing, and the best thing that could have ever happened to her son, and the best daughter-in-law she could have ever asked for. She'd bought Joanne's son out of the darkness and grief that had once consumed him.

Resting her palms on her thighs, Joanne stood up and everyone looked at her. "I'm going to retire to my room for a nap."

"Already?" Alex asked, looking up at her in surprise. "We haven't even finished unwrapping all the gifts yet."

"I'm tired. The knock to my noggin tuckered me out. Excuse me," she said, hurrying out of the room with Laryssa following her.

"I'm fine, hun. Go be with the kids while they open the rest of the gifts," she said, encouraging her to return to the family. "I'm just going to sleep."

"Are you sure?"

"Ya."

"I'll just see you to your room then, so you don't fall over," Laryssa said, winking at her. "Besides, I need a little breather. I haven't had any me time in far too long."

Joanne chuckled. "Sadly, that won't happen much until the kids grow up."

"Don't tell me that!" Laryssa complained. "Come on." She pulled Joanne's arm into the crook of her own, and they walked toward Joanne's new wing. Something Alex had been working on while she was away on the trip. It was her Christmas surprise.

"I still can't believe he did all this while I was gone."

"He had people working on it almost around the clock. Super noisy."

The addition looked like an apartment fit for a queen. Even her queen bed was a little too large for her, making her wish Nathan was here to enjoy it with her. Her mood fell even lower at the thought.

"Are you okay?" Laryssa asked again upon seeing her expression. "Alex told me what Nathan did."

Joanne sat down on the plump mattress topped with an ocean themed comforter. Did Alex tell her everything about Nathan? "I really can't make sense of it. We hit it off. We were planning a life together. I don't get it."

"Wow. He never told me that."

"He didn't know." That made her daughter-in-law quirk her eyebrows, but she said nothing, so Joanne continued, "I was going to tell Alex, but I never seemed to have the opportunity. But it's pointless now because we're not together anymore anyway."

"Do you want to talk about it?"

"We were doing great, you know. Everything was perfect. Oh gosh, he was even great in bed. He could make me laugh like nobody's business. He was even the one that said I love you first. Then suddenly, he's acting like he never cared about me and telling me to leave."

"Anyone who saw the two of you together could see that he cared about you. It was in his eyes for all to see."

"Right? And I thought I saw something in them, too, when I was fighting with him at the hospital, but..."

Laryssa brought her fingers up to her chin as she stared toward Alex's picture on Joanne's dresser. "I smell something fishy."

"Or he could be telling the truth."

"About?"

"That he was only with me to kill time."

"Kill time for what?" Laryssa asked, puzzled.

"While he waited to find out whether or not he was your father."

Laryssa plopped down on the chair by the window, dazed and confused. "Say what?"

"Oh, you didn't know. I'm sorry. I thought Alex would have told you."

"I heard absolutely nothing. Not from him or from Nathan. I thought he was going to stick around for a bit."

"Me too," Joanne said softly. "Shall I tell you everything?" She did have the right to know the whole story.

Laryssa nodded. "Start at the beginning."

Nathan was tired of laying around all day. Tired of being alone in a strange city where he didn't know anyone, and in a hospital, where the best tasting food was toast. He hadn't envisioned being stuck between four walls on Christmas day with a hole in his heart. His plan had been to return to Vancouver and spend Christmas with Joanne's family, but that thought quickly turned belly up.

It was hard not to pull her into his arms when her tears started flowing and tell her it was all a mistake. That he hadn't meant a single word he said, but he couldn't. It wasn't fair to her. And her son certainly didn't want him in her life. Nathan banged his head on the hospital pillow and groaned in frustration. He wanted to be with her. *Damn it.*

But Alex made it perfectly clear it could never happen—that the truth about him could never be made known. And that if he tried, he'd have him sent to jail for stealing Laryssa's DNA behind her back. Alex said that any guy willing to do that was probably lying about everything else, so Nathan wasn't someone he wanted around his mother. He'd already spent a long enough time in jail, dealing with the usual prison pleasantries, and refused to go back. He didn't want to die in jail.

He'd argued with Alex, but it was to no avail, and he hadn't wanted to upset Joanne's happy home life. He cared too much for her to do that. So, he did as Alex had asked and pushed Joanne away. Maybe it was the easy way out, but it was for the best. What hope did he have of a life with her anyway? As soon as Laryssa found out, she'd probably never look his way again anyway, and everyone would pick

---

at Joanne to get rid of him.

But, God, his stomach hurt, and his hands ached to hold her, to pull her close and whisper sweet words into her ears so he could see her eyes light up and see that smile play on her lips. Her spirit was so genuine and loving. It made him want to give her the sun, the moon, and every special diamond in the world.

And the more he thought about it, the more he wanted her back, and to hell with the wishes of her son. He would only live once, and no one should be able to dictate to him how he should live the rest of it. Joanne was his sun, his light. The bright part of his day, and without her, the rest of the world seemed dark. Pulling out his phone, he glanced at the picture of her on his background. It was the one she took when they were playing their card game.

Right now, she'd be with her family, probably enjoying Christmas day, while he was alone, sitting in a hospital bed with nowhere to go. Some of the nurses brought him Christmas cards and tried to brighten up his day, and for that, he was grateful, but they weren't her. He wanted to call but knew her son would probably pick up the phone, and he'd be hooped.

He couldn't even stop by the house because he was stuck here for another short bit. His body felt like it had aged a hundred years in the short time he'd been at the hospital. Joanne was the only thing that could make his body feel young again and help him forget that it was dying. He'd spoken with the doctors about chemo, but they said he had to speak with his doctor back in Calgary, where his primary residence was. Or at least, where his physical motorhome lot was. It's where he had to be at least six months out of every year to keep his medical coverage.

Soon, the service lady brought his lunch into the room, and the doctor followed behind her. He hadn't been in to see Nathan for the day yet. "Hey, doc."

"You're looking a little more wide-eyed today," Doctor Jacobs commented.

"I have a new mission, I guess."

"And what's that?"

"Win back the girl."

"The one you were with when you first got here?"

"Ya."

"Let's check your injury," the doctor suggested. "Have you tried calling her?"

Nathan covered himself with the sheet and then lifted his gown to reveal the bandaged side of his stomach. "Not yet."

Doctor Jacobs peeled back the bandage and smiled. "Looks great. May I propose a surprise visit when you get back on your feet?"

"You mean drive there and surprise her?"

"Ya, I'm sure she would love it."

"I've really made a mess of things."

"She'll forgive you. She sat with you day and night and wouldn't leave your side. That one's a keeper."

That's what he thought, too. After the doctor finished poking his injury and taking his vitals, he looked at Nathan and smiled. "You've made a remarkable recovery in such a short amount of time, Nathan."

Joanne was probably the reason for that. He often heard her voice and felt a pull toward it, like being pulled toward the light in every near-death experience. She lit up his world, and it's something he couldn't let go of. And the longer he went without seeing her, the more unsettled he had become. He'd gotten used to having her around. And with all she did for him, she deserved to make her own choices, not have someone else make them for her. Not him. Not her son. She was a grown woman, and it was time everyone treated her like one, including him.

"I think by tomorrow or the next day we should be able to have you on your way, be there in time for New Year's."

Nathan grimaced as he sat back up in bed, the bandage pulling at the skin on his stomach. As much as he wanted to travel immediately, he knew he wasn't ready for a trip of that magnitude yet. He'd have to hang around for a little while until he felt up for it.

But when he could travel, he had one objective and one alone...

"Joanne, I'm coming to win you back."

Chapter Thirty-Seven

"Alexander Michael Richards," Laryssa said as she stood in front of Alex with her hands on her hips, looking and sounding much like his mom would. He swallowed hard. She looked awfully cute with her hair done up in a bun. She had perfected the momma glare and stance.

He sat back in his seat, staring at his beautiful, angry wife, realizing that his plans for the evening were probably on the rails now. "What can I do for my gorgeous wife?"

"I know you called Nathan the day before he broke up with Mom."

"Have I said how much I love your hair like that?" he said, trying to avoid the subject at all costs.

"Don't change the subject. What did you tell him?" she asked, taking a menacing step his way. "And don't even think of lying. I have momma radar now."

He slumped in his seat. "What makes you think I did anything?"

"You've never liked him, so I'll bet you a week of diaper changes that you're the reason for Mom's unhappiness."

"She'll be fine. There are better people out there for her."

"But who are you to make that choice for her?"

"I'm protecting her and you."

"Why do I need protecting?"

"He's the man that killed your parents," he snapped, a little harder than he had intended.

"And I was the one that got your brother so mad he killed himself, yet you married me."

"That's different."

"How so?"

"It just is. I don't want to talk about this anymore."

"You know what's funny about all this? I'm the one that should be acting like you right now. He's the man who had sex with my mother while she was married to his own brother. He's the one who got into a fight with my dad, and between them both, they made the engine explode, killing everyone but him. He never came back for me, even though he knew there was a possibility that he was my father. He isn't, but if I've learned anything after all this time, it's that people change. Maybe not all the time, but they do. You did. I did. And ya, I don't know Nathan, but there is a woman in that other room who does."

"But he spent time in jail for killing them. That's proof enough for me of the type of person he is. He even stole your DNA, so he hasn't changed."

"It's a darn piece of hair. It's hardly intellectual property to steal."

"Why the heck are you sticking up for the man? I really don't understand you sometimes."

"That's why. How can we judge someone on something we don't understand yet? And if your mother accepted him after everything he told her, could he really be so bad?"

"How can you be so accepting of him? You were abused. What if he's as bad as Aidan?"

Laryssa wandered over and took a seat on her husband's lap. "Yes, I was abused, and I married a man who looks exactly like him, even acted like him a time or two, if I remember. But you changed and found your happy place. Now don't you think your mom, who's had a hard life, deserves to find that, too?"

Alex pressed his lips closed. His wife was making sense.

"I think it's sweet that you are trying to protect her, but did you watch her tonight? Did you see the sadness in her eyes, and the pain as she watched us together?"

He dropped his chin to his chest and groaned. No, he hadn't noticed. Sad to say, he'd missed it all because he was so focused on his own family. God, he felt like a heel. In trying to help his mother, he'd made her more miserable.

"It's not like I'm asking you to marry them. Only to let them have a chance to figure out what they want. I think after they all have been through, they deserve it."

"But what if he cheats on her?"

"What if I cheat on you?"

Alex laughed, his laughter echoing off the hallways outside the open office door. "You wouldn't."

"There is this nice guy at work. He does say hello to me every morn—."

Alex dug his finger into her side, making his wife squeal. She struggled to get away, but he held her firmly on his lap, relentlessly tickling her until her face turned red.

"Mercy. Mercy," she cried, pushing against his hands.

Just then, Ashley came barreling into the room, eyes full of tears. The head had come off her Barbie doll. That seemed to be the biggest nightmare in her little daughter's world. She ran straight toward her dad and tried to pull Laryssa off his lap. Alex was the fixer in their family, and she gladly surrendered her spot to her daughter. She wanted her kids to look up to him, as she never had a father to look up to.

Sometimes she wondered what her life would have been like had her parents survived. Would they have gotten a divorce, or would they have stayed together for her? She had sensed something different when they left for the boat that day. Her dad hadn't given her his usual hug before heading out the door. He seemed preoccupied. She had thought maybe it was something she did, but now all the pieces of the puzzle fit together in her mind.

Laryssa firmly believed it was just the one time. Her mother never disappeared at strange hours during the night, never went anywhere without anyone knowing about it. Never kept her phone locked. Never hid in the bathroom. She had treated Laryssa's father as a treasured man. They rarely fought. Never argued. Her mother treated her father like a king. She taught Laryssa what it meant to love someone. Now she had an amazing man to love, who loved her kids, too.

"There! All better, love bug," Alex said, kissing his daughter on the cheek before putting her back on the ground. Her Barbie was fixed. It was such a weird conundrum to be in. She was his niece, yet an adoptive daughter, too. He'd formally adopted the twins as his own after they got married. But not before they almost broke up for good because he hadn't been ready to accept his new fatherly role. Too broken to even hold the girls. But they made it through, and she wouldn't have it any other way. The man was an amazing father.

The funniest thing was that if Alex had a DNA test with her girls, it would tell them that he was their father, being that he was the identical twin of their father. Life didn't get any more complex than that. Well, at least until now. She still couldn't believe Nathan stole her DNA. He could have just told her the truth and asked for a paternity test. But then again, people do strange things when they're worried or afraid of the answer. And she wanted to give him a chance to explain himself. Regardless of whether he was her father, he was still the one and only person she knew from her family. She wanted to know more, especially after hearing about Joanne's trip.

But more importantly, Joanne wanted him. And she was going to make sure her mother-in-law had the chance to follow her heart, just as she had encouraged Laryssa to follow hers.

∼

"I don't want to celebrate," Joanne grumbled, pulling the sheets up over her head. "You guys go."

"No. We're not letting you mope around. You're coming and celebrating with us," Laryssa demanded.

Everyone was getting ready to go to the New Year's Eve bash being hosted by Richards' Enterprises. It's what they did every year and was like a tradition in their house. But Joanne wasn't into the idea. She wanted to go to sleep and forget that another year had gone by, and that she would be a single old lady for the rest of her life.

Laryssa grabbed the sheets and yanked them off. "Nope, you can't hide from the world today. You're coming."

"I don't wanna," she whined, sounding very much like a disgruntled teenager being forced to do something by her parents. "You guys go. I'm not up for it."

Why did it suddenly feel like she was the kid? She was older than they were and had the right to make up her own mind whether she wanted to go or not. They needed to stop bossing her around.

"People are going to miss you if you aren't there."

"No one will miss me. They'll be too busy drinking to care."

"I will. Please, Mom," Laryssa begged. "You won't regret it, I promise."

Grumbling, Joanne pulled her achy body out of bed. "The things I do for you guys."

"Great." Laryssa clapped her hands before heading to the closet to get her something to wear.

Her daughter-in-law rushed about Joanne's room like a cyclone. She got tired just watching her. Laryssa was a bundle of energy, and she wished she could harvest it somehow. It would be lovely being that age again, full of life, love, and energy. Laryssa almost had the energy of two people.

Were they going to announce that they were pregnant again? Is that why she had to go? "You aren't pregnant, are you?" she blurted.

"Oh, me?" Laryssa laughed, looking down at her existing post baby belly. "Nu uh, no way. I think three is enough for me. Here, put this on." Laryssa grabbed out the same outfit Joanne wore the first time she went out with Nathan.

"Picking my clothes now, are you?" Joanne grumbled as she snatched the dress. "Do you think I'm too much of an invalid to dress myself?"

Laryssa took no offense to her words and smiled. "Your girlfriends are downstairs, too, so don't be long."

After thirty minutes, her hair was done, and she had touched up her lips with lip gloss, slipping on the long red dress. Her appearance wasn't perfect, but it would do for a Christmas party. She wasn't trying to impress anyone. Her son was the boss.

They owned a tall office building that overlooked English Bay. It had a large balcony with which they could adjourn to, to watch the fireworks. She was getting a little old for all night New Year's Eve events. It would be the usual people in attendance, plus a few of the new hires that Alex had made recently and their families, minus kids. Every year she went with her girlfriends, but this year, she'd rather not go anywhere.

Joanne left her wing, noting her leg was aching more than usual, so she took the elevator down instead. When the doors opened into the big living room foyer, everyone was waiting for her, and her cheeks turned red, knowing she kept everyone waiting. "Why didn't you guys go on without me?"

"Because we aren't giving you the chance to back out. You need to be there," Grace said with a sparkle in her eye.

"It's not like I'm the center of the show," Joanne grumbled.

"I intend to be," Grace said, flaunting her new hip hugging dress. She was the only one of them who could show off flashy curves.

Joanne laughed. "Feel free."

She intended on grabbing a table by the big bay window so she could look out over the water, and let her friends dance their evening away while she got lost in her own world. A world where she and Nathan were together. Her dreams still featured him and their bizarre sexual games. She missed them. Everything about him. His humor. His laugh. His smile. The twinkle in his eye when he looked at her made her feel like the only woman alive.

She still couldn't understand why he had the sudden change of heart. It just didn't feel like it came from him. The man she spoke to the last time seemed different. His words didn't ring true in her head. And typically, she was an excellent judge of character. Her gut was normally spot on about people. She hadn't expected him to be so cruel. But he had been, and there wasn't anything she could do.

"It's time to go, everyone," Alex announced.

They slowly filed out to the party limo that could hold their entire family, and then some. Alex wanted to keep everyone together tonight. He probably thought she'd try to sneak out early, and now she couldn't. She usually left before everyone else, too tired to stay up until midnight.

In the limo, Joanne sat beside Laryssa, who looked stunning in her silk black dress, her hair pulled back with baby breath in it. Her other two friends had three-piece skirt suits on. One was in a lavender colored suit and the other in a black one. She desperately wished she had one on, too. Suits were more comfortable than her red sequin dress.

Her son had on his fancy tuxedo and looked every bit like the businessman she knew him to be, his face glowing with happiness and pride. Joanne held a hand to her chest, tears gathering in her eyes. She was so proud of him for overcoming most of his ghosts. Some still remained but Laryssa had brought him to a place where he was a proud family man.

Alex looked over her way and suddenly his eyes saddened, yet he seemed strangely hopeful. He looked like he wanted to say something, but the vehicle was buzzing with excitement, and he didn't get a chance. Grace couldn't wait to get out on the dance floor. Sharon would probably stay at the table with her, not wanting to make her husband, who couldn't come, jealous. Colleen would have a few drinks and then be out on the dance floor, too.

After about twenty-five minutes, the vehicle pulled up to the front of their office building. People were already going in, being greeted by the hosts at the entrance prior to going up the elevator to ensure they'd been invited. It was a closed party and pre-organized, where people had to pick up their tickets beforehand. The host had a list of whom to expect and knew most of them already. Alex had always used the same group that catered to his events. They often sent the same crew to serve them.

The six of them stepped into the elevator, and Laryssa squeezed Joanne's shoulder. "You're going to have a blast. I can just feel it."

Joanne glanced over at Alex, who was typing a message on his phone, his expression one of concern. "Is everything okay?"

His head snapped up, and he stuffed his phone into his pocket. "Ya, why?"

She pulled her lips to one side, her stomach twisting in knots. The man was lying. "What's going on?"

When the elevator doors opened, a person greeted them in the small lobby and took their jackets before they entered the main meeting room, which was the size of an auditorium. The dance floor was currently empty. Well, almost.

One lonely gentleman stood in the middle of it in a fancy tux. And she meant tux, tails and all. The rest of the people formed a line around the dance floor. When the man turned, Joanne gasped and brought her hands to her mouth, tears swirling in her eyes. "Nathan!"

"Go," Laryssa said, giving her a light push after Joanne continued to stand in her spot, staring.

She looked up at Alex, and while his face was more reserved, he nodded at her to go to him.

"Did you guys plan this?"

Her son put his arm around his wife as Laryssa said, "We couldn't stand to see you so sad. You deserve to be happy."

"But what about...you know."

"I'll be fine. I promise," her daughter-in-law said. Alex grumbled under his breath until Laryssa squeezed his hand reassuringly. "The past is in the past. I'm looking forward to getting to know my *uncle*."

Laryssa had gone through a lot and was a majorly strong woman now. She could even put Alex in his place if she wanted to, which was good, because he needed someone who knew how to be assertive so he wouldn't bowl them over.

Tentatively, Joanne walked toward Nathan, who remained where he was, his hands stuffed in his pocket. As she walked over, he mouthed an "I'm sorry."

Her heart pitter pattered, and her cheeks heated under everyone's close watch. She wished Alex would get the party started, but they all seemed content on watching the two of them. Joanne stopped two feet away from him, and that's when the music started.

"May I have this dance?" he asked, holding out his hand.

"I don't dance," she whispered.

"Then we'll just sway side to side. I just want you in my arms again."

"I think I'd like that, too."

"But I have something I need to do first," and with that, he got down on one knee and opened a jewelry box containing a small diamond ring. "Joanne Richards, will you marry me?"

She couldn't help but look back at her family and friends. Most were smiling and appeared to be genuinely happy for her, even Laryssa. Alex had reservations, you could see it on his face, but he mouthed, "Say yes."

And that was enough for her. "Yes. My gosh, yes!"

The audience squealed with delight and clapped their hands, and her son whistled. "Let's get this party started! Mom, consider this my Christmas gift to you," he said, popping a bottle of champagne.

She had received no greater gift in her lifetime, aside from her kids, of course. And it was a gift she wanted to spend the rest of her living days unwrapping, starting right now. She took him by the hand and led him out of the room. They found a quieter room down the hall. When they entered, she shut the door and locked it, closing all the blinds, then turned to him, her body humming with need.

"Here? But what about the party?" Nathan asked, pointing back the way they came.

"We could always go back if you want," she said, backing him up to the nice comfy chair in the corner. "If you aren't up for it..."

"What if someone comes looking?"

"Weren't you the one who didn't mind the guy peeking in the motorhome window?"

"Well, you're going to be my wife now. Only I get to look at you naked."

"And only I get to look at you," she repeated right back.

"I'm all yours, and yours alone. I'd want it no other way."

"Hm, I like that sound of that," she said, shoving him into the chair and straddling him.

"Don't you think we should wait until we get married?"

"Okay?" she said, pretending to get up.

He grabbed her arm and pulled her back to him. "I'm kidding. I'm kidding."

She linked her hands behind his neck and looked at him as she played with his hair. "I'm curious. What made you change your mind?"

"Your son. He came back and apologized for what he did."

"What did he do?"

"Threatened to send me back to jail if I didn't stay away from you."

"I'm gonna kill him."

"I think Laryssa whipped him into shape for you because he begged me to come tonight and gave me permission to propose. Mind you, it wasn't without stipulations."

Joanne growled, "Of course."

"He asked me to wait to marry you and to court you like you deserve."

"I say we run away and elope."

Nathan swallowed hard. "God, I so badly want to do that, but

I've never been married in my life. I want to do it right by you and by your family. Make it special."

She cupped his cheeks in her palms. "Anywhere with you is special."

He gave her a lopsided grin, letting his fingers trace the neckline of her dress. "Aw, shucks."

Raising her dress a little more so she could rest comfortably on his lap, she said, "So, are you going to take me or what?"

"Gladly," he said as he allowed her to undo his belt.

That's when she knew her bad luck had finally ended and love still existed, even for her. No one could have predicted that it would have been with Nathan, of all people, but life apparently wanted to keep their family together in more ways than one. Alex had married his brother's widow, and now Joanne would be tying the knot with her daughter-in-law's uncle.

Might be strange, but she wouldn't have it any other way.

The End

About the Author

Patricia Elliott lives in beautiful British Columbia with three of her children and her amazing, incredible partner. Now that her kids are all adults, she has decided to actively pursue her passion for the written word.

When she was a youngster, she spent the majority of her time writing fan-fiction and poetry to avoid the harsh reality of bullying. Writing allowed her to escape into another world, even if temporarily; a world in which she could be anyone or anything, even a mermaid.

Dreams really can come true. If you believe it, you can achieve it!

For more titles and to join her newsletter, please visit Patricia Elliott's website:

https://patriciaelliottromance.com